INSIDE WORK

Snow is on the ground, frost is in the air, and the Yule log, helped by the odd bucket of coal, burns cheerily in the grate. The old grandfather's eyeballs burn, too, but not so cheerily, and without any coal to help them along. All he asks of life is peace and quiet and a bottle of brandy; but as the festive season gets into swing he begins to feel like a spoonful of jam with wasps on top. He is in the grip of the old and honoured custom of getting together for Christmas—and what a grip! To his fevered imagination it seems that grandsons and granddaughters, and sons and their friends and private secretaries, are arriving on the scene in a thundering herd; and almost before he can reach for a lucky charm the famous (and valuable) heirloom has disappeared as if into a hole in the ground. Could Fate have struck a crueller blow? You bet it could!

INSIDE WORK

by

JOAN BUTLER

STANLEY PAUL AND CO. LTD
London   Melbourne   Sydney   Auckland
Bombay Johannesburg New York Toronto

First published 1956

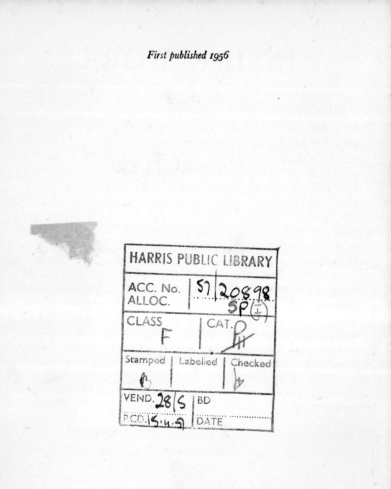
*Printed in Great Britain
by The Anchor Press, Ltd.,
Tiptree, Essex*

CHAPTER ONE

EARLIER in the afternoon Beale, the butler, who had been with the family for generations, had piled fresh logs on the fire. Now dusk was falling, together with a little snow, and the glow from the wide hearth was reflected in polished mahogany and shining mirrors—and, from time to time, when the lid lifted momentarily, in Mr. Oliver Blair Leigh's left eyeball. His right eye rested firmly against the upholstery of the arm-chair in which he reclined. Now and then a low snort, such as might be expected from a man on the verge of sleep, echoed through the room.

As noted above, dusk was falling, and, from a sky that had sunk down to balance on the chimney-pots, a little snow. Silently the flakes came drifting down, settling on roof and road, field and woods. Had Mr. Leigh been aware of this, he would have stood in the window, staring up; for he was still a boy at heart, and the sight of snowflakes falling from the sky stirred something deep down within him, and stirred it good.

The glowing embers settled on the hearth, and a few sparks shot out. The old coot's left eyelid rose briefly, showing a little of the white beneath, then sank again like the lid of a cockle. The book—doubtless of an improving nature—slipped from his right hand and thudded to the floor, but he scarcely stirred. Meanwhile the world outside grew dark, and all sounds faded.

Beale came in again, switching on the light. Smoothly he advanced, bearing a laden tray, which he deposited on a low table beside the armchair. This done, and pausing only to clear his throat just in case it had become clogged with foreign matter on his run up from the kitchen, he issued a bulletin.

"Tea and muffins, sir."

"Hunh?" Mr. Leigh muttered, without stirring.

"Tea and muffins, sir," the old butler repeated, patiently waiting for it to sink in.

At this, Mr. Leigh sat up, and without further delay reached for a muffin and bit down strongly, taking it as all part of the

5

game when a spoonful of melted butter ran down his chin. Satisfied that his message had been received and understood, Beale moved over to the window and drew the curtains.

"It is snowing, sir," he remarked, rightly judging that this not altogether unexpected development might have escaped his employer's notice.

"Haw?" said Mr. Leigh, wiping the butter from his chin and then licking the finger he had used for the mopping-up operation. "Snowing, what?"

"Yes, sir. It promises to be quite a heavy fall."

"Is that so?" Mr. Leigh reached for another muffin with one hand, while pouring a cup of tea with the other. "A heavy fall, what? Well, there would appear to be little or nothing we can do about it, Beale."

"Nothing whatever, sir," the old butler agreed.

"What I always say is that we must take these things as they come. Never doubt for a moment, Beale, they are sent for some good purpose."

"I can readily believe it, sir."

"Like these muffins," the old coot added. "Please inform Mrs. Chubb from me that she goes from strength to strength. Seldom or never has it been my good fortune to sink a tooth into a more delectable muffin."

"Very good, sir. Will there be anything else?"

"Not before dinner," Mr. Leigh answered with his mouth full. "Got to think of my figure."

Five minutes later he had finished the muffins, and was toying with the idea of forwarding an application for some more, when once again the door opened. This time it was his wife who entered. She came forward briskly, looking him over in that certain way she had, as if it would not surprise her to find he had forgotten to put on his trousers.

"You've got butter all over your chin," she remarked without wasting a moment. "You look like something basted for the oven."

"A little butter on the chin never harmed anyone," he replied amiably. "Take Tibet, for instance."

"*You* take it. I don't want it."

"In Tibet they put butter in their tea. And yak-butter, at that. Tell me, my dear, have you ever tasted yak-butter?"

"No, I have never tasted yak-butter, strange as it may seem."

"Nor have I," the old coot admitted, on a note of regret. "The yak would appear to be a most versatile animal. Not only does the female yak supply milk and butter, but——"

"I am not interested in the female yak."

"Well, in a country like Tibet I suppose one learns to make do with whatever lies at hand," the old coot remarked after a brief period of meditation, presumably about the female yak and its value to society. "Incidentally, the poorer classes get their milk from sheep and goats."

"I must remember that." Martha Leigh spread her hands to the warmth of the fire. "Let us postpone the lecture on the domestic animals of Tibet," she suggested. "I've just had a letter from Alfred and Marjorie."

"Ah! Alfred and Marjorie, what?"

There was little real pleasure in the yak-lover's tone. This news that a letter had arrived from his eldest son and daughter-in-law brought no sparkle to his eye, no flush of happiness to his cheek. Rather, it was with some reserve, and in a silence almost of foreboding, that he awaited the inevitable details. Meanwhile he wished he had something stronger than tea under his belt to steel him against the blow his every instinct warned him was about to fall—and fall from a height, at that.

"Alfred finds it necessary to go to Argentina for a few months."

As these good tidings bored in, the old coot uttered one short bark of laughter, biting it off in the middle and swallowing the bit that hadn't got out.

"Ha!" he snorted. "Have you ever remarked, my dear, that when Alfred finds it necessary to go abroad it is invariably about this time of year and to some sunnier clime? Last year it was South Africa. The year before, it was Morocco. Before that I seem to recollect a trip to Mexico, and, on another occasion, the West Indies. I can, of course, take it that his loving and beloved wife will accompany him, sacrificing her own desires to his happiness and welfare—and incidentally, of course, seeing that he keeps out of trouble?"

"Yes, she's going with him. What sort of trouble did you have in mind?"

"Dark-eyed señoritas?" the old coot mused. "No, no! Not Alfred! I can't imagine it—but perhaps Marjorie can. And what, may I ask, is to become of their two sweet little children while they go rolling down to Rio?"

"They're going to Buenos Aires, not Rio."

"The question is, where are the children going?"

"Most of the time, of course, they'll be at school."

"And the rest of the time?"

"Marjorie thought we might like to have them with us for the holidays."

"She is quite wrong," the old buffer stated, without any beating about the bush. "We would *not* like to have them with us for the holidays, and I trust you will tell her so at once, in words a child might understand, and no fiddle-faddle." He raised his right hand, and waggled a finger in his wife's face. "No, no, Martha! Let there be no weakening! This must not be! Christmas is bad enough at the best of times. Christmas with Derek and Alison about the house would be more than flesh and blood could bear—certainly *my* flesh and blood."

"You do realize you are speaking of your own grand-children, don't you?"

"I have no reason to doubt it. And behind it all, of course, I love them dearly; but the fact remains that as of above date they are a brace of unutterable young stinkers, and the thought of spending Christmas in their company, or for that matter any other time, makes my blood run cold."

"Nonsense!"

"It's not nonsense! I feel my temperature falling already."

"You haven't seen them for six months."

"If I hadn't seen them for six years, it would still be all too often."

"Derek can be a little trying," the fond grandmother admitted, after a brief spell of meditation. "But Alfred was a little trying, too, at that age."

"Derek is different," the old coot muttered, staring gloomily into the fire as if in expectation of seeing a vision. "I feel moved to prophesy he will end up either as Prime Minister, beloved of the people, or standing on a trap-door in Penton-ville with his hands tied behind his back and a bag over his

8

head." He took another look into the fire, and added, brightening a little: "Probably the latter."

"Alison is a sweet child."

"Alison is a little monster, and you know it. No doubt she will develop into a beautiful and affectionate young woman, an admirable wife and mother and an unfailing source of pride and joy to her family and a large circle of friends; but at the present stage of her development the prospect of spending even an hour in her company fills me with horror and revulsion."

"Then I am to tell Marjorie we refuse to take the children?"

"Briefly, yes."

"She'll be deeply offended."

"More than likely."

"You don't mind?"

"Not at all! I'd much rather offend her than put in three weeks of misery. Besides, you don't have to be so dashed blunt about it. Use a little tact, my dear. Tell her we've got measles in the district, or something."

"They've both had measles."

"They haven't had bubonic plague, have they? Or yellow fever? So long as you manage to keep her at bay, it's all one to me if you tell her we have typhoid right in the house. And I'd much rather have a little typhoid in the house than my two darling grandchildren. One can take something for a fever; but an antidote for Derek and Alison has yet to be discovered."

"Very well. I'll tell Marjorie that the thought of seeing her children fills you with revulsion."

"Ah!" said the old grandfather, turning that over in his mind. "A trifle outspoken, don't you think? Unnecessarily blunt, what? I don't mind actually *seeing* the little horrors. It's the thought of having to live with them for three or four weeks that rubs the salt in my wounds. Why not hint at an outbreak of rabies in the parish?"

"I prefer to tell the truth."

"Ah!" the old coot muttered again, on a sinking note. It was plain that, even without his glasses, he had seen the writing on the wall, and his backbone curved like a bow as he took a peep into the future. Nevertheless, futile as he knew it to

9

be, he lodged a protest. "If you had already decided to have them, my dear, why did you trouble to ascertain my views on the matter?"

"I hoped that perhaps, all appearances to the contrary, you might have mellowed a little, and that the prospect of having your grandchildren about your knees for the festive season would bring joy and anticipation into an otherwise empty life."

"My life is far from empty," Mr. Leigh remonstrated mildly. "And even if it were, my dear, I'd prefer it to remain a perfect vacuum than to have it filled to overflowing with a brace of inhuman fiends such as my darling grandchildren." He threw off a heavy sigh. "Some people whose lives are as empty as a politician's promise don't realize how fortunate they are."

"The children won't bother you."

"They had better not!" said the old coot, with a momentary gleam in his eye. "Old as I am, I still feel fully capable of dealing with a young reptile like Derek—more especially when his mother happens to be in Buenos Aires. Given just cause, my dear, I'll skin him alive, using what comes off to sole my shoes."

"It is unlikely that the need for such extreme measures will arise," the fond grandmother commented tolerantly. "Has it not occurred to you, Oliver, that almost certainly the children take an even poorer view of you than you do of them?"

"It didn't have to occur to me. Derek told me so, when he was with us last summer."

"He did?"

"Yes. He confessed that what baffled him was why I had been allowed to live so long, since obviously I served no useful purpose whatever. He further stated that among certain primitive tribes I would long since have been staked out in the jungle to be devoured by wild beasts, and I got an impression that this method of disposing of the village elders met with his unqualified approval."

"Why didn't you skin him alive, using what was left over after soling your shoes to make a tobacco pouch?"

"Because his mother was standing by—and you know how

I react when she's standing by. I feel like some small and helpless creature about to be swallowed by a snake."

"Christmas is the children's season," Mrs. Leigh mused. "We must make sacrifices for them."

"Or *of* them."

"Any unpleasantness will be largely your own fault. If you don't interfere with them, they won't interfere with you."

"Ha!" the old coot snorted, on a sardonic note. "Poppycock! That policy doesn't work with Derek. He takes it as a sign of weakness. But he had better be careful! I can be a fiend when roused. You haven't any more pleasant surprises for me, what?"

"As a matter of fact, I have. Claude will be with us, too."

The old grandfather jerked in his chair as if nipped by a scorpion. This news that his second son would be one of the party got in among him like a poisoned arrow.

"*Claude?*" he croaked. "You don't mean *Claude?*"

"Yes, Claude."

"But I understood he was snowed under with his political work! The last I heard of him, he couldn't leave London for a moment. I got the impression he spent most of his time at Downing Street, giving the Prime Minister the benefit of his advice on a variety of subjects, solving problems which had been the despair of the Cabinet for the past twelve months, and in general running the country from behind the scenes. The impression I had was that if he took a day off the Empire would go to pot. Without his guiding hand the government would topple, riot and civil commotion spread throughout the land, and a second Dark Ages stare us in the face. Don't tell me he has lost the Prime Minister's confidence!"

"As usual, you exaggerate. He has been working too hard, and now his doctor advises him that he needs a change."

"So he comes here?"

"Could anything be more natural?"

"Yes!" the old coot snorted. "It'd be a dashed sight more natural if he came to an arrangement with some nice young poppet and hopped off to the Riviera with her for a couple of weeks. I'll bet that's the sort of change the doctor had in mind for him, too—not a week or two buried in the country with nothing to look at but mud, slush and mud, pools of water and dripping trees, and more mud."

"That might be more natural for you," Martha admitted at once. "In fact, it appears to have been the first thought that sprang to your mind—if, indeed, it is ever out of it. But Claude is different."

"Ha!"

"What do you mean?"

"Just that. Ha!"

"Have you any reason to believe he is *not* different?"

"No, no! Nothing definite. He's a dashed queer fish; but some day he'll surprise you."

"After thirty-five years as your wife, my dear Oliver, it would take a great deal to surprise me. At any rate, Claude must mean to do some work while he is here, because he is bringing his secretary along."

"Another mouth to feed," the old coot commented, but without rancour.

"You didn't object to feeding her the last time she was here."

"'Her'? It's a female, what?"

"She looked extremely feminine to me; but perhaps you saw her from a different angle."

"Ha!" Mr. Leigh muttered, rubbing his chin. Suddenly he brightened. "Not Sally Henderson? That *was* the name, was it not?"

"Yes—and damned well you know it! Don't pretend you've forgotten her."

"It's coming back now. How long since she was here? Three years?"

"Three and a half. It was summer. The year Claude first became interested in politics."

"God help the country!"

"Your nephew Hugh was here at the time. Don't you remember, he spent a few weeks with us before going to Canada?"

"Dirty young dog!" the old coot muttered. "Haven't had a line from him for a year or two. Yes; I remember now. Seemed interested in Sally, didn't he? Not surprising, really—

any man with two eyes in his head, or even one, would be interested in her."

"Perhaps he was; but it came to nothing."

"You don't think Claude . . . ?" said the old grandfather, leaving the question half unspoken and raising his eyebrows in a most significant manner.

"No, I don't! Certainly not!"

"It was just a thought, my dear."

"Sally is a very nice girl; but you must remember she is only a private secretary, whereas Claude seems destined to be a Member of Parliament and a Cabinet Minister. If he decides to marry, he must pick someone who would be of help to him in his career."

"She may be only a private secretary; but he's only a skunk and she's a dashed sight too good for him," Mr. Leigh stated bluntly. "Yes, I know he's my son—don't remind me of it. That doesn't make him a paragon of all the virtues, my dear. Why should it? I was never one myself. Let me tell you, Martha, I feel that in politics he has found his true vocation. If ever there was a coldblooded, calculating reptile, selfish to a degree, ruthless and unscrupulous, a liar and a cheat and an all-round poisonous pill, Claude is that very character—and I've often told him so to his face, though it didn't appear to do any good."

"Your children don't seem to meet with your approval today," Martha commented tolerantly. "Simply because Claude is determined to carve a successful career for himself is no proof he's an unscrupulous scoundrel."

"He couldn't carve a chicken! Believe me, my dear, his constituents will see through him, if he ever has any. What was it some bird said about fooling some of the people some of the time? Claude won't fool them for a moment. He's a blown-up, conceited prig, and the youngest child could tell so at a glance. Ha! A Cabinet Minister, my eyeball!"

"Nevertheless he will be with us for Christmas, and I trust you will find sufficient strength to keep your opinion of him to yourself."

"He's not interested in my opinion of him or of anything else," the old grandfather replied, on a depressed note. "Nobody gives a toot for my opinion. I'm only a cipher about the

13

place. I don't want my grandchildren here; but they're coming anyway. I don't want Claude here; but he's coming, too. I'm not consulted about these things. I'm simply informed of what's going to happen."

"Consider yourself very lucky that you *are* informed," Martha replied amiably. "I was tempted to let the children arrive without a word of warning; but I decided it might do something serious to your heart. By the way, John is coming home, too."

This casual mention of his youngest son seemed actually to give the old coot some innocent pleasure. A smile settled on his aesthetic features, maintaining its position for some moments, the while his eyes, which a few seconds previous had smouldered in their sockets like a couple of lumps of punk, now glowed with childish happiness.

"Of course!" he said, keeping a firm hand on his emotions. "Naturally. Christmas wouldn't be the same without him. Strictly speaking, I suppose, he's a bit of a young flibberti-gibbet in his own way; but for some reason or other he reminds me very much of what I was myself at his age. Happy as the day was long, full of the joy of spring, and so forth. Bursting with life and good resolutions and all that sort of twaddle, and overflowing with confidence in the future."

"When you were John's age, you were already married."

"Was I? Married, what? Are you sure, my dear?"

"Quite sure. He's twenty-six, you know."

"God bless my soul! So he is! Ha!" The old grandfather did a few intricate calculations in his head, and came up with the answer as fast as any electronic brain. "That makes seven years he's been at Oxford, what?"

"Yes; seven years."

"Rather longer than usual, don't you think?"

"Perhaps. But by no means a record, or so I'm told."

"Who told you?"

"John. He says it's been known for men to spend their whole lives there, they became so immersed in study, like medieval hermits sunk in meditation."

"Indeed? An odd way to spend one's life, what? Not for me, I'm afraid. The pursuit of knowledge is all very well in its own way, and doubtless has its rewards; but there are other things to be pursued, and to my mind the rewards are sweeter. Tell me, my dear, has he any clue yet as to what he wishes to become?"

"If so, he hasn't mentioned it to me."

"Nor to me, either. Do you think I should broach the subject over the holidays?"

"Yes and no."

"Well, well! I suppose you're right, as usual."

"I mean, it certainly is time he came to some decision; but it might be disastrous to give him the impression we were rushing him."

"He could hardly accuse us of that, my dear," the old coot said mildly. "You must agree we've given him ample time to make up his mind. I've said nothing to him since the time, two years ago, that he decided to be a world-famous surgeon. Unfortunately, after thinking it over for a couple of months he abandoned the notion. It seems he looked in on a dissection class one day, and sight of the cadavers put him off his food for a week."

"That was three years ago. Two years ago he saw himself as a world-famous civil engineer, throwing bridges and dams across mighty rivers. But then he found that called for quite a lot of mathematics, and he never was good at maths."

"Then there was the time he thought he'd make rather a good barrister. I forget exactly what put him off; but it never came to anything. Nevertheless, my dear, I'm convinced that as soon as the boy discovers his true bent he'll make a success of his life. He has intelligence, drive, ambition, energy—everything, in fact, required for the successful career. The only trouble is, he doesn't seem to know what he wants to do. We must give him time."

"Of course. He's young yet. And he may have decided on something since we saw him last. He writes so seldom; and even when he does, I can scarcely read his letters. I do wish he'd use a typewriter! He said something about bringing a friend with him."

"For the holidays?"

"I think so. An American, or possibly an Armenian. Only a handwriting expert could tell."

"More likely an American, I think. Ha! Any friend of John's is always welcome here."

"He can have Alfred's old room. They'd like that, I'm sure."

"Indeed?" said the old coot, momentarily baffled. "Why should they like it, my dear?"

"Because there's a connecting door," his wife explained patiently. "They'll be able to talk all night if they wish."

CHAPTER TWO

IT WAS a fine, brisk winter afternoon, with snow on the ground and frost in the air and a wind that sliced to the bone like a surgeon's scalpel, when Master Derek Clayton Leigh, aged thirteen, and his sister Alison Patricia, aged eleven, arrived at Scumton station. This busy depot, serving Scumton village and parish, was in the midst of the Christmas rush, and two other travellers descended on to the windswept platform, while an even greater number embarked for the next leg of the journey. The guard waved his flag and blew his whistle; the locomotive snorted; couplings rattled, and the train moved off for foreign parts, while from without the station limits a couple of local urchins pelted it with snowballs.

This Derek Clayton Leigh, mention of whom had filled his grandfather with such horror and revulsion, was a well-developed lad of rather more than average height, and of considerably more than average weight, for his age. He appeared, also, to be of an unusually morose disposition for one of his years. His glance was reserved and unfriendly to a degree, and there was something in the curl of his lip which suggested that he held not only his fellow mortals, but the arrangement of things in general, in loathing and contempt.

This included his sister.

The lad was galled to think that he had been forced to travel for upwards of two hours in the company of an immature stinker for whom he had little affection and no esteem whatever. Most of the time, at school and surrounded by his merry playmates, he was able to banish from his mind all thought of her existence. Even at home, he had ways and means of dodging her for hours on end. The prospect now facing him, however, was one to wring a cry of despair and anguish from the stoutest heart. In Scumton Hall, with not a budding squaw of her own age for miles around, she would follow him like a dog.

Dark thoughts of this nature were stirring in the lad's mind as he stood in the snow beside his luggage, his hands in his overcoat pockets and his brows knit in a scowl. Alison Patricia waited at a respectful distance, watching him in a reserved sort of manner. She was a slender child, fair-haired and with deep blue eyes; and there was indeed little in either her appearance or her demeanour that seemed to justify her grandfather's description of her as a little monster.

"Hedgehogs eat snakes," she remarked suddenly, in a clear voice. It was as if some unseen spirit had descended on her from the darkling sky and borrowed her vocal cords to issue the statement.

Derek's eyes swivelled a few degrees in their sockets, and he bent on her an inscrutable glance. Silent and withdrawn, he waited for more. Plainly, though as yet he had no comment, his interest was aroused.

"They begin at the tail," Alison went on, still in the same clear tones, "and work up from there."

The lad shifted his weight from one foot to the other, but said nothing. Yet his glance, bleak as a reptile's, clung to his sister's attractive features as if glued.

"They keep going until there's nothing left," Alison concluded, her eyes wide in wonder at the strange ways of hedgehogs. "Here's Martin."

There had been no change in her tone. Derek turned, and saw the old chauffeur approaching. To his mind, Martin should have been staked out for the wild beasts twenty or thirty years back; but just at the moment he was glad to see him.

Martin greeted them in a manner by no means devoid of reserve, took up the luggage, and turned back to the car.

Viewed from any angle, Scumton Hall was an impressive gentleman's residence. Beginning as a modest mansion back in the days of Good Queen Bess, it had been added to and extended in all directions by almost every succeeding generation until now only the keenest and most experienced eye could trace the outlines of the original structure. The initial effect was overpowering, like a blow on the base of the skull with a cricket stump. Nevertheless the building was in the main dry and free of rats.

The devoted grandmother was waiting when Martin pulled up at the hall door, and actually came down a couple of steps to greet the children. She gave Alison a hug and a kiss, and was about to repeat the process with Derek when she caught his eye and drew back as if he had waved a horse-pistol under her nose. But she recovered her customary aplomb almost at once, and with her arm around Alison led the way indoors, at the same time remarking that they had grown so much she scarcely knew them. Alison reacted to this statement with a sweet and trusting glance; but Derek's upper lip lifted a fraction at one side, and he grunted to himself.

"Take off your coats and scarves," the old granny said briskly. "I've had tea set for you in the morning-room, where you won't be disturbed. You must be cold. Just for this once we won't wash our hands, will we? Come along, then."

She watched them eat, though the spectacle was one to turn many a stomach. Derek was a good, steady eater. He took a moment to decide what he wanted first, then reached out for it and got busy. In some ways, no doubt, he had been and still was a difficult boy; but he had never given his mother a moment's anxiety where his food was concerned. He simply took what came and tucked it away, then looked around for more. Nor was he at all fussy as to how he got it down, or if it made a noise on the way.

"Hedgehogs eat snakes," Alison announced suddenly, with a winning smile for the old granny.

The old granny started slightly. She had not been thinking of either hedgehogs or snakes.

"Indeed?" she said with polite interest. "They do, do they?"

"Yes. I learned that in my nature study. They begin at the tail and go as far as they can."

"That must be rather uncomfortable for the snake."

"Sometimes the snake is too big, and the hedgehog can't

finish it at one go, though he eats until he's practically sick. But he always comes back for what's left."

"I'm glad to hear they don't waste their food."

"There's nothing they like better than a good feed of snake."

"More than likely it's very good for them, too," the grandmother remarked with a shudder. "But what on earth made you think of that just now, dear?"

"I often think of snakes," Alison replied dreamily. "That makes me think of hedgehogs. Then I think of hedgehogs eating snakes, starting at the tail——"

"Yes, yes! You went into that before. Don't let it develop into a complex, darling. Try to think of something more pleasant."

"I can't imagine anything nicer than a hedgehog eating a snake."

"Then please don't talk to *me* about it!" the old granny begged, on a somewhat sharper note. "Tell your grandfather about it sometime. He'd be interested. Now I have something to say to you about your stay here. Of course, your grandfather and I will do everything we can to make your holiday enjoyable, and I needn't say we both love having you with us; but there are a few small points I'd like you to be clear about."

Here she paused briefly, staring at Derek. The lad was now replete. With admirable application to business, ignoring everything else, he had worked away steadily if not quietly, until now he had reached the stage where even another nibble might precipitate unthinkable disaster. A light perspiration dewed his noble brow, and for one horrible moment his eyes reminded the old granny of the eyes of a fried trout. He sat back in his chair, and appeared to be on the point of relapsing into a coma.

"Do you feel all right?" she asked, wondering if it was the cream buns or the mince pies that threatened his downfall.

"Fine," he replied on a confident note. "Swell."

"He always looks like that when he's had as much as he can eat," Alison volunteered. "You'd think he was going to be sick all over the floor, wouldn't you, Granny?"

This was exactly what the old grandmother had thought—

and for that matter, she was still far from convinced she was mistaken.

"Please, dear!" she murmured, closely watching the lad. "If you feel unwell, Derek, it might be better——"

"I feel fine!" he said coldly. "Don't worry—I'm not going to be sick. I haven't been sick since some well-wisher gave me a four-pound box of chocolates on my birthday two years ago. And even then I wouldn't have been sick if I hadn't tackled a couple of tins of herring in tomato sauce immediately afterwards. I still think there was something wrong with that sauce. The flavour was a little off."

"Well, what I wanted to say to you was this. We'll all do our best to make this your happiest Christmas ever; but it can't be all one-sided, you know. *You*'ve got to do your bit, too."

"Such as what?" Derek inquired, without any enthusiasm whatever.

"You must consider others."

"Why?"

"In order not to make them unhappy."

"Suppose we want to make them unhappy?"

"If they are trying to make *you* happy, you'll want to make *them* happy, won't you? Especially if they're not too strong."

"Who's not too strong?"

"Your grandfather isn't too strong just now."

"I don't see how he could expect to be," the lad admitted frankly. "He's getting on. Must be hitting it up for ninety, huh? A man at that age is past his prime. He's about had it."

"He's not near ninety," the old grandmother replied, after a few moments devoted to mastering her emotions.

"Still a year or two to go?"

"For your information, Derek, your grandfather is only a little over sixty."

"He looks more. He looks like a hundred. But maybe he's just breaking up sooner than most. Last time I saw him, I told myself it was only a matter of months."

"I love Granpa," Alison announced in a dreamy sort of tone. "I love *you*, too, Granny."

"Of course you do, darling! Well, as I've been trying to say for the past five minutes, you will do your very best not to irritate him, won't you?"

"If he keeps out of my hair, I'll keep out of his," Derek promised. "But the last time I was here he made a set at me. Everything I did was like driving skewers into his flesh. I couldn't raise my voice above a whisper or he'd blow his cork. Coming up to the end of the visit I had a pain in my jaw from keeping my mouth shut, and a cramp in my legs from creeping around on tiptoe. I don't think he likes me a lot."

"Don't be absurd! Of course he likes you."

"Then he must be the undemonstrative kind," the lad muttered. "The way he acts, you'd think his one ambition was to skin me alive and pour on salt with a liberal hand. He's a wizard at hiding his real feelings."

"All I ask is that you don't make too much noise while he's around," the old granny said patiently. "And it's not only your grandfather who has to be considered. Your Uncle Claude is here, too."

"Another nervous wreck, huh?"

"Your uncle is a very busy man. I'm afraid he might be annoyed if you did anything to distract him at his work."

"What's he doing here?"

"I don't know exactly what he's doing. Some sort of correspondence in connection with politics, I believe. But whatever it is, he wants peace and quiet for it. I'm sorry, darlings; but I gave him my word I'd mention it to you."

"Three weeks in the Bastille!" Derek muttered, squirming restlessly in his chair. "I can see I'm going to enjoy this holiday no end, going around with a clamp on my lip!"

"Now you mustn't exaggerate, Derek! I'm simply asking you to refrain from shouting and rushing around inside the house. If the weather is fine you can play outdoors. Have you brought your skates?"

"Skates?" The lad raised his eyebrows while at the same time pinning on a slight but contemptuous smile. "I don't skate."

"Oh! You don't like skating?"

"I see no future in rushing around like a madman, with or without skates," Derek admitted. "I leave that sort of thing to the bone and brawn merchants. Personally I prefer something a little more intellectual."

"Well, you could play in the snow, couldn't you?" the old grandmother suggested tentatively. "Or have you grown too old for making snowmen?"

"Yes," Derek confessed, on an aloof note. "I have. But keep up your heart—I'll find something to do, even if I have to read a book."

.   .   .   .   .   .

Claude Blair Leigh was a moderately tall and well-built young man measuring about six inches too much around the waist. Otherwise he kept himself in good shape, being always clean and neatly dressed, with his hair slicked down until it looked as if it had been gummed. He was a dark-complexioned type, and even after a close shave his chin and cheeks looked a little blue. He had a fine brow, an intent and searching glance which impressed persons of rather weak intellect, and a strong mouth. Here was a young man with a mission, and that mission was to make himself Prime Minister in the shortest possible space of time.

"The Empire needs men like me," he would often say, though he was by no means of a boastful nature. "In these dark and troublous times this mighty Empire of ours needs a firm hand on the helm—and I have it."

Of course, he admitted so much only to his most intimate friends and admirers, for in reality he was quite a modest young man.

This enforced absence from London irked him sorely; but what really got under his skin and burned like a mustard plaster was the discovery that his nephew and niece were to be among those present for the whole of his stay. It was some years since, through no fault of his own, he had met his brother's offspring, and it surprised him to hear that the boy was now thirteen and the girl eleven. Nevertheless he felt no pleasure at the thought of the reunion, for in his opinion all children under sixteen were stinkers, and it had occurred to him that almost certainly Alfred's children were greater stinkers than most. The possibility of getting any serious work done, with a brace of young savages howling around, receded sharply. He felt very bitter about it.

Nor was he overjoyed to learn that his young brother John, accompanied by an American (or possibly Armenian) friend, was to join the festive gathering. He regarded John as only a shade better than a half-wit. In more sombre moods he faced up to the fact that he had little regard for any of the family, including his old man. They lacked that driving ambition that kept him humming like a dynamo.

His mood was one of deep depression the evening Derek and Alison arrived, and an expression of dejection sat on his features as he gave himself a wash and brush-up before dinner. The children, he knew, would be on the premises now. It surprised him that he had not heard their shrieking and yelling before this. It was his belief that two or three children at play could make as much noise as a band of Sioux attacking a wagon-train, or possibly more.

He came downstairs a little early, without waiting for the gong, with in his mind a half-formed project of knocking back a couple of cocktails before dinner. He was not as a rule addicted to the consumption of alcohol; but he felt that on an occasion such as this a quick snort could do no harm. In fact, the thought cheered him up a little as it took definite shape, and he quickened his pace. Entering the drawing-room, he turned towards the small table where Beale was accustomed to set out the liquor, and at once perceived that another had got there before him.

That other was Derek, the boy wonder. He had mixed himself a brandy and soda, and was sipping it with every evidence of appreciation, when Claude arrived. Nor was the lad taken aback by this sudden appearance of an uncle he had not seen for years, and had not particularly wished to see, either. He gave Claude a distant nod, accompanied by one of his more inscrutable glances, and sucked in another toothful of the old snake-bite lotion.

"You're Derek, I take it?" Claude said, without any beating about the bush.

Although he had no clear recollection of how the boy had looked on the occasion of their previous meeting, it seemed evident that little improvement had taken place. Seldom or never, he reflected, had he seen so unprepossessing a youth; but in the next instant it occurred to him that this was only to be expected by anyone who had known his father at the same age. Yet something new had been added. It was, he thought, the coldly hostile, reptilian glance, such as might be looked for from a basilisk just waking up with a bad hangover.

"Yep," the lad admitted nonchalantly. "I'm Derek."

"What's that you're drinking?"

Derek's glance became a little colder, a shade more malevolent. Instinct seemed to warn him that the uncle was about to adopt a critical attitude. The prospect failed to fill him with dismay.

"Brandy and soda," he replied, and tipped another portion down the scuttle.

"You know perfectly well you have no right to drink brandy."

"Why not?"

"You're too young."

"A man is as old as he feels," Derek pointed out, maintaining all his customary sang-froid. "You want to make something of it, huh?"

Claude's neck swelled out over his collar like a soda-loaf in a tin, and if his eyes didn't become bloodshot there and then it was only because they were taken by surprise. But in a moment, as befitted an ambitious young politician who was determined some day to be Prime Minister, or at least Chancellor of the Exchequer, he had himself under control. That first blind urge, to leap on Derek like a hungry leopard and beat him into a thin paste, subsided. Beating schoolboys into a thin paste was no way to win votes.

"I shall certainly inform your grandfather about it," he said coldly, working a finger around inside his collar while waiting for his blood-pressure to drop. If he'd had a safety-valve, it would have been whistling like a runaway locomotive.

"Listen, brother!" Derek begged, in a tone that Claude himself might have used in discussing foreign policy with the village idiot. "Why don't you keep your nose clean? Does it bother you if I drink a little rot-gut? Is this your liquor, or does it belong to your old man? How can you be sure he didn't press me to help myself whenever I felt there might be a pinch of dust in my craw, huh?"

"I know perfectly well he didn't!"

"If you know what's good for you, chum, you'll leave me alone. I'm a peace-lover. I want no trouble with you or anyone else. I've got plenty to occupy my mind without a feud. But I'm not a guy who turns the other cheek when I get a poke in the eye. No, sir! I bide my time. To look at me, you'd think I'd forgotten all about it. But I haven't. I'm simply watching for an opportunity. And when it comes, in no time at all the other duck begins to wish he'd never been born."

This was a long speech for Derek, and at the end he flushed out his vocal passages, for he found this talking thirsty work. Claude, meanwhile, moving forward, had poured himself a little Scotch, tossing it off like one who has escaped some fearful fate by the skin of his denture, and takes the stuff purely as a medicine.

"Are you threatening me?" he asked incredulously, half-wondering if all this could be a horrible hallucination brought on by something he had eaten for lunch.

"No—I'm telling you. The story goes that you're anxious to do some work while around these parts. If you want to work, go ahead and work. But tangle with me, and you'll do no work while the feudin' is on—or afterwards, either."

Satisfied that he had stated his case clearly and without equivocation, and plainly ready to regard the matter as closed, Derek helped himself to a little more brandy, added a dash of soda, and sank into what appeared to be a spell of earnest meditation touched with melancholy. This encounter with his uncle had filled him with gloom and foreboding. It seemed to him that Uncle Claude, like all politicians, being convinced that he could run anything better than anyone else, was fundamentally incapable of keeping his nose out of affairs that were no concern of his; and with a duck like that around the place, friction was bound to develop.

"Suppose I take you by the ear and give you a good thrashing?" Claude suggested, having thought it over for a few moments, but without making any move to launch the programme.

Derek favoured him with a sombre glance.

"Try anything like that, and I'll break a decanter over your head," he replied coldly. "Maybe not now, when you're expecting it, but some time when your mind is miles away. And if I take a swing at you with a decanter, your mind will stay miles away for quite a while. You don't know me yet; but you will. I'm a dangerous duck to get fresh with. You just leave me alone, brother, and you'll have no cause for complaint. Try any funny stuff, and you'll rue the day. It's as simple as that."

Before Claude could reply, the old grandfather entered briskly, turning at once towards the table that held the liquor. Despite Derek's low opinion of him, he was a well-preserved citizen with a healthy colour in his cheek and a sparkle in his eye; and if, as his wife hinted, his nerves were frayed at the ends like a donkey's tail, this was by no means evident to the untrained eye. The thought of sinking a toothful of brandy had conjured a smile to his lips, and his step was buoyant as he entered the room.

Sight of the son and grandson clustered around the drinks wiped the smile from his face in short order, and his step lost much of its buoyancy. For the past hour or two, immersed in a good book, he had forgotten that Derek and Alison were scheduled to arrive for dinner; and now, as his glance came to rest on the lad himself, a sudden shiver ran through his frame, and he felt as if an ice-pack had been wrapped around his heart.

"Haw!" he exclaimed, still advancing, but more slowly. His attempt to pin on a smile of welcome met with indifferent success. "So there you are, what? My dear boy, how you've grown—especially around the stomach!"

This pleasantry, accompanied by what was meant to be a jolly laugh, earned him a brooding glance from Derek. Strangely enough, the lad was sensitive about his figure.

"You're looking remarkably well," the old coot added hurriedly, almost wringing the neck off the decanter in his eagerness to get something to thaw him out inside. He poured brandy into a glass, and tossed it off without bothering to add soda. Almost at once, he felt a genial glow radiating in all directions from his boiler-house. He laughed again, still a little off key. "Have some brandy, what?"

"I have some, thanks."

"You *have*?"

"Yep. What did you think this was—cold tea?"

"Haw!" the grandparent muttered. His eyes had gone a little blank, and he looked like some bold seer who, taking a quick peep into the future, saw himself being run over by a bus. Fumblingly, he replenished his glass.

"Haw!" he said again, and there was a world of misery in that single syllable.

CHAPTER THREE

BEALE, the butler, was a stout old character with a rather pink face, a smooth, shiny pate, and three or four spare chins hanging down over his collar. He had been with the family for several generations, and little of importance went on without his hearing about it. He had some secret way of coming by his information which for years past had on occasion turned the old grandfather purple in the face with fury and frustration.

At breakfast the morning after the children's arrival, it soon became obvious to the head of the family that Beale had something up his cuff. There was a twinkle deep down in the old butler's eye, and a certain jauntiness in his manner, that seemed to suggest he was chuckling slyly at some joke of his own.

It was the custom at Scumton Hall that everyone, family and guests alike, came down to breakfast at eight o'clock in the summer and nine o'clock in the winter. Unless in cases of illness, no meals were served in bed. This morning, Derek and Alison were first on the scene, and Derek had already tucked away a couple of sausages, holding them casually between finger and thumb, before his grandfather arrived. A few moments later Claude put in an appearance, looking as spruce as ever, or even sprucer. Then came Miss Sally Henderson, his private secretary.

This was a young woman to catch the eye, and hold it, like a fish-hook. She was just about the right height, and just about the right measurements everywhere, though nobody had actually gone over her with a tape. She moved with a certain

27

supple ease that commanded attention in any gathering. Her hair was a dark and coppery red, with glints of burnished metal, and her eyes were a sort of cross between green and blue, largely depending on her mood. There were little wrinkles of humour around her eyes and at the corners of her mouth, and when she laughed it was from deep down, not from behind the teeth. The old grandfather liked her very much, and seldom missed an opportunity to slip his arm around her waist and give her a big hug, at the same time remarking that he wished he was thirty years younger, though what he would have done under those circumstances he left to Miss Henderson's imagination.

The granny came in with a cheerful smile and word for all, and was about to take her chair and set the ball rolling when her glance, which missed little in her own department, became fixed. But only for a moment. She prized it loose again, and bent it on the butler.

"Two extra places, Beale?"

"Yes, madam." Beale raised the lid of a dish on the electric heater, peered at the contents, and nodded approvingly. "Oatmeal," he murmured, as if to himself. "Splendid for growing children."

"Whom do you expect, Beale?"

"Master John and his friend arrived last night, madam."

"God bless my soul!" the old grandfather exclaimed, looking a lot better pleased than he had before the news broke. "Last night, what? What time was this, Beale?"

"Actually it was a little after one o'clock this morning, sir. Master John had intended to arrive at a more reasonable hour; but, as perhaps you noticed, snow fell very heavily from about ten o'clock onwards, and unfortunately Master John went into a ditch some few miles from here."

"The devil he did! Were they hurt?"

"No, sir. Not in the least. It appears they sat in the car for some time, hoping to get a lift; but there was no traffic whatever on the road. Eventually they decided to walk the rest of the way, carrying their cases. It was either that or remain in the car all night, and they had begun to find it extremely cold. As I said, they got here a little after one o'clock, none the worse, I believe and trust, for their adventure."

"How did they get in?"

"Master John threw snowballs against my window, sir, until I awoke. I came down, let them in, and made them some rum toddy, which seemed to me the most suitable drink for the occasion. And indeed it appeared to do them a great deal of good, which is not really surprising seeing that I put in the better part of half a bottle of rum."

"You couldn't have done better," the old coot admitted, licking his lips. "Unless, of course, you'd put in the whole bottle. It revived them, what?"

"It certainly warmed them up, sir. I must say, considering the ordeal they had been through, they were in very good form when they arrived, laughing and joking and full of fun. When they had finished the toddy, and some sandwiches I made, I showed them to their rooms."

"It was stupid of John to try to drive home in a blizzard," Claude remarked. "He was lucky to get off so lightly, although no doubt the car is a wreck."

"Oh, come!" the old grandfather said mildly. "Couldn't really describe it as a blizzard, what? Anyway, so long as John and his friend weren't injured, there's no great harm done." He turned to the butler. "Tell me, Beale, Master John's friend *is* an American, what?"

"Oh, yes, sir!"

"I'm glad that's settled, anyway. For myself, the way he had it written, I thought it looked more like 'Armenian'."

"She is an American, sir," Beale stated positively. The twinkle in his eye had come a little farther into the open, though not much.

There was a brief silence, broken only by the sound of Derek munching the good food. He had taken advantage of all this yak-yak about John to replenish his stores of fodder, and was now working steadily through a plateful of assorted victuals, scarcely raising his eyes above the level of his fork. Nevertheless his ears were tuned in to the conversation, and he was aware that in some as yet undisclosed manner Beale had created a sensation. He listened more closely, reluctant to miss anything that might be turned to profit in the dark days ahead.

"Did you say 'she', Beale?" the old granny inquired at

length, slow to believe that her youngest son, whom she still regarded as a boy, had smuggled a female into the house. For that was how it looked to her at this stage of the business.

"Yes, madam. Master John's friend, it transpires, is a young lady, and a most attractive young lady, if I may say so."

At this, the old grandfather uttered a hoot of laughter, and in his delight pounded the table with both hands; but in a moment, catching his wife's eye, he broke off as if an unseen hand had taken him by the gullet. Having coughed a few times to clear his throat, he did his best to make it clear by his expression that while he had every sympathy with young people and their problems, this sort of hanky-panky could not be tolerated. But the effort proved too much for him, and the only impression he created was that something had gone down the wrong way, and something big, at that.

"And you put her in Master Alfred's room?" the granny asked in a low voice, staring at the butler with a dawning horror, or something very like it, in her eyes.

"Yes, madam. Those were your instructions."

"And Master John is in his own room?"

"Yes, madam. I understood that was the arrangement you intended."

"Of course," the old granny nodded. "But that, you bone-head, was before I knew John's friend was a young lady! Did it not occur to you, you dodderer!, that there's——"

She could not go on, but sat glowering at Beale, chewing her lower lip and looking as if only the fact that he was on the far side of the table kept her from sticking a fork in him.

"You are thinking of the communicating door, madam?" Beale ventured, raising his eyebrows.

"Yes, I am—and you know it!"

"It occurred to me that that might possibly be a source of embarrassment to the young lady," the butler continued, while a smile slid across his features like a shadow and was gone again. "So I locked the door, madam, and put the key in my pocket."

"Dashed good!" the old grandfather nodded. "Missed your vocation, Beale—should have been a Field-Marshal, or possibly an Admiral. Your tactics were perfect. Where's the key now?"

"Hanging in the pantry, sir."

The old grandfather was about to advise him to keep a close eye on it, because if Master John learned where it was it was liable to disappear under the most suspicious circumstances and with consequences none could foretell, when Master John himself entered briskly, leading his American friend by the hand. Master John was a clean-cut, athletic-looking, open-faced lad, bearing little or no resemblance to his brother Claude—which was, perhaps, explained by the difference in their ages, or something. Moving forward briskly, he kissed his mother; but although she returned his salute, and her eyes misted over to see him again, she spared him scarcely a glance, so eager was she to look over his companion.

And indeed, here was a young woman well worth looking over from any angle; and the old grandfather's eyes, too, were straining at their moorings as he took her in. She was slender and supple, yet rounded in the right places, and so far as the old coot could see from where he stood, nothing had been left out. Her hair was black and her eyes were next door to it. Her skin was a wonderful golden-brown, as if she had just returned from a couple of months in Florida. She was, he thought, one of the most attractive young popsies it had ever been his good fortune to lay eyes on, and his heart warmed towards John. In many ways the lad appeared to be a little left-footed, and indeed there were times when his future was so dim it was a virtual black-out; but as a popsy-picker he showed promise.

"Mums, I want you to meet Prudence Goodrich," John said proudly, almost as if he had designed her himself. He urged the young woman forward. "From Detroit, Michigan," he added, going into a little detail. "Where the cars come from."

"I'm delighted to meet you, my dear!"

"What was the name?" the old grandfather asked, moving around the table to grasp his son by the hand. "Goodrich, what?"

"That's right, Dad. Prudence Goodrich. Prue, meet the old man."

"It's a great pleasure to have you with us," said the grandfather, taking her hand in his and holding it much longer than was really necessary. "From Detroit, what? They say it's a big place."

"Thank you so much!" she murmured. "Yes, I guess it is kind of a big place, at that."

"Goodrich, what? Met a bird called Goodrich once. Believe he came from Detroit, too. Must be lots of Goodriches in a big city like that."

"Flocks of them," Prudence agreed readily. "You couldn't toss a brick over your shoulder on Woodward avenue without beaning a Goodrich—and a very good thing, too, in most cases."

"Prue studies political economy," John announced; and although he had by now grown quite used to the idea, just a little awe lingered in his tone.

"The deuce she does!" said the old grandfather, suitably impressed. "It's a subject I know dashed little about; but any time you feel like talking it over with an expert, my dear, Claude here is your man."

Miss Goodrich was introduced to Claude, who had been looking her over with a slight gleam in his eye since the moment she entered the room—and for Claude, even a slight gleam in the eyeball was something remarkable. But although the rising young politician seemed prepared to address her at some length, John gave him no opportunity, moving her on almost at once to meet Sally Henderson, and finally the children.

Then everyone sat down and tucked into the good food; and if the old grandfather kept darting keen glances at Prue from beneath his brows, and gave the impression of straining his ears to catch every word she said, there was nothing odd about that, for she was a very beautiful and glamorous young woman, apart altogether from her knowledge of political economy.

.   .   .   .   .

It was the old grandfather who, after lunch that day, took Miss Goodrich on a conducted tour of the house.

"It's not often you'll see a house like this, my dear," he told her, taking her arm and giving it a gentle squeeze. "It's a house of character—but what sort of character is another question." He looked at her in surprise as she hesitated. "Don't you want to come?"

"John said something about taking me for a walk."

"Nonsense!" the old coot snorted, increasing the pressure. "It's snowing, my dear—dashed regular blizzard. Can't go walking in a blizzard, what? Might lose yourself, and then we'd have to send out search parties, and dogs with brandy, and so forth. And besides, the conducted tour won't take long. Should get around in an hour or so if we don't loiter. Let John wait. Do him good."

He led her off without further resistance, pointing out various objects of interest on the way, and in no time at all had formed the opinion that seldom or never had he escorted so intelligent and charming a young woman. She hung on his every word, which was something that hadn't happened to him for at least twenty years, and not very often even then, and her questions showed she was taking a genuine interest in his discourse, even when he was inclined to ramble, which was most of the time. And when, from time to time, he slipped in a question about her life back home in Detroit when she wasn't studying political economy, she answered with the greatest possible frankness, so that before the tour was half completed he had learned practically everything about her and her family that he wished to know.

"Now here," he said, leading her into an apartment with tall windows all along one side, "we have the picture gallery." He gestured airily with his unoccupied hand. "Most of these old ducks, my dear, are ancestors, real or reputed, though if you want my honest opinion a few rogues and impostors crept in when nobody was looking. It has happened in the best of families. No foolproof method of keeping them out has yet been devised, nor ever will be so long as the ladies, bless them!, permit their hearts to rule, rather than their heads, We're by no means sure about some of the older portraits. Frankly, they could be anybody, and you can ignore the number plate beneath. But from James on up——"

"And there's the Rembrandt!" Miss Goodrich interrupted in hushed tones.

The old grandfather gave her a keen glance.

"Who told you about the Rembrandt?" he asked.

"John," she answered, pressing forward. "Oh, it's *wonderful*!"

"Not a bad piece of work at all," the proud owner admitted. "Of course, as you can see, we don't claim this bird as an ancestor. He was simply a prosperous merchant of Amsterdam, probably a personal friend of the artist, and the fact that he was painted by Rembrandt is his only claim to fame. Doubtless you will note at a glance that the portrait is in Rembrandt's second manner, the treatment of light and shade being——"

"It's *wonderful*!" Prue whispered again, her eyes shining.

"The treatment of light and shade being much superior to his early style," the old grandfather continued firmly. "And besides, it's worth a great deal of money. How it came into the family makes an interesting little story. It appears——"

"John told me."

"He did?"

"Yes, several times."

"Haw! Well, it can't be helped, I suppose. He always was a garrulous young twerp. You wouldn't care to hear it again?"

"Not just now, thanks."

"Some other time, perhaps. There could be a few nuances John overlooked."

Prue stood staring at the canvas, and the painted face stared right back at her, looking as if one of the eyelids might at any moment flick down in a quick wink. It occurred to the old grandfather that this girl obviously was keen on painting, and knew the genuine stuff when she saw it.

"It looks so *fresh*!" she said in wonder, after this had gone on for some time. "As if he'd finished it yesterday or the day before."

"I had it cleaned a few months ago," the old coot explained. "Took a little time, you know, and cost more, I'm sure, than the old boy himself was paid for it in the first place—if he was paid at all. But it was worth it. He was beginning to look a bit grey in the face, as if he had anaemia, and his clothes were merging with the background. A little longer, and we'd have had nothing but two eyes and a lace collar in the middle of a thundercloud."

"It must be worth a million."

"Oh, no! I've been offered a lot, but never quite that. But whatever it's worth, I wouldn't part with it for anything. I mean to say, it's an heirloom, and all that. Some things money

34

can't buy, what? Dashed few, admittedly; but this happens to be one of them."

The old coot paused briefly to clear his throat, and it could be seen that he was deeply moved.

"Chunk of family history, and so forth, you know," he went on nonchalantly. "Wouldn't dream of selling it. Last thing to go. Glad to say there's no need to look around for the right buyer. What I mean is, we may not be what we once were, but we still have our nose above water."

"But do you keep it here all the time—the picture, I mean?"

"Oh, yes! It's here all the time. Why not?"

"Are you not afraid it might be stolen?"

"Oh, no, no!" said the old grandfather, shaking his head. "Not the sort of boodle burglars go for, you know. No market. I suppose there may be a few odd nuts who'd buy it to lock it up in a back room and gloat on Sundays when everyone else is at church; but there can't be many characters like that around." He scratched his chin. "Or can there? At any rate, there's no future in worrying over what might happen, my dear. What is to be, will be, and you can't get around it no matter how you try. Come along—I've lots more to show you."

. . . . .

It was much later, and dusk was falling, when the old grandfather pushed into the library. A log fire burned in the grate; but that, he knew, was more to keep the books dry— most of them were too dry already—than because anyone was likely to come here to read. Consequently he was surprised, while still fumbling for the switch, to see someone stir in an armchair in front of the fire.

"Who's there?" he snorted. Then he saw. "Sally! It *is* you, what?"

"It is," Miss Henderson admitted, with a sigh. "But often I wish it was someone else."

"My dear!" said the old coot, closing in on her without bothering about the light. "You sound a little low in spirit, if you don't mind my saying so."

"I'm sunk," she agreed. "There isn't even a bubble coming up."

The grandfather settled himself in a chair beside her, and, leaning forward, did his best to peer into her eyes.

"It is at times like this that we should return thanks for our friends," he remarked. "Because what are friends for, if not to share our troubles? Tell me all about it. Why this deep depression?"

"It's really nothing. Nothing definite, I mean. Just one of these complex depressions. It'll pass."

"No doubt. Where's Claude?"

"He felt in need of exercise, so he went out walking with John and Miss Goodrich."

"Haw!" the old coot exclaimed, on a rather hollow note. "The devil he did! Well, why didn't *you* go, too?"

"For one thing, nobody asked me. And for another, he left me a pile of work to do."

"The dirty dog!"

"I got through that, then slunk down here like a wounded beast. I wanted to be alone for a while, to think things out. Somehow, the thought of those three going off together, as free as the air, while I stayed behind to work, opened my eyes to something."

"To what?"

"To my future," Sally said briefly. "It's not very bright. I can look at it without being dazzled. Claude knows where he's going, and sees his way; but no matter how successful he is, I'll still be only his private secretary."

"What would you like to be?"

"There are several things I'd like to be; but private secretary to a pudgy, conceited, egotistical, pie-eyed knucklehead of a third-rate politician isn't one of them."

"Are you referring to Claude?" the old grandfather asked incredulously.

"I'm sorry if I've hurt your feelings as a father; but that's how he rates with me."

"You haven't hurt my feelings. Claude is conceited, pudgy, egotistical, pie-eyed, and a knucklehead. He's also grasping, mean, cowardly, and a coldblooded fish. But you love him."

At this, Miss Henderson's shapely length stiffened from one end to the other.

"I do *not* love him!" she said in low, measured tones—they were measured to a fraction of an inch. "Don't you ever say that to me again, Mr. Oliver Blair Leigh! He's my employer, and he pays me a fair salary because I'm useful to him; but he's a pill and a worm, and if I let myself think about him at all I'd walk out on him here and now."

"Haw!" the old coot muttered, more than a little taken aback. "Then why the devil are you down in the depths because he's gone walking with Miss Goodrich?"

"That's not why I'm down in the depths. I don't give a damn who he goes walking with—and if he never came back that'd be soon enough for me. I'm in the depths because I suddenly caught a glimpse of my future. It was like someone sneaking up behind me and hitting me with a stuffed sock. I saw myself staying on as his secretary year after year, doing the same old routine stuff over and over again, with nothing to break the monotony and nothing to look back on, until eventually he became a Cabinet Minister because he'd worn everyone down to the bone. Then he'd cast me off like an old boot. I don't want that to be my life."

"Haw!" the old grandfather said again, seeking words of comfort, and finding none. The picture she had drawn was altogether too true for his liking. "But that's nonsense! You know very well some fine, handsome, worthy young man is going to throw himself at your feet and beg you to marry him—but before you commit yourself, my dear, make sure to find out how he's fixed financially. Having a little money makes it so much easier to remain in love, while on the other hand, if you do decide to get rid of him, he'll be in a position to pay the alimony."

"No young man is going to throw himself at my feet," Sally murmured, staring into the fire. "Certainly no wealthy young man. I'm only a working girl. I think I'll emigrate to America or somewhere. Maybe Canada."

"Canada?"

"They say it's a land of opportunity."

"That's where Hugh went."

"Who?"

"Hugh Massey. My nephew. Don't you remember—he was here three or four years ago, the first time you came with Claude."

37

"Oh, yes! Yes, I remember now, of course. He went to Canada?"

"That's right. He'd heard it was a land of opportunity, too."

"I hope he found some?"

"I don't know," the old grandfather admitted. "I had a few letters from him the first year; then they stopped coming. Must be two years since I heard from him—dirty young dog!"

"Maybe something happened to him."

"Always that possibility. Lots of things could happen to a feller in a place like Canada. Last time I heard from him he was in Alberta, and had some idea of moving on into British Columbia. So I looked up British Columbia in the encyclopedia, and it's one of these places with lots of high mountains and trackless forests and ferocious wild beasts and roaring torrents, so almost anything you care to imagine could have happened to him."

"What was he doing?"

"Some sort of prospecting, I believe," the old coot said vaguely. "Possibly panning for gold. He didn't go into detail. Maybe the wolves got him. My dear, you couldn't possibly go to a place like that!"

"Why not? I know how to deal with wolves, probably better than he did."

CHAPTER FOUR

THE shades of night had fallen even faster than usual, and but for the snow on the ground everything would have been as black as a shark's heart, when the young man came up the avenue. There was little of him visible beyond a vague outline and two suitcases; but that he was young was evident from the way he strode forward through the snow, as if he scarcely noticed the stuff. He stamped up the steps to the hall door, put down one case, and rang the bell. While awaiting a response, he occupied himself in removing some snow that had been doing its best to get inside his collar and slip down his spine.

The old butler opened the door, and peered uncertainly at

him, for the light was none too good and Beale needed spectacles though he was too proud to admit it. Then his face cracked open in a smile, and he uttered what would, but for a bothersome cold in the chest, have been a ringing cry of welcome.

"Master Hugh!" he croaked. "Is it indeed you?"

"It is," the new arrival admitted. "How are you, Beale? To my eye, you don't look a day older—or no more than a day, at any rate."

"I'm all the better for seeing you, sir," Beale replied courteously, reaching out for a case. "But do come in and warm yourself! Did you have to walk from the station?"

"I did," Mr. Massey replied. "They told me I'd never get here; but I made it. The rumour went around that the road was impassable. They've got an idea it's been snowing around here, I don't know why. Anyway, the walk warmed my feet— and believe me, Beale, after three hours in that train they needed warming."

By this time he was standing, steaming slightly, in front of the log fire in the hall. He was a tall and well-built young man with a keen eye and a look of the great outdoors; and it occurred to the old butler that seldom had he seen a character who with so little effort gave the impression of being ready, and even eager, to wrestle grizzly bears for the hell of it.

"Your uncle will be delighted to see you, sir. He mentioned you only a few days ago."

"What did he say?"

"He said you were a dirty young dog, and you hadn't written him for at least two years."

"It seems longer," Mr. Massey admitted. "How is he? Full of zest, what? Taking five-barred gates in his stride? What he should do is go out and climb a couple of mountains every day. Nothing like it for keeping fit."

"His health remains sound, sir."

"And Aunt Martha? Still the iron hand in the iron glove, but with a heart of gold behind it all?"

"There has been no significant change, sir," Beale replied with a slight smile. "If you will come with me——"

"No, no! Not yet. Brief me first. Is there a house-party in full swing?"

"Oh, no, sir! Nothing of the kind. Just a few of the family down for Christmas, as is the old family custom."

"I was afraid of that. Don't try to break it gently, Beale—let me know the worst."

"Master Claude is here, sir, and Master John. But if you insist on knowing the worst, it is that Master Alfred's children have been wished on us for the next three weeks."

"Derek and Alison, what? Nothing new has been added since I was last around these parts?"

"No, sir. I am very glad to say there are no infants on the premises."

"I seem to recall that Derek, even at a tender age, was a pretty revolting type."

"Quite so, sir. But only a pale shadow of what he is now."

"A worm-pill, what?"

"Not a really lovable child, sir."

"And the little sister? She was only seven or so when I saw her last."

"Unless I am greatly mistaken, sir, an even more dangerous character than Master Derek. Deeper, and a great deal more subtle, if you see what I mean? Admittedly I have nothing definite against the young lady; but my instinct, developed and honed to a razor edge over a number of years, warns me to be constantly on guard. In her I seem to sense a cold, calculating and thoroughly anti-social outlook; and it strikes me as being deeply significant, sir, that even Master Derek himself is afraid of her."

"The hell he is!"

"Yes, sir. I have been watching them closely, and that is the conclusion I have reached. She has some hold on him; but exactly what it is I have yet to discover."

"They're the apple of the granny's eye, huh?"

"I believe she has some slight appreciation of Master Derek's shortcomings, sir; but Miss Alison she regards as a little angel lacking only wings and a well-fitting halo."

"I'll keep an eye on them. Nobody else in the party?"

"Master John brought a friend along, sir, a Miss Prudence Goodrich, of Detroit, Michigan, in the United States of America."

"I've heard of it." Mr. Massey raised an eyebrow at the old butler. "Do I catch a slight fragrance of orange-blossom, Beale, or is this something else again?"

"Miss Goodrich is a beautiful and charming young lady, sir," the butler replied diplomatically. "She is a student at Oxford, where she studies political economy. It seems her father is an immensely wealthy person who manufactures motor-cars—a million a day, or something of that nature. Moreover, she is an only child, which by no means detracts from her charms. Master John may not be a second Einstein at his studies; but in my opinion he has what it takes to carve out a successful career, if only he can hold on to it."

"And that's all?"

"I beg your pardon, sir?"

"There's nobody else gorging on the fatted calf?"

"Only Master Claude's private secretary, sir."

"Of course," Mr. Massey said casually. "Never travels without one or two, does he? Last time I was here, he had a young lady with as fetching a head of red hair as it has ever been my good fortune to lay eye on."

"Quite so, sir. Miss Sally Henderson."

"That's right—Sally Henderson. Struck me as the sort of person who'd get married off to some discerning and lucky citizen without the slightest trouble."

"A most charming young lady, sir," Beale agreed. "A disposition of sunshine and laughter, if I may say so."

"You may put it to music if you wish." Mr. Massey produced a cigar-case and selected a smoke. "No doubt she's married long ago," he remarked, without even glancing at the old butler.

"Oh, no, sir!" Beale assured him. "She is still Master Claude's secretary."

"What a glutton for punishment!" Mr. Massey bit the end off his cigar, and lit up. "What you're trying to tell me, Beale, is that Miss Henderson is among those present?"

"Yes, sir. She is."

While coming out with this bald statement, the old butler took the liberty of watching closely for any reaction from Mr. Massey. He was disappointed. The news seemed to mean little or nothing to the returned wanderer, whose clean-cut features expressed only a polite interest. Suddenly he turned, and met Beale's glance.

"Then you can fit me in, what? I don't have to hike back to the village and book a room at the pub?"

"Heaven forfend, sir!" the old butler said in tones of horror. "Your room is vacant, and I shall see that the bed is made up at once. I'll have the fire lit, too, sir, to warm the room. You would, perhaps, like a little brandy left up?"

"Thank you. Not too little." Mr. Massey picked up his cases. "I'll go up now and get myself brushed off. I look like something the robins found in the woods and covered with leaves."

"Very good, sir. I'll bring the brandy up at once."

"You couldn't do better," Mr. Massey said approvingly. "I feel the need of a little something to take the chill out of my old bones. If you could see the marrow, Beale, you'd think you were looking at a yard of sugarstick."

.   .   .   .   .

Dinner, Mr. Massey seemed to recall, was laid on at seven-thirty, when the family pinned their whiskers back and let themselves go on the calories. He relaxed in his room, smoking a cigar and sipping a brandy and soda, then stood up, straightened his tie, and actually had his hand on the door-knob when there smote his ear a really high-class shriek. This was a yell that made him think of women and children being scalped in the old-fashioned manner; and it seemed obvious that mayhem of a very definite type was in progress just around the corner. Pausing only to button his jacket and grip his cigar more firmly between his teeth, he pressed on into the corridor.

As he did so, he caught a low, drumming sound, as of tribal tom-toms in the distant jungle. This enabled him to locate the scene of the disturbance, a bedroom at no great distance from his own. Moving forward rapidly, he threw open the door, and then for some moments stood at pause, drinking it all in.

On the rug beside the bed lay one of the housemaids, a young and comely blonde named Phyllis. She lay on her back, her framework straight and rigid; while her forearms, beating up and down almost too fast for the eye to follow, produced the drumming sound already noted. Her eyes were open, staring blankly at the ceiling, and so was her mouth. It was plain to Mr. Massey that for some reason best known to herself she was having a fit or something very like it; nor did this surprise him, for he had often heard that the Scumton people were much addicted to that sort of thing, and were, in fact, noted for it the length and breadth of the county.

He pushed on into the room, and knelt beside Phyllis, who was now breathing on a hoarse and laboured note and showing the whites of her eyes. This was a new experience for him; but he felt that the sooner the young woman was roused from this trance she was in, and restored to normal, the better it would be for all concerned. He was wondering if he should look around for a bucket of water, and try the popular shock treatment, when someone spoke from the open doorway.

"Okay, brother! Just stand up slowly, raise the arms above the head, and no funny business."

Mr. Massey took it that this development, which at the moment had him baffled, relieved him of his obligations to the popsy on the floor. He rose briskly, and turned, but without raising his arms above his head. To his way of thinking, that sort of stuff was out of place in Scumton Hall.

He found himself confronted by a young woman whom he at once identified as Miss Prudence Goodrich, of Detroit, Michigan, U.S.A.; and it occurred to him that Beale, in calling her beautiful and charming, had spoken the simple truth. She was indeed an unusually glamorous young woman, lovely in face and figure and with something in her eye. She also had something in her right hand, which she held steady against her hip. It was a small, compact automatic pistol, and it was trained unwaveringly on the Massey stomach.

"Up with them, comrade!" she said, watching him closely. "You know—like they do on television."

"This isn't television," Mr. Massey pointed out reasonably. "This is Scumton Hall. You'll oblige me by pointing that field-piece somewhere else. I get all strung up when people point guns at me."

It was at this juncture, when the situation looked like developing into an impasse, that Derek arrived. He shouldered his way past Miss Goodrich in a manner that made it plain this was his room, spared Mr. Massey an inscrutable glance, then turned his attention to the girl on the floor. She had by now relaxed a little, and was no longer beating the rug with her fists; and to Mr. Massey it seemed that the worst was over. Any moment now she would heave a long sigh, sit up, and ask where she was.

"What's going on here?" Derek demanded. He prodded Phyllis in the ribs with the toe of one shoe. "What's wrong with this dame?" His cold glance moved to the gun, then to Miss Goodrich's face. "You give her the heat, huh?"

"I guess this guy knocked her out," Prudence explained, keeping a sharp eye on Mr. Massey. "He must have come in through the window."

"I doubt it," said Derek. "He's my cousin."

"He's your cousin?"

"Yep. This here's cousin Hugh Massey. Is that a real gun you've got, huh? Were you going to plug him if I hadn't come along, huh? Huh?"

"I'm so sorry!" Prudence said. "I thought you were a second-storey man. "It didn't occur to me you were one of the family."

"It's not a thing I like to dwell on too much myself," Mr. Massey admitted, watching her slip the gun into her handbag. "Don't you think we should do something about this girl? So far as I can judge, she's in the throes of some sort of fit."

"I'm not too good on fits. What started her off?"

"Your guess is as good as mine, or maybe better. I heard a yell, and rushed in; and there she was, beating the floor like a drum."

"I've rung the bell," Derek announced, not without a slight curl of the lip. "Fit or no fit, I don't want her lying around my room all night."

A moment later, Beale arrived. He took a good look at Phyllis, then turned to Mr. Massey, raising his eyebrows in polite inquiry.

"She had a fit, or something," Mr. Massey explained.

"Indeed, sir? That is very strange."

"Is it? I understood the people around here had fits practically all the time."

44

"Some of them, sir," Beale agreed. "It is nothing unusual to see at least one victim stretched in the middle of the village street, as stiff as a poker—and if anyone runs to their assistance, you can be sure he is a stranger. But this young person is not of that class. She is a superior young person, sir, and in the three years she has been with us I have never before known her to behave like this."

"The heck with all that!" Derek said coldly. "Get her the hell out of here before she takes root."

At that moment the girl sat up, and, with Beale helping her on one side and Mr. Massey on the other, rose shakily to her feet. But to the butler's searching questions her only reply was a moan; and it was clear from the way her eyes rolled in their sockets that she was by no means back to normal. Expressing the belief that a cup of tea would put her right, Beale led her away, taking full advantage of this opportunity to put his arm around her waist.

Leaving Derek in his room, Miss Goodrich and Mr. Massey went downstairs together.

The old grandfather was already in the drawing-room, together with John and Claude. At sight of Mr. Massey his eyes stood out in wonder, and he uttered a cry of pleasure which seemed to come straight from the heart, though actually it may have had to make a detour here and there.

"*Hugh!*" he hooted, bounding forward. "My dear boy! Where on earth have you sprung from?" He did his best to reduce the nephew's fingerbones to a fine grit. "Why the devil didn't you let us know you were coming?"

"One of these sudden decisions," Mr. Massey explained nonchalantly. "Came to me like a flash. You're looking splendid, Nunk." He turned to Claude, who looked politely interested but by no means overjoyed. "And so are you, Claude. How you've grown!—especially around the middle. You're as sleek as a bear all ready to hole up for the winter."

"There's no need to be offensive about it," Claude replied coldly. "I'm a very busy man. I have no time to think about my figure."

"And why should you, when there are so many better figures to think about?" Mr. Massey agreed. "No offence meant, my boy. We can't all spend our time running up and down mountains with an eighty-pound pack on our back."

"Is that what you've been doing?" the old grandfather asked eagerly. "Sounds like dashed hard work to me. Tell me, Hugh, what did you hope to gain by it? You weren't doing it simply to keep your weight down, what?"

"A spot of prospecting," Mr. Massey explained casually. "Hoping to strike it rich, you know."

He would have said more, but at that moment Sally appeared in the doorway, and his vocal cords tied themselves in knots and splices. He stood staring at her. It seemed to him that something new had been added; and whatever it was, he approved of it.

She saw him, and for a moment stood quite still. Then she came forward, her eyes shining.

"Well, well, if it isn't old Dan'l Boone himself, back from the bear-hunt!" she greeted him, giving him her hand. "And it was only a few days ago we agreed the wolves had got you. I should have known you were safe. Wolf doesn't eat wolf."

"Not this wolf," Mr. Massey agreed. "Sally, you're as balm to the eye! Still at the old grind, what?"

"No change," she nodded. "It's nice to see you again."

Then the old grandmother joined the scrum, and a few moments later Beale made the welcome announcement that dinner was served.

Derek was the last to show up. This was so unusual that the old grandfather bent on him a glance designed to lay bare his soul like a cadaver on a dissection table; but, perhaps because there was nothing there, drew a blank. It occurred to him that the lad looked a little flustered and ill at ease, and that it might be wise to probe into the matter later on. Just now, however, he had to remember he was host.

.   .   .   .   .

Beale, who despite appearances had something of the bloodhound in him, ran his quarry to earth in the library. Mr. Massey had settled a log or two on the glowing embers, and flames were already licking up the chimney—and Mr.

46

Massey felt that if flames had been licking up the old butler's shanks that would have been no more than justice.

"Wouldn't you imagine," he remarked to Sally, who sat beside him on the couch, "that by the time a man reached the age of ninety-seven he'd have developed at least a little tact? But no! They go through life like wooden images—especially from the neck up."

"I beg your pardon, sir!" Beale said courteously, smiling slightly as he pressed on towards the fireplace. "I've been looking for you since dinner. There is something I think you should know."

"And there's something I think *you* should know—but we'll go into that later. What's on your mind, old horse?"

"It's about Phyllis, sir."

"Ah!" Sally murmured. "The other woman!"

"Make yourself clear, Beale!" Mr. Massey urged. "Who is this mysterious Phyllis?"

"The young person you found in Master Derek's room, sir."

"He doesn't mean what you think he means," Mr. Massey assured Sally. "This was just before dinner; and Derek wasn't there, anyway." He turned back to the old butler, who was waiting patiently. "Well, old horse, what about her? I hope she's better, what? Last glimpse I caught of her, as she staggered off with your arm around her waist like a rope around a bollard, she looked like a job for a good bone-setter."

"She is quite herself again, sir, apart from being so nervous that she leaps a foot into the air at the slightest sound," Beale replied. "In fact, I had the greatest difficulty in persuading her not to leave the house at once. She is, I understand, betrothed to an estimable and handsome young fellow; and the view she takes is that, apart altogether from her own wishes in the matter, she has no right to risk her life, which in the eyes of her betrothed is more valuable than rubies and pearls, by remaining under this roof one second longer than is essential. However, I took the liberty of giving her a little something to soothe her nerves, and before long she seemed more reconciled, and was, indeed, inclined to sing. Nevertheless she starts at sounds, and is constantly peering into corners."

"What does she expect to see?"

47

"Snakes, sir."

"Snakes, what?"

"Exactly, sir."

"Seems to be the imaginative type," Mr. Massey commented tolerantly. "She should be writing science fiction, that's what."

"Does she often see snakes?" Sally asked curiously. "Or is she only on the threshold of her career? I always thought her a very nice girl, though she never told me she was engaged."

"She is not in the habit of seeing snakes," Beale stated, the moment he got a chance. "She never mentioned snakes, so far as I am aware, until this evening. Now, however, she would appear to have a snake complex."

"What was the cause of her downfall?" Mr. Massey inquired. "Or perhaps only a psychiatrist could discover that, after an hour or two with her on a couch. May have been something that happened before she was born."

"No, sir. It was something that happened this evening. As perhaps you are not aware, Master Derek and Miss Alison retire at nine o'clock, and it is Phyllis's duty to put a hot-water bottle in their beds some time before dinner. She placed Miss Alison's bottle in position this evening, then went to Master Derek's room and thrust the bottle down between the sheets. As she did so, she felt something cold touch her hand. Thinking it was something Master Derek had left in the bed, she turned back the clothes. And what did she see?"

"Don't tell!" Mr. Massey begged. "Let me guess. A snake, what?"

"Exactly, sir. A large snake."

"How large?"

"It struck her as being extremely large, sir. Naturally, she screamed."

"What's natural about it? I've seen hundreds of snakes and I've never screamed once."

"Were they in your bed, sir?"

"No—and they weren't in hers, either."

"Don't get it more involved than it is," Sally begged. "And I don't blame her a bit for screaming. What did she do then, Beale?"

"The snake bit her, miss, and she screamed again. Then she pulled the bedclothes up, and fainted."

"It bit her?"

"So she says, sir. But I could find no mark on her arm."

"Maybe it bit her in the leg."

"No, sir. It is scarcely likely that she would push the bottle into position with her foot."

"I didn't think of that," Mr. Massey admitted. He glanced at his watch. "It's a quarter to ten. Can we take it that Derek is stiff and stark by now, punctured all over?"

"Oh, no, sir! On hearing Phyllis's story, my first thought was for Master Derek."

"I'll bet it was!" Mr. Massey agreed. "You hoped the snake would bite him, and bite him good, huh?"

"It was almost nine o'clock," Beale continued, evading the question. "There was not a moment to spare. I dashed up to Master Derek's room. He was already there. He inquired, in a very coarse manner, what I wanted. I informed him that I had reason to believe there was a snake in his bed. He replied, with a sneer, that I must have been drinking too much of his grandfather's brandy, and that if I kept it up I'd soon be seeing sea-serpents. Then, before I could stop him, he pulled back the bedclothes, and requested me to point out the snake —which he qualified by a most unsuitable adjective—to him."

"And you did?"

"No, sir. There was no snake. All I could see was the hot-water bottle."

"You're sure it *was* a hot-water bottle, and not some exotic species of snake?"

"Quite sure, sir."

"Then Phyllis imagined the whole thing?"

"Either that, sir, or the reptile had made its escape."

"Snakes don't move around in this sort of weather," Mr. Massey pointed out. "They're intelligent and sensible creatures, and highly sensitive to cold. When they're cold, they go torpid all over."

"So do I, sir," the old butler admitted, with a sigh.

"Perhaps; but you can take something for it. If there was a snake in Derek's bed, then it was Derek's snake."

"A pet snake, sir?" Beale said dubiously. "White mice,

yes. Rats, undoubtedly. Hamsters, by all means. But snakes, no."

"More than likely he's training it to balance balls on its nose," Mr. Massey added. "Probably sees himself making a million as the proprietor and manager of the only trained snake in captivity. He might have something there, at that."

"Then what would you advise me to do, sir?"

"You feel an urge to do something about it?"

"I'm afraid, if there is a snake, it may be poisonous, sir."

"No, no!" Mr. Massey said confidently. "Derek may not be one of our brighter intellects; but he knows better than to monkey around with a poisonous snake. If he has a snake— and personally I'm inclined to think Phyllis imagined the whole thing—it's a harmless type, and probably a most gentle and affectionate creature ready and eager to respond to a little kindness. So if you happen to meet with it on your rounds, Beale, don't be in too much of a hurry to beat it out flat. Tell yourself that there, but for an accident of birth, goes George Henry Beale—and the sooner he goes out of this room, the better I'll be pleased."

CHAPTER FIVE

IT SEEMED to John that he was being shadowed. At breakfast he caught Derek's gaze on him more than once, brooding, inscrutable, and vaguely disturbing, reminiscent of some medieval poisoner quietly waiting for the first spasm of pain to contort his victim's features. After breakfast the lad disappeared for a while; but now he was back again like a bad smell, mooning around with his hands in his pockets, whistling tunelessly, lifting small articles off tables and putting them down again, all without a word, and, so far as John could see, without a glance in his direction. It was slightly unnerving.

Only when Prudence went off with the old grandfather to look at his stamp collection, leaving John alone, did Derek close in on one flank.

"Hey!" he said, by way of opening the conversation.

"Hey!" John replied guardedly, determined to give nothing away.

50

"You know what?"

"What?"

"What you want is a key."

"A key?" said John, groping for the thread. "Pardon me if I seem a little dull, my boy; but what the hell are you yammering about?"

"Save you a lot of dodging in and out of doors," Derek explained patiently. "Everything would be so much more convenient if you had a key."

John took in a deep breath, and went purple in the face. Meanwhile, for good measure, his eyes became a trifle bloodshot and his fingers worked convulsively. Derek, a keen student of the drama, realized at once that his uncle, in the grip of some violent emotion, was fighting tooth and claw for self-control. Moreover, it looked like being a losing battle. John took a quick step forward and dropped a hand on the lad's shoulder. The fingers bit in like tiger's teeth.

"What do you mean, 'dodging in and out of doors'?" he growled. "Make yourself clear, polecat, before I take you in my two hands and stuff you up the chimney!"

Although it seemed that mayhem could be averted only by a miracle, and he had no great faith in miracles, Derek's calm remained unshaken. Indeed, his upper lip curled just perceptibly in a sneer, and in some subtle manner he conveyed the impression that he might at any moment turn his head and spit on the floor.

"You know what I mean," he said, without raising his voice. "When I talk about dodging in and out of doors, dodging in and out of doors is what I mean—and dodging in and out of doors is what you were up to, brother, about twelve o'clock last night. Yeah. You dodged out of your own door and into——"

"*Quiet!*" John snarled, his fingers biting to the bone. He advanced his face to within a few inches of Derek's impassive features, and breathed heavily all over them. "How would you like to be skinned alive, like an eel for the pot?"

Derek made no reply. Possibly he was wondering how it felt to be skinned alive; but it was much more likely that he considered the question beneath his notice.

"Because that's what will happen if you breathe a word to

51

anyone," John continued, advancing his face until their noses almost rubbed. "Make a note of that, Derek my boy! I'll skin you alive a bit at a time, and rub salt in—and what's more, I'll take a fiendish pleasure in the job. There must be a bucket of Red Indian blood in me somewhere."

"It doesn't mean a toot to me what doors you duck out of or into," the lad stated coldly, ignoring these veiled threats. "I'm broadminded. I'm tolerant. I take the modern view. But Granny's a bit old-fashioned in ways, and she wouldn't like it. That's why I say you ought to get a key, and make things easy for yourself."

John thought this over for a few moments; and it was obvious, from the way his grip relaxed, that he appreciated the wisdom of the suggestion. Plainly he had begun to look at the problem from another angle; but plainly, also, it hurt him to talk the matter over, as man to man, with his nephew.

"There always was a key," he remarked on a very distant note. "It was left in the lock. It's not there now."

"No," Derek agreed. "But it hasn't been melted down, either."

John moved off a pace or two in order to get a better look at him. For years past he had suspected that in Derek the family had produced someone worthy of apprenticeship to Nana Sahib or Burke the bodysnatcher. Now he knew he had, if anything, underrated the youth's promise. Derek would go far—probably with the police on his trail every foot of the way.

"You know where it is?" he asked in a low voice, having first glanced around to make sure nobody was listening in with an ear-trumpet.

"There's very little goes on around here that I don't know," Derek replied, not boastfully, but on a note of sober confidence. "I keep in touch."

"Never mind the song of praise! Have *you* got it?"

"No. But I know where it is."

"Where is it?"

Derek's only reply to this was a slight elevation of the eyebrows, accompanied by a scornful glance. He seemed to feel that no more was necessary; and John, on thinking it over, was inclined to agree.

"Would it be possible to get it?"

"All things are possible with Allah," Derek pointed out. "And I come a close second. Say the word, and the key is as good as in your hand."

"Would it be missed?"

"I'll hang another very similar in its place."

John nodded approvingly. He was not surprised that the lad had thought of everything. All the best gangsters, he reflected, were born that way.

"How much?" he inquired briefly, realizing that the time to get down to figures had now come.

"A fiver."

"*What?*"

"A fiver."

"Are you out of your mind? Where the hell do you think I'd get a fiver?"

"I don't give a damn where you get it," Derek admitted frankly. "It's all one to me if you cut a throat for it, brother. That's my price. A fiver or nothing. Only thing is, if you decide not to deal, someone is sure to hear of what I saw last night."

"What were you doing out of bed at that hour?" John asked, after a rather lengthy pause. (It had taken him some little time to overcome the urge to beat his nephew unconscious with the piano-stool.)

"I move around," Derek replied nonchalantly. "It's the leopard in me. Comes the night, I get restless. I have to get up and prowl. I can slink along without making a sound. How about that fiver? Wouldn't do for anyone to see you slipping it to me—especially that little pig-powder, Alison."

"I can read your future without any crystal ball," John said sourly. "There's a rope mixed up in it." He drew a fiver from his wallet and handed it over. "When do I get the key?"

"Soon," Derek assured him, pocketing the note without any perceptible change of expression. "Maybe this evening. Certainly tomorrow. I'm a man of my word. Meanwhile, my lips are sealed."

"They'd better be!" John growled. "If *you* don't seal them, *I* will!"

Derek pretended not to hear that. Turning, hands in

pockets, he moved off; and as he went, he whistled tunelessly to himself, presumably through his nose.

. . . .

Mr. Claude Blair Leigh, the rising (he hoped) young politician, had more than once been described by his own father, and in his hearing, as an anaemic codfish. Actually any resemblance he bore to a codfish was purely superficial, and he was far from being anaemic. The charge rested more on the fact that, at an age when all properly constituted males began to feel that the ideal place to be was in the presence of a glamorous young female, preferably with nobody else around, Claude was content to pass the day with his copy of *Hansard*, which, it seemed, he found more alluring than any popsy.

Naturally, this was a source of some concern to his parents, who longed to see him married and settled down, with little ones clustering around his knees. Nothing, however, appeared to be further from his thoughts. Beautiful girls were led before him at garden parties, at tea parties, at dinner parties (he saw it as part of his political training to mix with the people on their own ground); but though he was unfailingly polite, as befitted a prospective candidate who might some day solicit their votes, his eye remained cold, his blood-pressure continued at normal or rather less, and his heart beat on without a flutter. He was unstirred. He saw them, not as seductive creatures, the future wives and mothers of the race, but as so many electors who might, unless he made a favourable impression, turn to the opposition candidate on polling day.

To his father, he confided his views. It was, he explained, all very well for the average young man to let himself be guided by his heart when it came to the question of choosing a wife. For the rising young politician, however, that would not do. All hope of romance could be abandoned. The head must rule the heart. The young woman should be selected, not for her looks, not for her charm, not because his heart went bump-bump! at sight of her for this reason or that, but for her family connections and her wealth. Any young woman with first-rate family connections was good. A young woman with first-rate connections and lots of money was better. Best of all was a young woman with beauty and charm, first-rate connections, lots of money, and a title. These last, however, were scarce.

It must be admitted that Claude had lived up to this abominable creed despite all temptations—which was why his old man wrote him off as a coldblooded codfish. The lad had hitched his wagon to a star, and no young woman without the proper qualifications, however seductive she might be, was going to uncouple the traces.

Or so it seemed, until Miss Prudence Goodrich came up over his horizon, a new star of the first magnitude and with some strange fascination of her own.

The fact of the matter was that the moment Claude's cold and calculating glance came to rest on the person of Miss Goodrich, it lost much of its coldness, and something that might almost have been a sparkle crept into the old eyeballs. Something exploded within him like a hand-grenade, not even fizzing for a moment to give him warning. Emotions Claude had never previously experienced bubbled up in him like boiling milk, and it was as much as he could do to refrain from uttering a wolf-howl there and then. For him this beautiful girl, one of America's finest products, had something all the others lacked, and had it in gobs. Whatever it was, it reached out to him and stirred him to the depths; and when he learned that she was an only child, and that her father owned automobile factories and oil-wells and similar real estate, he became so stuffed with emotion he almost burst.

The only outward and visible sign of all this, however, was a slight gleam deep down in the eye. The future Cabinet Minister had himself well under control. And besides, there was the awkward fact that Miss Goodrich was John's guest, and John seemed to consider he had some claim on her company. They might even be secretly betrothed, or something of that nature. This possibility failed to give Claude pause. He had little regard for his young brother, whom he had long since written off as a good-for-nothing flibbertigibbet who would almost certainly come to a bad end and drag the family name in the gutter. It could well be, he reasoned, that John was suffering from an attack of calf-love; for, although he was twenty-six, in Claude's opinion his mental development had ground to a halt at about the age of twelve. John would not stand in the way—or if he did, he would be run down as by a ten-ton truck.

All of which explains why Prue, having been shown over the old grandfather's stamp collection, and making her escape with the appropriate expressions of gratitude and admiration, found herself ambushed by Claude. He charged out from cover like a wounded buffalo, and in a moment had her firmly by the arm.

"My dear Miss Goodrich!" he exclaimed in his most unctuous tone—and he could be as unctuous as anything when he tried, and sometimes when he wasn't trying at all. "Or may I call you Prue?"

"Sure!" the beautiful young woman replied agreeably, looking him over with her left eyebrow just a fraction higher than the other. "The hell with formality!"

This reply took Claude somewhat aback, and he spent a moment or two wondering how it would go down with a bunch of ambassadors and their wives. But in no time at all he had recovered from the shock. A course of patient and sympathetic tuition would cure her of such crudities, he reflected.

"I am sure the dear old man bored you to distraction," he remarked ponderously, massaging her arm by way of showing his sympathy. "Or are you interested in stamps?"

"Now and then I find myself thinking about other things," Prue admitted frankly, with a smile that shook Claude to his foundations. "I'm afraid I don't know a whole lot about stamps. But I do adore your pictures."

This abrupt switch failed to catch Claude on the wrong foot. No man who hoped to address public meetings, where a little heckling might confidently be anticipated, not to mention the odd overripe tomato, could be so lightly thrown off balance.

"Ah, yes!" he nodded. "Our pictures, yes. We have a few that are admitted to be not too bad. The Kneller, for instance; a couple of small Morlands; a Constable; and of course the Rembrandt. I think I may say, without fear of contradiction, the Rembrandt is the star of our humble collection. Would you care to look them over again?"

"I'd just love it."

Claude was only too happy to oblige, since the gallery was almost certain to be deserted at this or any other hour; and without a moment's delay—he was afraid John might show up—he set off. Actually he took little or no interest in art, and what he knew about it was largely inaccurate; but he was quietly confident that his knowledge was far superior to his companion's, and he was ready to propound at practically unlimited length without, as he would have put it himself, fear of contradiction.

He was still in good voice when they came to the Rembrandt. Before this magnificent work of art he stood well back, preparing to give of his best; but Prue gently squeezed his arm.

"No, please!" she said softly. "I just want to drink it in."

Claude was silent. He did not understand this urge to drink it in. For himself, he could see nothing remarkable in the painting, and privately he was of the opinion that Rembrandt at his best was just another pot-boiler; but if Prue wished to soak it in through the pores he was happy to keep her company while she did so. Tearing his glance away from the picture, he bent it on her profile, and his heart expanded in his breast as if blown up with a bicycle pump. The wonder of it all got in among him. This young woman had no connections whatever that were likely to help him in his career, and indeed seemed likely to need much grooming before she could take her place beside him at State receptions and so forth; yet so far as he could judge he was falling in love with her without even putting up a fight. Never again could he be accused of being a coldblooded codfish. Right now his blood was simmering gently in the old pipe-line, and the indications were that under really favourable conditions it would come to the boil.

"It's so *fresh*!" Prue murmured. "As if he'd painted it yesterday."

"I understand my father had it cleaned not long ago," Claude explained. "Quite regularly he sends it to London, and it comes back looking like new."

"But is that necessary?"

"He seems to think it is. He says there's something in the air here that dulls the finish, and only periodic cleaning can keep it looking its best."

"He's so proud of it!"

"Yes, yes. Of course, it has been in the family a long time. One of our most valuable possessions, and so forth. If the house were on fire, I really believe my father's first thought would be to preserve this painting, while his wife and children saved themselves."

Claude laughed heartily to show that this was not to be taken seriously, and would have moved on; but Prue hung back.

"Of course, it must be worth a pile," she said.

"It's not so much the cash value that weighs with him, my dear Prue. He could have sold it a hundred times over had he wished. He tells me wealthy collectors have gone on their knees to him, waving blank cheques in his face, and his only answer to their prayers was a scornful smile. He wouldn't part with that painting for a million pounds."

"Not for a whole million?"

"That was merely a figure of speech," Claude explained kindly. "I'm sure he has never been offered a million, and I'm equally sure he never will be. The point is, he wouldn't sell. He regards this canvas as part of the history of our house—a history, I might add, that goes back to the time of Edward the Confessor."

"And probably even farther, if only you could trace it," Prue added innocently. "That was before the Conquest, wasn't it?"

"Yes; that was before the Conquest."

"You must have got a knock when William came along, huh?"

"We got quite a knock," Claude agreed. "But we survived, we survived. We bore up under adversity in the good old Anglo-Saxon fashion. And after a while we fought back with tooth and claw. Once again we were on the way up."

"My dad always says you can't keep a good man down," Prue remarked. "*We* got a knock, too, from a guy called Burgoyne. Of course that's not going back as far as Edward the Confessor; but it's pretty far back for us. Detroit was only a fort then. Now look at it!"

"I'd like to, very much. I've never been to America."

Claude cleared his throat. "Your father is in business in Detroit, what?"

"Most of the time," Prue nodded. "He makes cars. Three or four thousand a day—I forget. Now and then he skips off to Philadelphia. He has a steel-mill there. Sometimes he has to take off for Texas, too."

"What has he got in Texas?"

"Couple of oil-wells and a refinery," Prue added casually. "Oh, yes—and a cattle ranch. Then there's a pulp-mill in Oregon. He keeps on the jump."

All this warmed Claude's heart. He approved of multi-millionaire fathers-in-law who kept on the jump. That, as he saw it, was the function of fathers-in-law. There was much to be said for a father-in-law with political influence; but a father-in-law with motor factories and oil-wells and steel-mills had something to recommend him too—more especially when he had only one child to inherit all this heavy industry.

"I, too, believe in keeping on the jump," he said. "As you may have gathered, I have chosen politics as my career. I am to be the Tory candidate in the next by-election, should one come before the General Election." He gestured airily with one hand. "After that, who knows?"

"Who knows what?"

"Who knows to what heights a man might aspire?"

"That's right," Prue nodded. "Who knows? The prospects are good, huh?"

"The prospects are dazzling—for the right man, of course. A few stirring speeches, a little hard work, a readiness to support the Party on every occasion, right or wrong, and in no time at all the foot is on the first rung of the ladder and the glittering prizes are almost within reach."

"Prime Minister?"

"Not at once, no. The ascent is more gradual. Rung by rung. First, perhaps, an under-secretaryship, followed in due course by the secretaryship. More hard work, more selfless endeavour, and comes the reward—perhaps the Chancellor-ship, pehaps even the Premiership itself." Claude raised his glance to the ceiling, and his eyes gleamed with ambition, or something. "There is a prize worth the winning!"

"That's as far as you can go?"

"By no means! One serves one's country and the Empire honourably and devotedly, without consideration of self, striving only for the common weal; and at the end of one's service, with any luck at all, one is made an earl. Sometimes this honour is accompanied by a lump sum in cash in an effort to express the public gratitude for services faithfully rendered; but not always. And although it is a touching old custom one would be sorry to see abandoned, it should not be really necessary; because no man who has been prominent in politics for a number of years, dedicated to the people and thinking only of their good, should stand in need of financial assistance at the end of his term. On the contrary, he should be comfortably fixed financially by the time he retires."

"We have a lot of that at home, too."

"Honours are showered on him," Claude continued, choosing to ignore this rather unfortunate remark. "His name is on every lip, his photograph in every magazine. He is beloved of the people—with the possible exception, of course, of labourites, socialists and communists, and exponents of Free Trade. From all sides a cry of dismay goes up when he announces his decision to lay aside the heavy burden he has borne so long. He has become a figurehead, a symbol. His name will be remembered for ever. Humble though he is, he cannot but feel a little quiet pride in his achievements—not because he has an earldom and perhaps a hundred thousand in cash; not because he has risen to be the most powerful subject in the land; not because his family and friends share his good fortune; but because the people, the voiceless, inarticulate masses, love him. There, I say again, is a prize worth the winning!"

At this point, Claude knocked off to clear his throat and dart a keen glance at his audience. He found her staring at him with wide eyes, obviously impressed.

"You'd sacrifice yourself like that?" she asked in wonder. "You'd give up your whole life, or the best part of it, to serve these bums who throw rotten eggs and dead cats at election meetings?"

"Certainly!" he answered without hesitation. "And that without asking a reward. Let them throw their cats, dead or alive! Let them throw their rotten eggs! It was for the right to throw dead cats and rotten eggs that our ancestors fought throughout the ages. There are those who feel that the best way to serve humanity is to retire into a monastery, or even into a cave in the desert, and there pass the years in prayer and meditation, meanwhile making things even more difficult for themselves by donning a hair shirt, or wearing a couple of fathoms of chain around the waist, as a means of keeping the mind on matters spiritual. I am not of their number. My desire to serve the people is no less sincere than theirs; but I approach the problem from a different angle. My aim is to raise their standard of living here and now, rather than to ensure their spiritual wellbeing in the next world. Who is to say that I am wrong?"

The words may have been trembling on Prue's lip; but if so she pulled them in again, for at that moment John put in an appearance, bearing down on them in a very purposeful manner indeed.

"Been looking for you all over the place," he said to Prue, and took her free arm—Claude still hanging on to the other. He gave his brother an inscrutable sort of glance, which was accounted for by the fact that now, for the first time, he was seeing Claude as a human being, or at least as something with pretensions in that line. "Nice of you to show her around."

"We were talking about art," Claude replied lightly. "Something, perhaps, a little beyond your understanding."

He added a hearty laugh to take the sting from his words, and, releasing Prue's arm, moved off in a dignified manner, though only by exercising the greatest self-control; for it would not have surprised him in the least if John had leaped in pursuit and given him a brutal kick to help him on his way. Something in the lad's eye had seemed to suggest that that very thought was in his mind.

CHAPTER SIX

IT WAS the old grandfather's custom, when conditions were normal, to spend an hour or two in the late afternoon sunk in meditation, though anyone who didn't know him well would have sworn he was sound asleep. For this period of contemplation and soul-searching he preferred his favourite armchair in front of the drawing-room fire; and the more complete the silence, the better he liked it, for the problems to which he bent his mind were of a very abstruse nature indeed.

Nowadays, however, with the house so full of people that he seemed to be shouldering them out of his way most of the time, the chances of undisturbed cerebration in the drawing-room were negligible, so he slunk off to his study, a small and cosy room in a sort of backwater in the west wing.

Here, having fortified his spirit with just a toothful of brandy, and thrown a little coal on the fire, he settled himself as comfortably as he might, closed his eyes, took in a deep breath, and relaxed.

He had been in this condition for some time, stirring now and then, and uttering the odd snort, when some unnamed sense, dating back to the days when his ancestors lived in caves and had to keep one eye lifted for bears, gave him so sharp a prod that he sat up, quivering all over. Nor had he been roused without just cause. Sitting in the chair opposite, looking not so much at him as through him with that horribly aloof gaze, and with features as expressive as the back view of a stone image, was his grandson, Derek.

"The power of the human eye," Derek remarked, displaying no unseemly triumph. "I looked at you, and willed you to wake up, and you did."

"Be very thankful that there are limits to the power of the human eye," the old coot replied, wondering how best to nudge his heart back into position. (It gave every indication of having jumped the points.) "Otherwise, my boy, you would now be little more than a smoking cinder, rapidly burning a hole in the seat of your chair. How the devil did you get in here?"

"I opened the door and walked in. You were asleep."

"I was not asleep! I was thinking deeply!"

"Okay, you were thinking deeply. You were snoring deeply, too."

The old grandfather decided not to pursue the question further. He saw no profit in it.

"You had no right to open the door and walk in," he said coldly. "This is my study. My purpose in coming here was to get away from persons like you, to enjoy a little peace and quiet, if only for an hour. Whether or not I fell into a doze is quite beside the point. I should be justified in boxing your ears—and believe me, the urge is there. But I wish to be reasonable and patient and understanding. This is the season of peace and goodwill and all that sort of tosh, and I am reluctant to be the first to start a brawl. Just oblige me by stating briefly what the devil it is you want, and then be good enough to remove yourself out of my sight, for I must admit I find you a repellent spectacle, and one, indeed, likely to put me off my food."

There were sensitive souls who would have been hurt by this plain speaking; but Derek gave no sign that the old grandfather's words had raised a blister on him, either inside or out.

"Touching on this season of peace and goodwill and so forth," he said. "I'm glad you brought that up. At this time of year grandparents should have only one problem—what to give their grandchildren that might at least approach to being worthy of them."

"You mean I should be wondering what present to give you, and fining myself down to skin and bone in the process?"

"You're getting the idea."

"The problem is one which has not engaged my attention to the exclusion of all else," the old grandfather confessed, without looking in the least ashamed of himself. "As a matter of fact, my boy, I haven't given it a thought. I am more than content to leave it in the capable hands of your grandmother, who, perhaps, has a higher regard for you than I have."

"*I'm* not."

"No? But why? Has she not done right by you on former occasions?"

"She thinks I'm still a child!" Derek's upper lip curled a little. "I shouldn't be surprised if she trotted up with something in the cuddly teddy-bear line."

"Cuddly teddy-bears are out of favour, what? I can recall the time you wouldn't go to bed without one." The old coot rubbed his chin, at the same time keeping a sharp eye on Derek. It had occurred to him that there was something behind all this, and he was feeling his way. "Perhaps you'd prefer a clockwork train, what?"

"I don't play with trains," Derek replied coldly. "And if I did, they'd be electric."

"Come, come, my boy! You can't sit there all evening running through a list of the things you *don't* want. That's what they call the negative approach. Could you not drop a hint as to what *would* meet with your approval?"

"A twenty-bore shotgun and a rook rifle," the lad answered without batting an eyelid. "And stacks of ammo."

The old grandfather poured himself a tot of brandy. He felt he needed a quick bracer.

"God bless my soul!" he muttered. "A shotgun and a rifle, what? Dashed lethal weapons, both of 'em. Either you'd put a bullet through someone, or blow his head off, beyond a shadow of doubt. Life and limb would be in constant danger until the inevitable happened and a charge of shot, or perhaps a dum-dum bullet, buried itself in your person. No, no, my boy! You'll have to wait a few years before finding shotguns and rifles in your Christmas stocking. Just how long you must wait is a matter for your father to decide. You'll settle for an electric train, what?"

"I'll settle for a shotgun and rifle."

The old grandfather took another spoonful of moral uplift. His mind raced as it hadn't raced for years. How right he had been, he thought, to suspect there was something behind all this. The lad had an ace up his sleeve—and with a young thug like Derek, that could be anything. As readily might one hope for the sporting approach from a hungry tiger.

"I'm very much afraid it's for your father to decide, my boy," he said reasonably. "I could not shoulder the responsibility. And besides, I have no wish to spend the next couple of weeks dodging dum-dum bullets. I'm too old and stiff in the joints to enjoy the pastime. Pray oblige me by thinking of something else. Firearms are out."

"Sure!" said Derek, without any visible change of expression. "I'll think about the Rembrandt."

At this, the old grandfather started as if a scorpion, which had been lying dormant in the seat of his pants, had suddenly come to life and nipped him on a tender spot.

"You'll think about *what?*" he croaked, though knowing all too well that his ears had not deceived him.

"The Rembrandt."

"Haw! The Rembrandt, what?" Aware that Derek was watching him like a rattlesnake poised to strike, the old grandfather pulled himself together and tossed off an airy laugh. (Even to his own ears, it sounded like a bullfrog croaking in a swamp.) "Add a few footnotes, my boy," he begged. "I seem to have lost the thread."

"No, you haven't," Derek said coldly. "And you know damn' well you haven't. If I can't think about a rifle and shotgun, then I'll think about the Rembrandt—and you know what I'll think about it, too!"

"I didn't realize you were interested in art."

"I get an American art magazine every month." The lad smiled slightly, as at some inner vision. "It costs plenty; but it's worth it. Anyway I hire it out to the other grubs, and sometimes I show a profit."

"You derive pleasure from studying the reproductions, what?"

"I derive pleasure from studying the nudes."

"God bless my soul!" the old coot muttered to himself. "You certainly *are* past the cuddly teddy-bear stage. It's something else you'll be cuddling . . ." He took a few moments off to brood, then raised his head and bent a searching glance on his grandson. "While looking for these dashed nudes, you came on something of interest, what?"

"That's right. I came on a reproduction of the Rembrandt."

"Why should that surprise you? It's a famous picture."

"There was quite an article about it," Derek added, showing his teeth in a smile that somehow made the old coot think of wolves. "I read every word. I knew you'd like me to be able to give you the gen. Or if you weren't interested, I guessed Granny would be."

"Your grandmother would not be at all interested. Nor, for that matter, am I. Now be good enough to take yourself off." The old grandfather gestured towards the door. "Run along, my boy! You've taken up too much of my time. Make yourself scarce before I leap to my feet and peel you like a banana."

Derek seemed to realize that the interview was at an end. Rising heavily, he prepared to take his departure.

"You'll remember about the gun and rifle?" he said in a most significant tone.

"Let it be understood at once that I am not going to buy you either a gun or a rifle, now or at any foreseeable time in the future," the old coot replied crisply. (He seemed to have regained much of his customary nonchalance.) "Furthermore, if you attempt to give me any argument about it I'll do what lies in my power to bone and roll you with my own hands. More than likely you regard me as a spent force. If so, my boy, you have never suffered from a more dangerous delusion— and 'dangerous' is a word I use advisedly. You follow me, what?"

Derek nodded. He had halted with one hand on the door-knob and his glance fixed on the old grandfather's features, which were a little richer in colour than usual.

"Yep," he said, on a flat note. "I've got all that. So you won't do business, huh?"

"There is no question of doing business," the old gran'pa replied. "Nor do I see that it is imperative for you to speak like some tobacco-chewing Western sheriff with a drooping moustache. But having resolutely refused to present you with a brace of lethal weapons, let me add this by way of salving your wounds—I am quite prepared to let you have a little ready cash in place of some present you might not appreciate."

"How much?"

"That is a matter calling for lengthy deliberation, and possibly even a little prayer. What you might do with the cash after you leave here would, of course, be a question for your father."

"Yeah," Derek agreed, without the slightest change of expression.

"Yeah," the old grandfather nodded.

The interview was at an end.

.　　　.　　　.　　　.　　　.

Oft in the stilly night Beale, the old butler, developed a touch of insomnia, lying awake for hours on end with his eyes closed and his mind flowing over with gloomy thoughts. On these occasions every unpleasant episode in a career stuffed with them came up for review, until the butler's soul writhed in torment like a salted slug. The only treatment he had found to be at all efficacious was to get up and move around a little, more especially in the direction of a bottle of brandy put aside for such emergencies.

One of these occasions was now with him. For an hour or more he had lain awake, while scenes from his youth, few of which redounded to his credit, passed before his inner eye. Embarrassing moments from as far back as his childhood were suddenly resurrected from his subconscious; and so starkly realistic were these visions that more than once he groaned aloud. Finally, unable to bear any more, he dragged himself out of bed, pulled his trousers on over his nightshirt, thrust his feet into his slippers, and began to pace up and down the length of his modest room, muttering to himself, shivering a little, and cracking his finger-joints.

There was no need for him to switch on the light. The moon had not yet risen; but the sky was crusted with stars, all twinkling and blazing away to the top of their bent, and from the snowy ground and laden trees a cold, comfortless light stole into the room. Beale could not have read his prayer-book by this diffused lighting. It was good enough, however, to let him see beyond a shadow of doubt that the brandy bottle was empty. As he put it himself, there wasn't what would pickle a flea; and he now recalled having made a mental note that his stock needed replenishing.

Muttering an oath or two, he opened the door and stood listening a moment; for although the hour was now long past midnight he was well aware that someone might still be moving around. With such a crowd in the house, almost anything could happen. Yet though he stretched his old ears until they vibrated under the strain, he heard nothing that struck him as suspicious; and, allowing his ears relax into their normal shape, he shuffled off towards the kitchen.

The first indication he had that all was not well came in the form of a beam of light projected through the keyhole of the side door and shining on the opposite wall. This was a door used only by the staff, and Beale had no scruples about bending down and applying his eye to the keyhole, for there was little danger of his being taken from the rear.

It was a large keyhole, cut for a key of the old-fashioned style and weighing about four pounds—the ideal key to slip down an epileptic's back. Though the attitude threw a strain on both his spine and his knees, and there was a draught coming through that threatened to freeze his eyeball solid, Beale was richly rewarded for his pains. The view was good. It took in all of the far end of the kitchen. In the middle of the screen was the table.

The principal actor in the drama currently unfolding itself was Derek. Wearing pyjamas and a dressing-gown, he was seated at the table, with the refrigerator at his back. To Beale, it became plain at a glance that the refrigerator had been raided. A roast chicken left over from lunch now occupied the place of honour on the festive board. Even as the old butler watched, Derek nonchalantly tore off one leg and fell to gnawing it with evident appreciation. It occupied him but a moment. Two or three crunching sounds, a gulp or two, and the bone was bare. The lad dropped it to the floor, and without wasting a moment, using his bare hands, wrenched off the other leg. His teeth sank into the tender flesh, and his cheeks and chin developed a greasy polish. A moment later the second femur had joined its brother, and Derek, using a fork, was excavating the stuffing from the body of the bird and transferring it to his own capacious gullet, swallowing it, so far as Beale could judge, in solid blocks and without chewing. It was like watching a hungry shark laying in the carbo-hydrates.

Beale was on the point of stepping into the kitchen and having a fatherly talk with the lad, for this sort of conduct did not meet with his approval, when he noticed a peculiar phenomenon. The door across the kitchen, giving access to the central part of the house, had opened a little. He watched it swing back slowly, so slowly; and then he saw what he took to be an eye applied to the crack, staring in. After that, there were no further developments for some moments. Derek continued to strip the flesh from the framework in the manner that seemed most convenient, careless if a little grease worked its way into his hair. But this pleasure in the good food had not thrown him off guard.

"You can come in," he said abruptly; and Beale almost jumped out of his skin.

It was not to the old butler, however, that Derek had spoken. Still stuffing his craw with chicken, he turned his head a little towards the far door and watched it open. Slowly, Alison entered. She wore her nightie with a dressing-gown thrown over, and presented a most appealing spectacle—but not to Derek.

"Shut the door!" he grunted, first spitting out a fragment of bone. "You want everyone in the parish to know we're down here?" He looked the skeleton over, found nothing more to eat, and laid it aside. This done, he turned a cold and hostile glance on his little sister. "What the hell are you following me for?"

Many a young woman would have replied that nothing was farther from her mind, and that actually she thought she had dropped something around here; but Alison was of a different stamp. Apparently she believed in telling the truth, even if it hurt—and if it hurt Derek, then virtue was indeed its own reward.

"To find out what you're up to," she replied, without any beating about the bush. "You should know by now you can't get away with anything unless you cut me in."

"I'd like to cut you in all right—in little pieces."

"What *are* you up to?"

Derek's only answer to this was a curl of the lip. He had now finished the chicken, inside and out. The mice were welcome to what was left on the denuded framework. He looked around for something to eat, and in a moment was spooning up the remains of a large custard, sucking in the yellow mess with the sounds of a sludge pump at work. Plainly he had no intention of suffering from night starvation.

Advancing to the table, Alison stared at the pile of bones left over from the orgy.

"Is there another chicken?" she inquired, though with no real hope.

"If there was another chicken, I wouldn't be eating custard."

"Oh! You're *eating* it?"

"What did you think I was doing?"

"I thought you were snuffling it up your nose."

Derek deigned no reply. If his little sister didn't like the slurping noises, she was at liberty to withdraw. He finished the custard, cleaning the bowl by running one finger around the inside and licking off the gleanings. Clearly it was his wish to give the staff as little trouble as possible.

"You didn't come down here just to eat," Alison said. "You had something else on your mind. You'd better tell me."

"Run along and play with your dollies!" Derek replied tolerantly. "All young stinkers should be in bed at this hour. Young stinkers caught out of bed at this hour get their bottoms smacked."

"You'd better tell me."

"They get their bottoms smacked until they can't sit down for a week."

There was a brief pause in the conversation; and when Alison went on the air again it was to introduce a new subject.

"Where's Joe?"

To the old butler, watching enthralled through the key-hole, it seemed that Alison, with this innocent question, had pierced Master Derek's guard. Not that the lad betrayed anger or any other emotion; but there was a certain edge to his tone when he replied.

"He's in a place of safety—and if you try to find him I'll skin you alive!"

"Little boys shouldn't lose their temper!" Alison said sweetly. "And little boys shouldn't tell lies. Little boys who lose their temper and tell lies go to hell—even fat little boys who are really nothing but a sort of walking stomach."

"Aw, shut up!" Derek growled.

It was a weak retort, and he knew it. Though he could be scathing at times, and was a master of coarse but blistering invective, long and frustrating experience had taught him that even his best efforts were of no avail against his little sister. No words, however hurtful or insulting, could penetrate her defences. It was as if she could shut her ears with a couple of built-in plugs; but invariably her reply, though it might have no bearing on the subject, was as gall and wormwood to a proud spirit. The only way to get the better of her was to

70

smack her over the head, always being careful to ascertain, before launching hostilities, that she wasn't carrying a concealed weapon. Derek's recollections of the occasion when she had fleshed a nail-scissors up to the hilt in his thigh were as clear as if it had happened only yesterday. There was one scar he would bear to his grave, though luckily it was in a spot seldom on view to the public.

Rising heavily, he pushed back his chair and closed the refrigerator door. This done, he turned again to the little sister, bending on her a glance that would have sent a shiver through an Arctic seal.

"You lay off Joe!" he said in a low voice.

"I'm not laying on him."

"You leave him alone!" The lad's voice rose a little, for he was deeply stirred. "Keep away from him, or I'll—I'll——"

"You'll what?" Alison smiled sweetly. "What will you do, Derek?"

"I don't know," Derek admitted, for the question was one to which he had as yet given no thought. "But I'll do something awful. Just to hear about it will make people's blood run cold. So you'd better be very careful."

"And you'd better tell me what you came down here for."

"I came down to get something to eat. I'm a growing boy. I need lots of nourishment. It's inhuman to expect a boy to go without food for thirteen or fourteen hours. That's how people gets rickets and things. Can't I come down for a snack without you following me like a bad smell?"

"It's too bad about Joe."

"What's too bad about Joe?"

"It's too bad he has to suffer."

"How is he going to suffer?"

"I wouldn't like to tell you," Alison whispered, her eyes wide. "Poor Joe!"

"You keep away from him or I'll murder you!" Derek said between his teeth. Then, with a superhuman effort, he salvaged a portion of his customary aplomb. A sneering smile twisted his features, though purely temporarily. "Aw, why do I waste my time on little girls?" he wondered scornfully. "I should know better. Little girls have no brains. Little girls have no intelligence at all. Little girls are just a nose and a big mouth that's always going yak-yak-yak! They're a sort of primitive organism, like something in a drop of pond water."

"Your face is all greasy," Alison remarked. "You look as if you'd rubbed it all over with a piece of fat bacon."

"I rubbed it all over with a roast chicken" the lad replied, moving towards the door. "It's good for the skin, and for the stomach, too. I'm going up now. You can stay if you like— and if you get frozen to the floor, and perish miserably of exposure, I'll hang out bunting."

With these few words he pushed off, sparing his little sister not so much as a glance.

Left alone, Alison stood quite still for a few moments, lost in thought. Then she turned to the refrigerator, opened the door, and peered in. Finding nothing to tempt her appetite, she shut the door again and followed her big brother, switching off the light as she left the kitchen.

Beale straightened up with a sigh of relief. It took him a few moments to get the kinks out of his spine. Meanwhile his eye watered freely, the fluid trickling down the side of his nose and on to his upper lip, at which point he brushed it off with the back of one hand.

Presently, however, having massaged as best he could the small of his back, he opened the door and shuffled forward, laying a course for the pantry.

CHAPTER SEVEN

DEREK, on his way back to bed in sombre and pensive mood, noticed that Alison had attached a length of black thread to his door by means of a drawing-pin. Presumably this, leading to her room, had in some way conveyed to the little sister warning that he was on the move. Feeling rather ashamed of himself that he had not noticed it earlier and taken steps, he now broke it at a point roughly midway between the two doors, in the hope that she might be deceived into thinking it was still functioning. This done, he entered his room and switched on the light.

John, in pyjamas and dressing-gown, was relaxed in the only armchair, smoking a cigarette.

Derek took this unexpected development in his stride, and the only greeting he gave his uncle was a grunt and a morose glance. He felt pretty low. All the way up from the kitchen he had been brooding about Alison; and the thought now uppermost in his mind was that it must have been wizard to live in the good old days when a man could hire an assassin to do odd jobs around the house.

"Well?" said John.

He had laid his cigarette-case and lighter on the table beside his chair. Before replying, Derek helped himself from the case and lit up. John, watching this, was conscious of an urge to spring up and give his nephew a brutal kick in the pants. It was a powerful urge, and he had difficulty in fighting it down. He comforted himself with the reflection that a day of reckoning would come—and when it came, would stick like a mustard plaster.

"Well?" he said again. "Did you get it?"

"No."

"Why not?"

"Alison followed me." Derek pulled strongly on his cigarette. "Some day she'll go too far!" he muttered. "Some day she'll step across the danger-line, and I'll fall on her like a thunderbolt. There'll be nothing left but a smell of sulphur and brimstone."

All this was of little interest to John. So far as he was concerned, Derek was welcome to fall on Alison, thunderbolt style, whenever the spirit moved him.

"Why did she follow you?" he asked idly.

"She couldn't rest unless she knew what I was doing. She'd be all burned up if she thought I was getting away with anything. It's a sort of complex. Springing from a sense of inferiority, no doubt."

"No doubt," John agreed. "I often get it myself when you're around. She didn't discover what you were after?"

"Nobody ever discovers what I'm after except by accident," Derek replied coldly. "I told her I'd gone down for a snack, something to keep body and soul together."

"You look as if you'd smeared your chops with rancid

73

butter in some pagan rite," John observed. "A touch of realism, what?"

"I happened to find a surplus chicken in the 'frige. It served to throw her off the scent." Derek smiled fleetingly, though his mood was far from sunny. "And I can't imagine a more pleasant way of throwing anyone off the scent, either, unless two of the same. I could have gone another round."

"So the key is in the kitchen?"

"The key is not in the kitchen," Derek replied, with an aloof glance. "And even if it were, and you went straight to it and lifted it off the hook, you wouldn't get your money back. The bird who could get his money back from me has yet to be hatched. They tell me the medieval moneylender would much rather have his toenails torn off, or lose all his teeth, than forfeit his profit. I can understand that. It's an attitude I respect. That's the sort of duck I am myself."

"I had no intention of demanding my money back," John assured him. "Are you going to try again?"

"Not tonight. I have a hunch it's a bad night to be moving around. I'm psychic that way."

"What way?"

"I get these hunches. Something rings a bell inside me, and I know it's time to lie low."

"If you're not psychic, you're certainly something," John admitted. "Maybe a psychiatrist would have a name for it. You think someone else is prowling around tonight?"

"That's right. It's something in the atmosphere. Like a shock-wave."

"Then I'd better go down and get the key myself."

"That's up to you, brother," Derek replied agreeably. "So long as you don't expect to get your money back, what you do or don't do is a matter of indifference to me. If you leave the job to me, I'll undoubtedly deliver the goods. If you decide to do it yourself, you have my blessing. You'll find the missing key somewhere in Beale's pantry. He removed it to a place of safety when he discovered your American friend was a squaw."

"Miss Goodrich is not a squaw—she's a young lady!"

"Then you shouldn't be trying to get your hands on that key," Derek pointed out, curling his upper lip in a most offensive manner. "Wipe that gleam out of your eye, chum! I know you'd like to kick me plumb in the teeth; but always bear it in mind you're in my power."

"I am?"

"You're tootin' you are!"

"I didn't know I was tootin'. So I'm in your power, what?"

"You wouldn't like the old folks to know what *I* know, would you?" Derek helped himself to another cigarette. "It doesn't bother *me*," he added tolerantly. "Once the deal goes through I won't give it another thought. You've got your key and I've got your fiver, so everyone's happy."

"I wouldn't like the old folks to know what you know," John admitted, rising to his feet. "For that matter, I wouldn't like anyone to know it." He laid a fatherly hand on Derek's shoulder. "So it will be a secret just between us two, what? And if you breathe a word of it, you slug, I'll do things to you that were never done to a medieval moneylender! Make a note of that on the fly-leaf of your hymnal."

With these few words, to which Derek's only reply was a contemptuous smile, he left the room, and in a matter of moments was on his way to the kitchen. He moved confidently but quietly along the twilit passages, for he remembered from his boyhood the location of every floorboard that could be expected to squeak at the least desirable moment.

He was not surprised to find the light on in the kitchen. Doubtless Alison, a sweet child he regarded with a sort of veiled horror, had forgotten to switch it off before returning to her room. Quietly closing the door, he pressed forward to the pantry, hoping Beale was not so low-minded as to keep it locked.

This fear was unfounded. The door opened readily, and he stepped in.

By this time Beale was feeling a little better, though his spine still creaked like a rusty gate when he stooped. He had switched on an electric radiator to warm his old shanks, and was settled comfortably in front of same with a glass of brandy in one hand and a vacant look in his eye. His mind, however, was far from being a blank. He was wondering what had brought Master Derek to the kitchen at this time of night; why Alison had followed him, obviously by stealth; and who was the mysterious Joe mentioned in their conversation. This last intrigued Beale most of all, because it appeared that Joe was in danger of meeting with some horrible fate—a danger, in the old butler's opinion, by no means remote for anyone having dealings with Master Derek and Miss Alison.

The sudden opening of the pantry door, and the equally sudden appearance of Master John, derailed the old butler's train of thought. Moreover, it went a long way towards making him jump out of his pants and nightshirt. So violent was his reaction that he came as close as a toucher to slopping the contents of his glass into his lap.

"Master John!" he croaked, struggling to his feet.

"What ho!" John exclaimed, no less taken aback. "It's you, what?"

"Yes, indeed, sir. Did you think it was somebody else?"

"I didn't think it was anyone at all. I mean to say, I didn't expect to find anyone pottering around here at this time of night."

"I was not exactly pottering around, sir," the old butler pointed out courteously. "As perhaps you are not aware, I suffer from insomnia."

"You do, what? That's bad!"

"Yes, sir. On occasion I lie awake hour after hour, tossing and turning, while scenes from my past life float before my inner eye."

"It's not so bad when they float," John commented, gazing around with interest. "You've really got something to worry about when they begin to sink. So then you slip down here and pin on a quick one to cheer yourself up, what?"

"Precisely, sir. I find that a quick one, as you term it, dispels these dark and gloomy visions and allows me to sink into refreshing slumber."

"What's that cure-all you have there?"

"This, sir, is brandy. It is my experience that when it comes to dispelling unwelcome visions, from the past or anywhere else, you can't beat brandy. The very thought of it brightens one's outlook and fills the bosom with gladness and song. Ghosts from the dead past are driven underground, and joyous fancies come tripping in to take their place. There is no room for gloom and melancholy where a toothful of brandy has been added to the system."

"And it helps you to sleep, too?"

"Oh, yes, sir! And furthermore, such dreams as may follow are of a very pleasant and agreeable nature, though admittedly bearing no relation whatever to anything experienced by me personally. No doubt they spring from the subconscious, sir."

"No doubt," John agreed. "Practically everything does. And the more brandy you take, the better it springs."

"And the more gracefully, sir."

Here the conversation, which had been going so well, languished a little. It occurred to John, who was one of these slow but dogged thinkers, that despite all this yak-yak about insomnia and visions from the past and the beneficial effect of a little brandy upon dreams, Beale was staring at him in a rather piercing manner, as if awaiting an explanation of his presence here in the butler's sanctum at this hour of night.

"You're not the only one who suffers from insomnia, Beale," he remarked on a sombre note.

"No, indeed, sir! Due possibly to the pace of modern life, it is a common affliction. We can take it that at this very moment thousands upon thousands are lying awake, staring into the darkness with burning eyes, wooing in vain the slumber that comes so readily to others—and few among them, sir, can afford the snifter of brandy that would make all the difference."

"You're looking at one now."

"Oh, no, sir!" the old butler exclaimed, assuming an expression of incredulous horror. "Not *you*!"

"Yes, Beale. Me."

"You've got insomnia, sir?"

"It comes and goes," John answered nonchalantly. "Sometimes it comes and stays. I've had it for months at a time. Then again I've been free of it, and sleeping like a babe in its mother's arms, for the better part of a year. It's insomnia has me here just now."

"Yes, sir?" Beale said politely, waiting for further detail.

"The moment I was in bed I knew I was for it. The mind began to race, Beale."

"Invariably fatal, sir."

"Very soon the eyeballs were burning."

"I am familiar with the sensation, sir. There are times I get the impression my own are smoking like a brace of boiled potatoes just out of the pot."

"I found myself listening for sounds. And I heard them."

"You heard them, sir?"

"Distinctly. There seemed to be a certain amount of traffic around and about the premises. Not heavy, Beale, but steady. Coming and going, you know. Now a creak, now a muttered word, now a muted thud as of a closing door. All of which conveyed the impression that the inmates were restless and moving about."

"Very odd, sir," the butler agreed. "But we must bear it in mind that your father frequently moves around the house, no doubt for some very good reason, at all hours of the night."

"He does?"

"Yes, sir. If I may say so without offence, he slinks around like a beast of prey."

"A leopard or something, what?"

"Precisely, sir. Or possibly a panther."

"What's the difference?"

"The difference is negligible, sir," Beale admitted handsomely. "Let us settle for the leopard."

"He must have insomnia, what? I mean the old man, not the leopard."

"That may be so, sir; but it does not seem to affect him in the afternoon."

"Anyway I looked out, saw nobody, and decided to do a little prowling in my own right. And here I am."

"Here you are, sir," the old butler agreed cordially. "And now that you're here, perhaps you'd join me in a glass of brandy?"

"If you have a glass big enough, nothing could please me better," John replied, with that old-world courtesy that made him so popular everywhere he went.

.　　　.　　　.　　　.　　　.

Claude, the rising young politician, had retired to his room shortly after dinner to put in a spot of work; and he hadn't been long there before sending for Sally to take some notes. She went under protest from Mr. Massey, who strongly advised her to tell Claude to go jump in the lake.

"See you later," she said, laughing. "Perhaps we could take a walk. I haven't had a sniff of fresh air for a week."

"That's what comes of working with someone whose proper place is under a flat stone, or maybe a rotten log. Let's take a walk now, and the devil take Claude."

"Oh, no! This is part of my contract."

"He must think he's the Prime Minister!" Mr. Massey muttered. "And with the Empire facing a crisis, at that. The devil scald him!"

"You'll wait?"

"Yep. I'll wait."

He waited, smoking a cigar and sipping his brandy. Then he smoked another cigar, and sipped more brandy. He got the impression that everyone else was shunting off to bed. The house seemed to be settling down for the night. Finally Beale looked in.

"Are you all right, sir?" he inquired solicitously.

Mr. Massey glanced at the decanter. There was still a good pint to go.

"I'm fine," he said. "Have no fears for me, Beale—I'll last through the night. Don't bother to bolt and bar the hall door. I may be going for a walk."

"The snow is very deep, sir."

"Ha! I've been out in snow so deep, Beale, I had to burrow through it like a rabbit, using a compass to keep on course."

"Indeed, sir?" the old butler said politely. "Permit me to remark that you are welcome to my share of it. Good night, sir."

He shuffled off, warmed and sustained by the Massey blessing; and the house became as quiet as if it had been laid under a spell.

Presently, however, came the sound of quick footsteps, and Sally entered. She was dressed for the open in a fur coat and fur-lined boots, with a woollen cap that came down over her ears.

"Are we going?" she asked, her eyes sparkling. "I know it's

late, and all good people are off to bed; but unless I get out for an hour or two I'm liable to burst."

"That unsightly clot has no right to keep you working until this hour," Mr. Massey commented. "And I'll make a point of telling him so, too. What I'd like to do is pick him up by the ears and shake him out of his skin—and if he gives me half an excuse I'll do it without a qualm. What he needs is firm handling."

"Where's your coat? Or are you so tough you don't need one?"

"In the cloakroom. Have a toothful of brandy to keep the frost out of your bones?"

"Not now, thanks. Perhaps when we come back."

They went out, Mr. Massey quietly closing the hall door. It was a still, frosty night, the stars twinkling in a sky as black and polished as an old-fashioned iron range. The snow was crisp and crunchy underfoot, but not deep enough to make walking laborious. Mr. Massey took Sally's arm, and they stepped out briskly.

.   .   .   .   .

Having dismissed Sally, the rising young politician yawned, stretched as well as he could without popping a button, lit a cigarette, and for some time sat relaxed in his chair, letting the wheels run down. As he would have been the first to admit, he had been driving himself hard. So hard, in fact, that now the wheels refused to run down. The great brain continued to function as if still goaded to give of its best. Brilliant phrases dealing with this and that topical subject flashed into his mind; and had his secretary still been with him he would have told her to get them down on paper for future reference.

With an effort he switched his train of thought on to a branch line. Summoning before his inner eye a vision of Miss Prudence Goodrich, he gave it his personal attention. His blood, reputed to be sluggish, stirred a little, and his eye brightened. Something out of the ordinary was needed to take his mind off politics, for he had dedicated his life to the service of the people; but Miss Goodrich managed it without straining a muscle. There was something about her, Claude reflected, that called to the very depths of his being. Nor did it, whatever it was, call in vain. Something from the very depths of his being answered her right back.

Thoughts of this nature were surging through his mind like a tidal bore when suddenly it seemed to him he heard voices in the night. This was nothing unusual at Scumton Hall; but these voices were coming from outside. Leaving his chair, he stepped to the window and drew the curtain aside just in time to see two dark figures, arm-in-arm, disappear beneath the avenue trees.

"Ah!" Claude murmured, on a note of deep significance.

He had caught no more than a glimpse of the pair moving off across the snow, but he was satisfied as to their identity. The fact that John and Miss Goodrich should go walking together at this time of night and in this wintry weather seemed to him conclusive evidence of some understanding between them; and for the first time, striking into his vitals like an arrow, came the thought that possibly they were betrothed, or something of that nature. To him it seemed incredible and fantastic that any young woman in possession of her senses should allow herself to become betrothed to John, whether secretly or any other way; but he was aware that young women in love could scarcely be regarded as intelligent entities. The brighter the light in a young woman's eyes, and the sweeter the song in her heart, the emptier her head. Miss Goodrich was a beautiful, glamorous, polished and intelligent girl, the only child of a doting father, at present unattached, who obviously was not only in the multi-millionaire class but near the head of it. The sort of girl, in short, who could have had her pick of the eligible bachelors of England and America. Was it possible, Claude asked himself, that a girl in so strong a position could so completely lose her sense of proportion as to become engaged to John? Gloomily, he conceded that it was. Beautiful and wealthy young women were doing it all the time. What was stranger still, they seemed to like it.

Yet what had John to offer any woman? Undeniably he possessed a certain boyish charm, and came equipped with regular features, wavy hair, white teeth and flashing eyes; but closer investigation revealed that behind this attractive façade was a skull, so far as could be ascertained without opening it up, as solid as a cannonball. Up to date he had given no proof whatever of having a brain, even in the most rudimentary form. Nor had he shown any genuine desire to redeem this deficiency by working himself to skin and bone.

These reflections, and others of a very similar nature, ran through Claude's mind in a matter of moments. It took him another moment or two to convince himself that, if only for Prue's sake, it was his duty to cut John right out of her affections. The boy had no future. She must be made to see him in his true colours, whatever the true colours of a drone might be. Her attention should be drawn to his complete unworthiness, as also to the fact that he had no money now, and the indications were he never would have any. No girl with a spoonful of common sense would hesitate when it came to a choice between a total loss like John and a rising young politician who would one day be Prime Minister, an intimate friend of kings and queens and visiting potentates.

Without delaying a moment, Claude attired himself like some fearless explorer about to make a parachute jump at the North Pole—for he had to be careful of his health—and quietly made his way downstairs. The fresh night air flowed into his lungs, filling him with zip and zest. He felt as if he could mush off across the snow like some tough trapper of the North setting out on his rounds, returning to his lonely cabin laden with choice pelts and with frostbite in his toes. The stars twinkled down at him, and the snow crunched beneath his feet. It was years since he had done anything like this, for life to him had always been real and earnest and No. 10 Downing Street was the goal. The urge to utter a few piercing yells rose in him, only to be crushed. It was all very well to feel like a boy; but to start acting like an idiot was another matter entirely.

The possibility that he might have difficulty in following the trail had not occurred to Claude. He mushed strongly down the avenue, darting keen glances from side to side, though there was no real necessity for this, it being scarcely likely that his quarry had climbed the fence and struck off across the fields. Nor was he perturbed to note that the snow on the middle of the avenue was well trodden down, though to either side it lay like a sheet just back from the laundry. Only when he came to the gates, and saw how the traffic had laid a dark and icy surface from ditch to ditch, did he pause a moment, fingering his lip.

He was not one to stand around all night, fingering his lip. The conviction that he could follow a trail in the snow as well as any trapper, if not better, filled him with quiet confidence. Darting a keen glance first to one side, then to the other, he satisfied himself that John and Prue were out of sight. He saw only the dark hedges and the gaunt shapes of trees, motionless in the frosty air. He listened, and heard only the distant bawling of a cow with insomnia, or possibly the stomach-ache.

Still full of confidence, he began to cast about for the trail. All he needed to know was whether the pair had turned left or right. There should be one set of large footprints, he reasoned, and one of small, close together and proceeding in the same direction. Nothing could be simpler.

Within a few moments he had found what he sought, and struck out as briskly as conditions would permit, a song in his heart mixed with a stern resolve to save the glamorous Miss Goodrich from herself.

Unfortunately, the trail he followed had been laid by Phyllis and her boy friend.

CHAPTER EIGHT

FAMILY breakfast was at nine o'clock, for those who liked to eat with their elbows on the table. Mr. Massey came down at five minutes to zero hour, and found the scene already crowded. Sally and Prue had arrived, also John, the old grandfather, and Derek and Alison. A *pot-pourri* of appetizing fragrances filled the room; and the genial host, leaving it to someone else to say grace, was loading his plate from the dishes on the sideboard.

"Another kidney and I'm right," he murmured to himself, then glanced briefly at Mr. Massey. "How are you, my boy? Tell me, did you sleep well?"

"Like a log," Mr. Massey replied cheerfully. "And you, Nunk?"

"I had a disturbed night."

"Who disturbed you?"

"There seemed to be people moving around all night. I'd open my door and peep out, but there'd be nobody on view. It was dashed odd."

"Spooks, what?"

"I don't think so. Haven't seen a ghost for years. Used to be a couple of good types around the place; but they seem to have moved on. Too quiet for 'em here, no doubt."

He would have said more, though his mouth was now filled with a rich mixture of sausage and kidney and fried egg; but at that moment Claude entered, limping slightly. There was something about Claude's bearing that diverted the old coot's thoughts. To his dim eye, the young statesman looked as if nothing could please him better than to bite someone in the flank. To all cheery greetings he returned only a morose grunt; and even when his glance fell on Prue, who looked as fresh and lovely as a summer morning, it warmed up only a few degrees. This gain was immediately lost when his brooding gaze switched over to John.

"What have you done to your dashed leg?" the old grandfather asked, all interest. "Fall out of bed, or something, what?"

"I am not in the habit of falling out of bed," Claude replied coldly.

"Then you must have turned over a new leaf. As a child, you were in the habit of falling out of bed. You fell out of bed so regularly we had to leave a mattress on the floor for you to fall on in case you'd break a bone or two. Almost every night it was the same thing, a thud and a yell. The unfortunate nurse never got a full night's sleep. For myself I favoured strapping you in; but expert opinion was against it. You've outgrown the weakness, what?"

"Yes."

"Then why are you limping?"

"Because I slipped on the icy road, and almost broke a leg," Claude replied, with a glance that should have warned the old coot he was on dangerous ground, but didn't.

"You slipped on the road? When was this, my boy?"

"I cannot give you the exact time; but it must have been about one o'clock this morning. My hip is black and blue."

"Let us leave your hip out of it for the moment, if you don't mind. We'll come back to it later. What were you doing on the road at one o'clock in the morning, may I ask?"

"Walking," Claude answered, on a sour note. He seemed to feel some further explanation was called for, and went on. "I hadn't been outside the door for days."

"So you go walking on an icy road at one in the morning?" The old grandfather eyed him very closely, making it clear that in his opinion something was being held back. "Dashed odd!"

"It was a beautiful night for a walk."

"Permit me to remark that to my way of thinking you must have been out of your mind," said the old grandfather, slicing up another sausage. "Also that you were dashed lucky to escape with a bruised hip. It's a miracle you weren't found frozen to the road this morning, by some peasant on his way to work, with a fractured leg and your teeth showing in a grin. Frankly I find your account of the matter very hard to believe, because I had reached the conclusion, from watching you closely, that walking was for you almost a lost art."

"You don't believe me?" Claude said—and there was more ice in his tone than there was on the road.

"I didn't say that. This isn't an election meeting, so there's no need for you to twist my meaning. I said I found it difficult to believe you. And frankly, my boy, I suspect you came by that bruised hip in some manner or other that reflects no credit on you whatever. Let us leave it at that."

"Certainly not!" Claude snorted. "This may be your idea of a little leg-pulling; but I am not accustomed to being called a liar."

"Then you had better get accustomed to it, because if ever you become a politician you'll be called a liar every day of your life, and with good reason."

"What reason have you to doubt my word?" Claude asked, adding a tolerant smile though the effort nearly dislocated his jaw.

"Because nobody but a halfwit would have gone walking

on the road at one in the morning. I'd prefer to put you down as a liar."

"Then there are two halfwits in the family. John was out, also."

"Me?" said John, raising his eyebrows. "No, no! Not me, brother. You must be thinking of some other hoddy-doddy."

"You deny it?" Claude demanded between his teeth, his control slipping for a moment, but not very far. "You have the temerity to deny it?"

"You bet!" John nodded. "And hand on heart, at that. I didn't leave the old log cabin after dinner last night."

"I cannot imagine why you should wish to conceal the fact," Claude admitted, first fighting down an urge to hurl his breakfast in John's face, plate and all. "And I am sorry that I mentioned it in the first place. But I have gone too far now to retract. I saw you leave the house last night at about twelve o'clock."

"Not me," said John again. "Some other duck."

At this point, Sally would have spoken; but Mr. Massey, sitting beside her, gave her a little nudge with his elbow, and she held it back.

"Why all this to-do?" Mr. Massey asked tolerantly. "Is it a crime to leave the premises, or what? So far as I know there's no law against it. So why bare the gums and grind the teeth at each other like a brace of grizzlies getting ready to rassle?"

"I have been called a liar," Claude pointed out on a very cold note.

"So have I," John said cheerfully. "But I don't mind, because I know I'm in the right. I don't doubt for a moment you saw some bird or other venture out into the frozen wastes, taking his life in his hands and a flask of firewater on his hip. Only thing is, it wasn't me."

"No doubt you were in bed and asleep?" Claude sneered. "Or possibly reading a chapter of your bible, as is your nightly custom?" He fixed his brother with a glittering eye. "Were you in bed at twelve o'clock?"

"Where I was or was not at twelve o'clock or any other time is no concern of yours," John replied equably. "The point is, I wasn't outside the house, whatever you thought you saw. So let's talk about something else, what? I mean, before you go just that inch too far, and I bung you in the eye with a sausage."

"Comes of working too hard," the old grandfather explained to Claude, on a kindly note. "You're a little off the beam, my boy. Suffering from delusions, and so forth. More than likely it was a shadow."

"What was a shadow?"

"This thing, whatever it was, you took for John."

"Then the shadow was arm-in-arm with Miss Goodrich!" Claude snorted, goaded beyond endurance.

At this, John started slightly, and, turning his head, bent a searching glance on Prue. That glamorous young woman, for her part, stared across the table at Claude as if he had suddenly turned into a horse.

"You saw Miss Goodrich, too?" the old grandfather asked politely.

"Yes!" Claude replied, at his most dogged. "She was with John."

"How could she have been with John, when John wasn't there?" The old coot tossed off a tolerant laugh. "Rather difficult for her, what?" He turned to Prue. "Were you out walking at midnight, my dear?"

"Oh, no!" she said, widening her eyes a little more, though it had seemed scarcely possible. "You'd have to be a penguin, or maybe a Polar bear, to enjoy walking out there—and I don't suppose even a penguin or a Polar bear would enjoy it unless there were a few fish around."

"I had overlooked that point," the old coot confessed. He turned to Claude. "Well, my boy? Are you convinced that what you saw was the shadow of a branch, or something, or are you going to cast doubt on this lovely young lady's word?"

"You'd better not," said John, on a note of friendly warning. "I mean, you'd better not cast doubt on Prue's word. Not unless you really want a fork stuck in your eye."

"Go on!" Derek urged, unable to restrain his enthusiasm. "*Stick* your fork in his eye and see what happens!"

"I have no wish to cast doubt on Miss Goodrich's word."

"You have no wish to have a fork stuck in your eye, either."

"I must have been mistaken," Claude said stiffly, ignoring Derek, who had become all keyed-up at the prospect of bloodshed. "I must have——" A sudden thought struck him, and he fixed a keen glance on Mr. Massey. "It wasn't *you*, was it?"

"It was."

"You were out walking with——" Claude pulled himself up just in time. "You were out walking with someone?"

"I was out walking with Sally."

"Then why the devil didn't you say so?" Claude inquired on a rather grating note.

"Why should I? You said you'd seen John and Prue. You were dogmatic about it. Not until you awoke to the danger of having a fork stuck in your eye did you admit you could have been mistaken. And I don't blame you a bit. It must be a sore thing to be prodded in the eye with a fork."

"You could have prevented a great deal of unpleasantness by speaking up."

"So could you, by keeping your mouth shut," the old grandfather pointed out. "But I suppose that's too much to expect of a budding politician. Every politician seems to consider himself under an obligation to keep yap-yap-yapping without a break—most of the time on matters about which he knows nothing whatever. How I hate them! The only creature that can at all compare with them is the vampire bat, and even the vampire bat has the decency to attack its victim's big toe, whereas the politician, mouthing platitudes about the public good, goes for the throat every time." He bent an inquiring glance on Mr. Massey. "Tell me, my boy, did I get a bit mixed up there, or have I made myself clear?"

"You don't like politicians?"

"No, I don't."

"You'd prefer the vampire bat?"

"Definitely! The dashed bat flutters off when he's had enough—but a politician *never* has enough."

"Then we've got your message," Mr. Massey assured him. "For myself, I'm inclined to regard politicians as a separate species. They're not just normal human beings. Seldom or never are they in touch with reality. They exist on another plane; but whether it's higher than ours, or lower, is not for me to say. When the first politician was put together, something was left out. Or possibly something extra was put in. They can't face facts. They can't get anything straight— possibly because they're so crooked themselves."

He would have continued at some length, for the question was one to which he had devoted much thought and prayer; but at that moment Beale rushed into the room at top speed, which came to about four miles an hour when the going was good. It became evident at a glance that the old retainer was in a state of considerable agitation, and that his boiler-pressure was dangerously high. There was unwonted colour in his cheeks, which normally looked like a dried-out grapefruit, and his eyes protruded a little from their sockets, but not so much that they seemed likely to fall out.

"Sir!" he croaked, fixing a wild gaze on the old grand-father, who appeared to be quite unstirred by this startling development. "Sir!" He took off a moment or two to draw some air into his lungs, for he had not spared himself in his dash with the news, and his gullet felt as if it had been rubbed down with a wire brush. "Sir, something terrible and dreadful has happened!"

"I don't doubt it for a moment," the old coot admitted, remaining calm. "Somewhere or other, something terrible and dreadful is happening practically all the time. What with floods and earthquakes and volcanic eruptions, not to mention train wrecks, air crashes, storms at sea and the toll of the roads, the feller who dies in bed, or even with his boots off, must be accounted fortunate indeed. What is it this time, Beale? Has some thriving town been levelled by a typhoon? Is some stately ocean liner at this very moment sinking with all hands? Come, come, Beale! Don't hold us in suspense! Tell us the worst."

"The Rembrandt has been stolen, sir!" the old butler hooted, swinging his hands.

"*Stolen?*" Claude bawled, rising to his feet and drawing himself up to his full height, meanwhile bending a stern glance on Beale. "Nonsense! How could it have been stolen? There must be some mistake."

"That's what they said when the Mona Lisa was swiped, too," Mr. Massey remarked helpfully.

"There is no mistake, sir," Beale said, absentmindedly

pouring himself a cup of tea. He drank with loud slurping noises, for his vocal cords felt as if they might at any moment burst into flame, and to his mind prevention was better than cure. "The canvas has been cut out with some sharp instrument, and removed entire. I discovered the theft just now, when I went to the gallery to draw the curtains. I have not touched anything, knowing that the police will be looking for fingerprints. I hurried out, locked the door, and came straight here, sir."

All this time the old grandfather sat as in a trance, staring straight before him with a vacant look in his eyes, giving a wonderful impersonation of one struck over the head with a stuffed sock. Plainly the news had come as a blow, though no actual loss of life was involved. No terrible disaster at sea could have produced so powerful an effect. The tidings of some convulsion of nature, burying thousands in the rubble of their homes, might for a moment hold the old coot's interest and cause him to purse his lips and shake his head in disapproval, but could never leave him shocked and silent as he was now. This was something personal, something right in his own home; and the old grandfather's silence, and his glazed eyes, could be taken as an indication that the worst was still sinking in. So far, shock had dulled the pain. Later, he would really suffer.

"We must call the police at once!" Claude snorted, taking over. "Now, this very moment! There is not a second to waste. Beale, call the police!"

"The police, sir? You mean, the local constabulary?"

"Certainly! If I had meant you to call Scotland Yard, I would have said so."

"But, sir!" the old butler protested, wringing his hands until they seemed in danger of coming off at the wrist. "The local constabulary are quite unfit to handle a problem of this nature. The entire establishment, sir, consists of a sergeant and a constable, both elderly men soon to be retired, stationed here because there never has been any crime worthy of the name in Scumton parish. The only thing at which the sergeant displays even a glimmering of intelligence is the culture of onions; and the constable, I understand, has little interest in anything but fishing."

"Fishing?" said the old grandfather, suddenly rousing himself from his trance. "Who the devil mentioned fishing? What the deuce do you fish for at this time of year, what?" He glared at the old butler. "What was that you said about the Rembrandt, Beale? You did mention casually something about its being stolen, did you not? Let us stick to that, and leave the fishing out of it. A shining example of your warped sense of humour, no doubt."

"Alas, no, sir!" Beale moaned, pouring himself another cup of tea, though his hand shook so much that he poured most of it on the table. "It is only too true. The Rembrandt has been stolen, and Master Claude has instructed me to call in the local police, who, as you are well aware, are a pair of fools."

"Nonsense!" the old grandfather said briskly. "You'll do no such thing. If ever there was a bubble-brain it's that sergeant what's-his-name, and the constable is worse. They couldn't find a pig in a parlour. Be so good, my dear Claude, as to leave this matter entirely in my hands."

"You mean you're not going to call in the police?"

"Not at the moment, no. And if I do, it certainly won't be the local boobies. Tell me, Beale, did you notice anything unusual on entering the gallery just now?"

"I noticed that the Rembrandt had been removed from its frame, sir."

"No, no!" the old grandfather said irritably. "Not that, you fool! Was there anything *else*?"

"There may have been, sir," Beale replied, looking offended. "I am a butler, not a detective, and quite possibly I overlooked something. Perhaps several of the other paintings were removed at the same time, though I can assure you that the portrait of your grandmother still hangs in its accustomed place."

"The devil take the portrait of my grandmother!" The old coot thought that over a moment, then added: "In fact, I wish he would. I never could get hardened to the dashed thing. Those eyes of hers, jabbing into me like a couple of rapiers, have haunted me since boyhood days. There was a tough old battle-axe for you! She always reminded me of the crones who did their knitting around the guillotine, watching the heads roll into the basket, at the height of the Terror. One plain, two purl and another coconut. My grandmother would have been at home among them. I can hear the click of her needles now."

"It is the Rembrandt, not the portrait of your grandmother, that has been stolen," Claude reminded him.

"More's the pity, my boy! As I hinted just now, I could get along without the old granny. She always makes me feel as if I had jam on my face."

"What are you going to *do*?" Claude insisted, restraining with difficulty a coarse comment that sprang to his lips—some relic of his schooldays, no doubt.

"I'm going to look into the matter myself," the old grandfather informed him, thoughtfully dissecting a kidney which had cooled off to some extent, but was still fit for human consumption. "As he says himself, Beale is a butler, not a Pinkerton agent on the trail of a bank-robber. He's sure to have overlooked something. You admit, Beale, you dashed from the room like a startled fawn the moment you noticed that the Rembrandt had been removed from the frame?"

"I must confess, sir, I left the room at once. Whether or not I resembled a startled fawn I am not in a position to say."

"The point is this—you did not pause to assure yourself that everything else was in order?"

"No, sir. As perhaps you can imagine, the discovery had come as quite a shock. I was in no fit condition to crawl around on all fours, with a magnifying glass to me eye, looking for clues. Besides, I had no magnifying glass."

"Your sight may be poor; but you would scarcely need a magnifying glass to see if one of the windows was open."

"Every evening, sir, without fail, I put the shutters across the windows, bar them, and draw the curtains."

"I know," the old grandfather nodded. "I've been watching you do it for the past sixty years or so. You should be getting pretty good at it by now."

"Before putting over the shutters, sir, I satisfy myself that the windows are latched."

"Can you satisfy *me* on that point?"

"The windows were latched, shuttered and barred before

dark yesterday afternoon, sir," Beale continued imperturbably. "The two farthest from the door are still, so far as I know, in that condition. I had drawn back the shutters from the window nearest the door, and was moving on to the next, when I noticed the empty frame."

"That took you aback, what?"

"Yes, sir. It reminded me of a dark day in my youth when the demon bowler of our village cricket team caught me between the eyes with one of his most bullet-like deliveries."

"Never mind your dashed youth!" the old grandfather said impatiently. "And besides, I don't believe the game was played so long ago as that. Let us dispense with these boyhood reminiscences, Beale. Some other time I'll gladly listen; but just now I feel more interested in the fate of my Rembrandt. Tell me, do you lock the gallery door at night?"

"No, sir. I have never been instructed to lock the door."

"You were never instructed to put the shutters across, either; but you do it every night. Then the position is that anyone could walk in whenever the spirit moved him, run around the canvas with a razor blade, and push off with the painting under his arm like a roll of oilcloth?"

"That is the position, sir," Beale nodded. "Provided, of course, that the miscreant came from inside the house. Otherwise he would first have to effect an entry."

"No trouble about that, what? I mean, there must be three or four hundred windows in the place. Given patience and perseverance, he'd be bound to find one unlatched. Furthermore, Beale, I don't believe a latched window is going to stop a really determined burglar, a feller trained to the profession and with years of experience behind him. I have no doubt there are methods of opening a window from the outside, with which these lawless types are familiar, short of heaving a brick through the pane."

"You know what?" Derek said suddenly.

"Be quiet, boy!" said the old grandfather, giving him one of his best armour-piercing glances. "One more word from you, or even an animal grunt, and I'll shoot you off to a dogs' hospital for the remainder of your holidays."

Derek was not abashed. Already life had hardened him to harsh words and chilling glances; and if the old grandfather thought to succeed where better men had degenerated into nervous wrecks, it was time he got his penny back.

"What you've got to do is offer a reward," he went on in his stolid way. "One of these handsome rewards we read about. You'll be surprised——"

But the old grandfather had turned to Mr. Massey.

"Oblige me, my boy, by removing this budding sleuth-hound, at present more hound than sleuth," he requested courteously. "And should it happen that you break a few of his bones in the process, I'll gladly pay the doctor's bills."

"Consider it as good as done," Mr. Massey replied, rising to his feet.

"Keep your hands off me, brother!" Derek said, without stirring, but somehow injecting into his eye the mean expression of a snake about to strike. Then, as Mr. Massey closed in, he raised his voice. "Keep your paws off me, you bum! Nobody lays a finger on me——"

He said no more. Mr. Massey had grasped him by the back of the collar and the seat of the pants and swung him to his feet. Next moment Derek found himself moving rapidly towards the door, which Beale, ever on the job, had already opened. Nor were his indignities ended. Suddenly he was released, and a powerful kick helped him on his way.

"Always do as your grandfather tells you," Mr. Massey advised him, turning back.

"You'll pay for this!" Derek bawled, his voice going squeaky with rage. "I'll see the colour of your blood if it's the last thing I do!"

"It's blue," Mr. Massey said, and closed the door.

CHAPTER NINE

MR. MASSEY stood in the snow, staring up at the front of the house. Sally stood beside him, not staring at anything in particular, but awaiting a bulletin. The meeting in the dining-room had broken up in disorder, with Claude demanding that the police be called in, and the old grandfather telling him to mind his own business, over and over again. The debate had given Mr. Massey many a hearty laugh; but nothing constructive had come of it.

"And for a man who loved his Rembrandt, he's taking it very well," Sally remarked suddenly.

"You mean Nunk?" Mr. Massey continued to stare up at the imposing façade of Scumton Hall. "What did you expect him to do—break down and cry like a child? Or run to the kitchen for some ashes to rub on his scalp? No, no! We have our pride. Nunk may be all broken up inside; but he won't show it. And besides, I'm sure he had the picture adequately insured. He wouldn't be so nonchalant if he hadn't. This should solve his financial problems for a year or two."

"I didn't know he had financial problems."

"We all have. Some have too much money, some have too little. Either way, you've got problems. You know what?"

"What?"

"This was an inside job."

"Oh, yes!" Sally agreed. "I came to that conclusion ten minutes ago."

"You did?"

"Yes. There's been a light fall of snow since we came in last night; but though we've been right around the house we haven't seen a fresh footprint."

"The burglar could have come and gone before the snow fell," Mr. Massey pointed out. "You don't know what time the snow was laid on. It might have been just before dawn."

"Oh! I hadn't thought of that. Well, what makes *you* think it was an inside job?"

"Just a hunch. I'm sensitive to hunches. I should have been a great detective."

"*I* get the odd hunch, too," Sally admitted. "And I've got one now. Watch out for Derek."

"You think he's pining for vengeance, what?"

"I think he'd stick a knife in you if he saw his chance."

"Not Derek!"

"Yes, Derek."

"You're afraid I hurt his pride?"

"I think there's nothing he'd like better than to stand by while you were skinned alive—unless it was to do the job

95

himself. I caught him watching you, and it sent cold shivers down my spine."

"Let him try anything like that, and I'll send cold shivers down *his* spine," Mr. Massey said confidently. "I've handled tougher types than Derek. What do you think he might do?"

"I don't know. Put an infernal machine under your bed, or something."

"Carries infernal machines around with him, does he?"

"I don't suppose he has them ready made. But he could fix one up for the occasion."

"What made you think of infernal machines under the bed?"

"I heard him telling your uncle how easy it would be to blow someone to pieces that way."

"He explained the scheme in detail, what?"

"He seemed to know how to go about it," Sally admitted. "And the way he told it, it sounded simple and effective. So perhaps you'd better get into the habit of looking under the bed at night."

"I've got it already. I always take a peep before getting in. Tell me, how did Nunk take it?"

"He listened with the closest attention. You could almost say he hung on every word."

"The hell he did! That's not like him at all. Normally he avoids his grandchildren as if they had all the symptoms of bubonic plague. Tell me, did it strike you that Derek might have been threatening the old grandfather in a quiet way, letting him know what could happen to him under certain circumstances? Or would you say the lad was simply doing his best to carry on an interesting conversation?"

"I don't know. They were both quite calm about it. Derek went into all the technical details, and described what was likely to happen when the bomb went off. That was a messy bit, like an eyewitness account of a train wreck; but your uncle didn't seem put out. I attached no significance to it at the time. It seemed a perfectly normal conversation."

"No conversation with Derek is perfectly normal," Mr. Massey commented. "Unless he has something to say, he doesn't talk. I have a hunch his lecture on the design and construction of infernal machines was intended as a friendly warning. Furthermore, I have a hunch Nunk knew it. Otherwise he'd have advised the lad to go address a public meeting some place."

"I thought I'd mention it, to put you on your guard."

"It was a kindly thought, and I appreciate it," Mr. Massey replied courteously, taking her arm. "Now let's move on. I've seen enough here."

"You won't forget about the infernal machine, will you?"

"Have no fear. I'll bear it in mind."

"It might not be under the bed at all."

"There's always that possibility."

"I mean, he might hide it somewhere else."

"I'll be on the alert."

"Better to be on the alert than spread on the ceiling like jam," Sally remarked. "He said that's what happens when an infernal machine goes off under the bed."

"No doubt he speaks from experience." Mr. Massey turned into the avenue, and stepped out briskly. "Keep your eye open for clues."

"I wouldn't know a clue unless it had a label on it."

"If this was an outside job, the bird who swiped the painting had transport waiting, what?"

"I don't believe he'd walk all the way to the station and wait there for the milk-train," Sally agreed.

"There'd be a high-powered car waiting somewhere, with the engine ticking over, like they have in the best bank robberies. That's what we're looking for now."

"The car?"

"No. The place it was parked."

"What makes you think you'd know it if you saw it?"

"If it's there, we'll pick it out," Mr. Massey replied confidently. "The man at the wheel would be tossing cigarette-butts out of the window all the time, wouldn't he? He's keyed up. He's chain-smoking. His eyeballs ache from staring into the night. He thinks the other duck will never come. He takes four or five pulls at his cigarette, tosses it away, and lights another. So what we have to watch for is a collection of half-smoked cigarettes on the side of the road."

"Maybe he doesn't smoke," Sally objected. "Maybe he chews gum."

"In that case, what we watch for is the half-chewed wad of gum. We're not licked just because this hoodlum doesn't like tobacco."

"And suppose we find nothing at all? That means the Rembrandt is still in its frame, does it?"

"It means the Rembrandt is still in the house, which is what I've suspected all along," Mr. Massey replied. "But don't mention to anyone that I said so."

.　　　.　　　.　　　.　　　.

"I beg your pardon, sir!" said Beale.

"Don't mention it!" the old grandfather replied, continuing on his way. "Dashed if I know what you're apologizing for, anyway," he threw back over one shoulder.

"May I have a word with you, sir?"

At this, the old grandfather halted, turned back, and bent on Beale a glance that went through him like a harpoon.

"Eh, what?" he snorted. "A word with me? What about? Let me tell you, Beale, I'm in no mood for idle chit-chat. If you have some observations to make on the weather, or the behaviour of the under-housemaid, be advised by me and keep them to yourself. My mind is fully occupied with more important matters, as you'd know without being told if you had the sense of a dashed mealie-bug. And don't ask me what a mealie-bug is, because I don't know."

"There is something I feel I should tell you, sir," the butler said in a low voice.

"I'll bet there are lots of things you should tell me. Doesn't concern the under-housemaid, does it?"

"No, sir. It has nothing whatever to do with the under-housemaid."

"You surprise me," the old coot admitted. "She's a seductive-looking wench, and I've been expecting news of her ever since she came. Of course, I don't mean what you think I mean, Beale. That didn't occur to me at all."

"Of course not, sir," Beale agreed politely. "Did you suspect anyone in particular?"

"I didn't suspect anyone of anything! If you have anything important to say, say it! I can't stand here all day listening to kitchen gossip."

"Not here, sir!" Beale whispered, glancing around. "We might be overheard."

"Haw! This is top secret stuff, what?" The old grandfather turned away. "Come along, then—we'll go to my study. Should be fairly private there, unless Derek walks in. What a horrid little bastard the boy is!"

Without expressing an opinion on this final observation, Beale shuffled along at the old coot's heels, and presently they were alone in the study. Not at once, however, did the old grandfather lock the door. First he went on his knees and peered sharply under the settee and chairs, a performance Beale watched with polite interest, but without comment.

"Always as well to be on the safe side, what?"

"Yes, indeed, sir."

"Found Alison here yesterday," the old grandfather went on, rising to his feet. "Dashed if she wasn't stretched out under the settee, as flat as a flounder and as quiet as a corpse in the coffin. Believe me, Beale, I'd never have suspected her presence if I hadn't dropped my matches, and as I was stooping to pick 'em up I caught a glimpse of her dress. So I grabbed her by the leg and hauled her out, and demanded to know what the devil she was playing at, because I don't mind admitting there was a dashed fishy look about it to my way of thinking, and for two pins I'd have turned her over my knee and smacked her bottom until it glowed like a fiery furnace. But she explained that she was involved in a game of hide-and-seek with Derek, so for lack of proof to the contrary I let her go. What do *you* think, Beale?"

"I cannot imagine Master Derek playing hide-and-seek, sir. I should say a fast game of poker would be more in his line." Here, Beale took time off to clear his throat, because it could be he was venturing on to dangerous ground. "If I may say so, sir, they do not appear to be on the best of terms."

"You may say that again. Doesn't surprise you, does it? How could anyone be on good terms with either of 'em? Kublai Khan must have been like Derek when he was a boy. Or am I thinking of Jenghiz? Anyway, I mean the character who massacred practically everyone he met. But if it wasn't a game of hide-and-seek, Beale, why *was* she lying under the settee?"

"I have no idea, sir."

"Unless she hoped to overhear something not meant for her little ears," the old coot muttered. "Something dashed odd going on around here, Beale, if you want my worthless opinion. What could she hope to hear? Well, she's not under the dashed settee now, and the door is locked, so unless there's a tape recorder hidden somewhere we can speak up."

With these few words, the old grandfather poured himself a tot of brandy, for he had had a trying morning and felt in need of something to lend him courage. Adding just a dash of soda-water out of consideration for his liver, which had seemed to be a little scorched of late, he leaned against the mantel-piece and let the heat of the fire play pleasantly on his rear. Meanwhile Beale cleared his throat several times in a rather suggestive manner.

"Nasty cough you've got," said the old grandfather, giving him a sombre look, as if wondering how much longer he might last. "Better be careful, Beale—you're not as young as you used to be. Well, what's this big news you were bursting with a few minutes ago? Something to do with the crime, what?"

"Possibly, sir, and possibly not." Beale barked like a seal, and tenderly massaged his throat. "I feel as if my bronchial tubes were on fire, sir."

"Take a glass of water and put 'em out. What's all this 'possibly and possibly not' stuff? Must be one thing or the other."

"Last night, sir, at about twelve o'clock, I had occasion to go to the pantry for a bottle of sedative, being, as you know, a martyr to insomnia."

"Don't sleep in the dashed pantry, do you?"

"No, sir. I had forgotten to take the medicine to my room. Picture my amazement when I perceived that there was a light in the kitchen!"

"I don't want to picture anything about it!" the old grandfather retorted impatiently. "Say what you have to say without all these dashed flourishes."

Thus encouraged, Beale obliged with a brief account of what he had seen and heard, the old grandfather listening with the closest attention.

"Who's this feller Joe they were talking about?" he asked at the first opportunity.

"I have no idea, sir."

"That doesn't surprise me," the old coot muttered, on a morose note. "You're one of the majority around here. Did you get the impression that this character was actually in the house?"

"If not in the house, sir, then somewhere very close at hand."

"Lurking under cover, what?"

"Precisely, sir. Miss Alison claimed to know his hiding-place; but I have a suspicion she was bluffing. Also I got the impression that she meant him no good."

"Then he had better keep his fingers crossed, dirty dog though he undoubtedly is. If she means him no good he'll be lucky to escape with his life." The old grandfather rubbed his chin, then darted a keen glance at Beale. "You think this character Joe may have had a hand in pinching the Rembrandt, what?"

"There is that possibility, sir. What occurred to me was that this Joe person, being a friend of Master Derek's, is morally certain to be a scoundrel of the very lowest type, and that, if at all possible, he should be located and handed over to the police. I do not accuse him of having stolen the Rembrandt; but nothing could be surer than that he will steal everything small enough to be removed on a lorry unless he is speedily apprehended."

"You think Derek has gone into partnership with this bird, what?"

"That did occur to me, sir," Beale admitted frankly. "My theory is that either Master Derek has smuggled him into the house, which would not be at all difficult, or has him hidden in one of the outhouses. Presumably Joe will be able to dispose of such valuables as are stolen, and Master Derek is to get his share of the proceeds."

"Are you suggesting my grandson is a dashed crook?"

"Yes, sir; I am."

"And you're perfectly right," the old grandfather nodded. "He is, and always will be unless we can do something about it now. So far as I can see the only hope is that he becomes a politician, like his uncle. That's bad enough; but I suppose it's preferable to having him spend the better part of his life as a dashed convict, cracking rocks. Just at the moment, however, I feel we should concentrate on Joe."

"Who is certain to be a dangerous character, sir," Beale mentioned, on a warning note.

"Yes. Very probably you're right."

"More than likely he is armed, sir."

"Haw! You think so, what?"

"Yes, sir. Nowadays a great many criminals carry a lethal weapon of one kind or another, and sometimes both. Nor, I may add, are they slow to use same."

"You're in a dashed cheerful mood!" the old grandfather commented sourly. "Must be those burning bronchial tubes of yours that give you the sunny disposition. Are you suggesting, Beale, that I should go in search of this dangerous criminal, who is almost certainly armed to the teeth, and get myself shot, or possibly bludgeoned into a state of insensibility, for my pains?"

"By no means, sir! You have two sons and a nephew who should be only too happy to undertake the job for you."

For some moments the old grandfather turned this proposition over in his mind, meanwhile sipping his brandy in a manner that made Beale run his tongue over his lips, which felt scorched and blackened to the touch.

"Claude is scarcely the man for the job," he said at length. "I am afraid the fighting blood of the Leighs flows only sluggishly in his veins, if, indeed, it hasn't congealed entirely. It is my considered opinion, Beale, that Claude would run from any moderately resolute rabbit that bared its teeth at him. The mere suggestion that he should undertake a search for a dangerous criminal armed with everything short of the atomic bomb would chill him like a fresh-frozen fillet of fish. It hurts me to say it; but you can leave Claude out."

"No doubt you are right, sir. Master Claude is not a man of action."

"No. John wouldn't do, either. Everyone in the parish would know what he was up to, and Joe would get ample warning. The man for the job, Beale, is my nephew."

"I agree, sir!" Beale said heartily.

"You couldn't but agree. Did you ever pause to ask yourself what it feels like to be stalked by a man-eating tiger?"

"No, sir. I am glad to say the question is one to which I have devoted no thought whatever."

"Yet you'll admit it must be an unpleasant experience?"

"Very unpleasant indeed, sir. I can scarcely imagine anything more unsettling."

"Unless, of course, being stalked by my nephew Hugh. There you have an even more blood-curdling experience, Beale, and one to turn the hair white in a matter of moments. If I allowed myself to think about it from that angle, very soon I'd find myself feeling sorry for Joe."

"Surely not, sir!"

"Yes, Beale. You may not know my nephew so well as I do. Should he find this feller Joe, and should Joe offer any resistance, I shudder to think what might happen. Certainly Joe would be fortunate indeed to escape with more than two or three sound bones in his wretched body—and if he has one limb still functioning, he can count it a miracle."

"Then I should consider Master Hugh the ideal man for the job, sir."

"Oh, yes! Yes, he is. Only thing is, it keeps popping into my mind that Joe, too, has a mother."

"He should have thought of that, sir, before embarking on a career of crime. And more especially, before going into partnership with Master Derek."

"Yes, yes!" the old grandfather sighed. "No doubt he has only himself to blame. Yet one cannot but feel sorry for his poor old mother, who still loves him, we may be sure, despite everything."

"I have no sympathy whatever for his poor old mother, sir," Beale admitted frankly. "Almost certainly she is a person of the very lowest type, and it would not surprise me in the least to learn that she was largely responsible for her son's choice of a criminal career."

"You could be right," the old grandfather admitted, though not without a sorrowful shake of the head. "To the devil with her, anyway! What is she but a raddled old doxy, pickled in gin? Very well, Beale—I'll put my nephew on the job. It's one after his own heart. Meanwhile, not a word to anyone!"

"Certainly not, sir."

"If it got to Derek's ears—and it's amazing how much *does* get to his dashed ears—he'd have Joe out of the place before you could wink." The old grandfather laid a friendly hand on Beale's shoulder. "How fortunate that you had insomnia last night! Otherwise we might never have learned about Joe."

"Very fortunate indeed, sir," Beale agreed, on a note of some reserve. "Nor was I the only one who could not sleep."

"Ha! Someone else was moving around, what?"

"Yes, sir. Master John had insomnia, too."

"The devil he had!" said the old grandfather, staring hard at Beale. "Then it's the first time he's had anything since he had measles as a boy. You met him wandering around, what?"

"He walked into the pantry while I was there, sir."

"What the deuce did he want in the pantry?"

"He had heard noises in the kitchen, sir—which could be explained by the fact that Master Derek ate a cold roast chicken just about then. Master John came down, saw the light in the pantry, and investigated. We talked for perhaps half an hour, then separated and went to bed."

"I see," the old grandfather said slowly. "Hugh and Sally Henderson went out walking at about midnight, and weren't back until two. Claude followed them, and wasn't back until about one-thirty. Derek and Alison are in the kitchen around midnight. John is in the pantry at approximately twelve-thirty. The only guest who went to bed and stayed there was Miss Goodrich, bless her tender heart!"

"Pardon me, sir! Miss Goodrich also was out of her room."

"She was, was she?"

"Yes, sir. Having separated from Master John in the kitchen, I went up by the back stair and took a quick look around to satisfy myself that everything was in order."

"Yes, yes?" the old grandfather said eagerly. "And what did you see?"

"I saw Miss Goodrich at one of the front windows, sir. So far as I could see, she was peering forth into the night. And she had something in her hand that could have been an electric torch."

"Come, come, Beale! What are you suggesting?"

"I am not suggesting anything, sir. I am merely telling you what I saw. Miss Goodrich stood at the window for quite five minutes while I watched her, then moved off quietly in the direction of her room."

"Did you see her go into her room?"

"No, sir. I could not have followed her without being detected. I remained where I was a few moments longer, but saw or heard nothing unusual. Then I went to bed."

"It hurts me even to think of this, Beale—but was she signalling with that dashed torch?"

"Not while I was there, sir," the old butler replied, failing to look at all shocked. "But who can say how long she was at the window before I arrived?"

CHAPTER TEN

THERE was still a quarter of an hour to go before dinner when the old grandfather took Beale by one arm and drew him aside.

"Have you seen Master Hugh around?" he asked in a low voice.

"Around where, sir?"

"Around the house, you old fool!"

"Not since some time this afternoon, sir," Beale replied, refusing to take umbrage. "He was then accompanied by Miss Henderson, and for some reason or other I got the impression he was searching the premises from top to bottom, leaving no stone unturned; but why he found it necessary to be accompanied by Miss Henderson I have no idea."

This was followed by a slight wrinkling of the jowls which could almost be taken for a smile; and the old grandfather, who had been functioning under something of a strain all day, came very close to bursting a blood-vessel as he fought for control.

"Take that grin off your face!" he snorted. "Don't you

realize he may have met with an accident? He's not in his room, and neither is Miss Henderson."

"One would scarcely expect to find Miss Henderson in his room, sir."

"I mean, she's not in hers. It's no laughing matter." The old grandfather lowered his voice another foot or two, until it seemed to come from the bottom of a well, at the same time advancing his face until his lips almost brushed Beale's ear. "He was looking for that dashed dirty dog—the Joseph feller, you know."

"Indeed, sir?" said Beale, jacking up his eyebrows and assuming a disapproving expression. "That had indeed occurred to me; but I decided that Master Hugh would be most reluctant to take a young lady along on so dangerous an excursion."

"He didn't consider it dangerous. To begin with, he laughed heartily when I told him my theory about Joe. Or was it yours?"

"I am quite ready to share the honour with you, sir."

"Dashed nice of you! Anyway, he laughed heartily, and it took me some time to convince him I was serious. Then he said that if I turned out to be right, and this character Joe was indeed lurking somewhere on the premises, he'd lift him up by the ears and shake him out of his skin. At no time did it seem to strike him that there might be any danger involved —except, of course, for Joe."

"Did you warn him, sir, that Joe would almost certainly be armed?"

"I did," said the old grandfather. "I told him Joe was the sort of bird who carried concealed weapons, and lots of 'em, about his person. But it didn't seem to make an impression. So far as I can remember, he said something about taking Joe's concealed weapons and ramming them down his gullet, though frankly I find it hard to believe he would go to such lengths. Making a man swallow a brace of six-shooters, a knife or two, and possibly a set of brass knuckles, scarcely comes under the heading of 'self-defence'."

"And now, sir, you fear that Master Hugh, stumbling upon this desperate character's hiding-place, has fallen victim to one or more of the weapons you mention?"

"Something like that, though I'm dashed if I can imagine how it happened. I'd have backed him against a team of man-eaters. But it's the first time I've known him to be late for a meal, so something's wrong somewhere."

"Perhaps we should put dinner back half an hour, sir?"

"By no means, Beale! I see no need for such extreme measures. If he doesn't turn up, we can take it he has met with a mishap, and is stretched in some unfrequented corner with a lump on his head the size of a grapefruit."

"And Miss Henderson, sir?"

"We can only hope this Joseph feller has a spark of chivalry somewhere in his composition," the old grandfather replied, on a dubious note. "Though I'm dashed if I'd know where to look for it. Meanwhile, Beale, we know nothing."

"Absolutely nothing, sir."

"I mean, we simply express surprise if they don't turn up —not that there's any need for you to express anything at all, of course. Above all, there must be no mention of Joe."

"Certainly not, sir."

"He's an unmentionable type, anyway," the old coot added, moving off. "No bird who knocks a young lady stiff with a stuffed sock can claim to be a gentleman as I understand the term."

.   .   .   .   .

Neither Sally nor Mr. Massey showed up for dinner; but there was no panic. It seemed to the old grandfather, peering around from beneath his eyebrows, that all present were wrapped up to the ears in their own little problems. Public reaction to the two empty chairs was negligible. All John's thoughts and glances were for the beautiful and glamorous Prue, who was—as even the old grandfather would have agreed if taxed—particularly eye-filling tonight in a strapless evening gown that revealed to the best advantage her satin-smooth shoulders and her equally silky back.

Claude, too, seemed fascinated by this vision, and ate in an abstracted manner, pushing the rich food into his mouth and dropping it down the chute as if it had no more flavour than a forkful of hay. His gaze, reserved and brooding, seldom strayed from those flushed and animated features; and it would have become plain to anyone who bothered to think it over that the sudden and mysterious disappearance of his secretary had up to the present occasioned him little alarm and less despondency, and if he had been shocked at first he was getting over it now.

The old grandfather's glance, still probing from underneath the eyebrows, moved on, coming to rest on the delicate and faintly wistful features of his little grand-daughter, Alison. This sweet-faced child appeared to pay no attention whatever to what was going on around her. Most of the time her gaze remained fixed on her plate; and the old grandfather noted, not for the first time, that in a quiet and ladylike way she was stowing away the grub like a hungry anaconda. From time to time, while waiting for the next course, she raised her glance and looked around the table; and if she chanced to catch anyone's eye, a sweet smile curved her lips and wrinkled her nose, making it plain that her heart was swelling with happiness and goodwill to all, as might be expected in one of so lovable a nature.

The old grandfather shuddered slightly, and turned his attention to Derek.

As usual while feeding, the lad had nothing to say for himself. He was a solid worker, sitting close to the table, keeping his face well over the plate, grunting a little from time to time to express his pleasure and appreciation. It was not a delightful performance to watch, but it was one to warm a mother's heart, banishing all fears that her boy might suffer from malnutrition. Yet though his main interest was in the food, and he had no time for idle chit-chat, he listened closely to everything that was said; and even while his jaws worked in powerful and almost unbroken rhythm, his glance roved from face to face as if he hoped, by catching an unguarded expression, to learn something to his advantage.

So far as the old grandfather could judge, there was no reason to suspect that Derek attached undue significance to Mr. Massey's absence. He appeared, indeed, to have no interest in the matter; and the old grandfather rapidly came to the conclusion that if Mr. Massey actually had been set upon by Joe, and beaten unconscious, Derek had as yet learned nothing of it. Certainly there was no sign that the lad was gloating over some secret knowledge, hugging to himself the thought that in the course of the afternoon his cousin had sustained a fractured skull.

.   .   .   .   .   .

The old grandfather was in his study, standing in front of the fire with a glass of brandy in one hand and an enormous revolver in the other, when Mr. Massey knocked and entered. It at once occurred to the old coot that there was something dashed furtive in his nephew's bearing, and instead of raising his voice in gladsome cries he had already lowered it almost to a whisper when he spoke.

"Where the devil have you come from, what?" he inquired, noting how careful Mr. Massey was to close the door with scarcely a sound. "I was on the point of setting out to look for you as soon as I had this dashed gun cleaned. Dashed thing was positively stuffed with dead spiders. Every chamber had at least one corpse in it, and there must have been a dozen in the barrel."

"What's the idea of the artillery, Nunk?" Mr. Massey asked, pouring himself a toothful of brandy. "You're sure it's not loaded?"

"Only with spiders. I thought I might need it if I met Joe—I mean, to blow his leg off with." The old grandfather waved the revolver in Mr. Massey's face. "I tell you, my boy, I'd have shot him like a dirty dog!"

"Be careful you don't shoot *me* like a dirty dog!" Mr. Massey begged. "Put it down, Nunk. I can't really relax with guns being waved in my face."

"I was looking forward to blowing a hole in him." The old coot laid the gun on the table, but only with reluctance. "I felt a sort of blood-lust rising up in me like a gusher. It was frightening, but dashed pleasant at the same time. Primitive, you know. Primordial, and so forth. Sort of urge the dashed caveman felt while creeping up behind his next-door neighbour—the bird with the good-looking wife. But you haven't told me where you've been all afternoon and evening. And Sally—is she safe?"

"Quite safe," Mr. Massey nodded. "Why shouldn't she be? Did you think we'd met with an accident, or what?"

"I thought you'd met with this feller Joe, and he'd knocked you senseless with some type of blunt instrument. That's why I was so keen to shoot him. You didn't bump into him, what?"

"No." Mr. Massey helped himself to a little more brandy. "This talking is thirsty work," he said apologetically.

"Help yourself, my boy. There's plenty for both of us—or there was a few moments ago, anyway. If you didn't fall foul of Joe, then where the devil have you been?"

"In the hayloft."

"Haw! In the hayloft, what?"

"That's right. In the hayloft."

"Seems an odd place to spend the evening," the old coot remarked after a significant pause. "Especially, if you don't mind my saying so, with a young lady. Sally *was* with you, was she not?"

"She was. We were looking for Joe."

"You spent hours and hours in the hayloft, looking for Joe?" The old grandfather raised his eyebrows a little, but not quite enough to be offensive. "What the deuce do you think he is—a dashed earwig, or something?"

"There's a lot of hay up there," Mr. Massey explained. "The thought came to me that Joe might be lurking under it, trying to pass himself off as a cockroach, so I took up the fork and gave it a few prods. I expected to hear from Joe if he was there. It takes a man of sterling courage and resolution to lie mumchance under a wisp of hay while someone prods around with a fork. Must be difficult to choke down the cry of alarm while every moment expecting the tines of a fork to slip in between your ribs and tickle your liver. Calls for an iron self-control, what? The early martyrs had it, too."

"Let us leave the early martyrs out of it!" the old grandfather begged. "Are you trying to convince me that you spent five or six hours prodding this dashed hay in the hope of tickling Joseph's liver, while Sally stood by with a lantern in her hand? Because if you are, my boy, I'm dashed if I believe you."

"I'm not. You're familiar with the hayloft?"

"I am familiar with the hayloft—but not, it would appear, so familiar as *you* are."

"One climbs a ladder to get up, and enters through a trap-door in the floor."

"I am aware of that. After all, I've been around here a matter of sixty years."

"You don't look a day over forty," Mr. Massey remarked politely. "While I was poking around with the fork, hoping to feel a sudden check as it came up against Joe's liver, some wellwisher snuck up the ladder and bolted the trap-door. There I was, caged like a wild beast! And was I wild!"

"Indeed?" said the old grandfather, on a note of considerable reserve. "And Sally caged with you! Did it not occur to you to open the large front doors, through which the hay is loaded, and shout for help?"

"They were padlocked."

"How unfortunate! Or was it? So nobody heard your cries?"

"I'm not in the habit of crying when I get in a jam," Mr. Massey admitted. "I'm self-reliant, that's what."

"Well, how did you get out?" the old grandfather asked, though in a tone that made it clear he was asking only from politeness, and not in expectation of receiving a truthful reply. "Someone came along and drew the bolt, but you don't know who it was, what?"

"No. I cut a hole in the trap-door with my knife, and drew the bolt myself."

"The devil you did! A slow job, what?"

"It took time. The wood is about two inches thick."

"How fortunate you had your pocket-knife with you! Otherwise, my boy, you could well have been there for the night, in which case Sally would have been hopelessly compromised. For that matter, she may be compromised already. I'm not well up on the finer points of the question; but your aunt will put you right if you're in any doubt. I'm sure Sally heaved a sigh of relief when you got the trap-door open. It must have been an anxious time for her."

"She was rather nervous of rats and mice."

"I don't blame her at all. If I'd been in her shoes I'd have been in a state of nervous prostration—purely because of the rats and mice, I mean." The old grandfather threw off a snort of amusement for no clear reason, but cut it short on catching his nephew's eye. "Tell me, my boy, who do you suspect of playing that particularly low trick on you?" he inquired with genuine interest.

"It must have been Derek."

"Certainly a vision of Derek springs to the mind; but have you proof?"

"No," Mr. Massey admitted. "Do we need any? The lust for vengeance burns in him like a fireball. What surprises me is that he didn't put a match to the place when he had me cooped up."

"Possibly the fact that you had Sally with you made him hold his hand," the old grandfather mused. "Nevertheless, my boy, you cannot descend on him with loud cries, brandishing a thin and pliant cane, with the intention of making it hell for him to sit down for a month to come, until the weight of evidence points to his guilt. Or can you?"

"I thought I could."

"No, no! We must play the game, my boy! The urge to promote Derek's spiritual welfare by removing a few square inches of skin from his ample stern may rise strong within us; but justice must be served. The moment you have proof his was the hand that shot the bolt, by all means lay on with a will—and if you feel in need of any assistance, such as holding his feet, call on me. Until we have proof, however, we must hold our hand."

"You're taking a very narrow view of the matter, Nunk," Mr. Massey commented. "Who else could have done it?"

"Has it not occurred to you that Joseph himself could have been the culprit? Perhaps it was Joe who dogged your foot-steps with murder in his heart and two feet of lead pipe in his right hand, watching for his chance to strike. I know it seems rather unlikely; but the whole dashed business is un-likely, what?"

"For a man who has just lost a painting worth thousands, you're bearing up well," Mr. Massey remarked, going off at a tangent. "Almost anyone would think you had it insured for double its market value."

"It's insured," the old grandfather admitted, without

going into figures. "Yet even if it were insured for treble its value, my boy, its loss is going to break my heart—in a manner of speaking, you understand. What is mere money compared to a thing of beauty that has been in the family for generations?"

"Forgive me, Nunk! I didn't realize you felt so deeply about it. Why don't you call in the police?"

The old grandfather did not reply at once. He sat silent, brooding, his gaze fixed on the decanter—which, he regretted to note, was almost empty. When at length he looked up, his eyes were brimming with emotion.

"Why don't I call in the police?" he mused, twisting his features in a mirthless smile. "Yes, indeed, a natural enough question, and one I am likely to be asked by the insurance company if I let it go much longer. But does one call in the police, my boy, when one suspects that a member of one's own family is the thief? What? No, no! Under those circumstances one puts off the evil hour until the last moment, hoping against hope that events might prove one wrong."

"One understands," Mr. Massey nodded, rising to his feet. "It hurts me to say so, Nunk; but I've had much the same idea myself."

"The devil you have!" The old grandfather leaned forward eagerly. "Just between us two, my boy, and in the strictest confidence, who do you suspect?"

"No, no, Nunk! One must play the game. One must have proof. You said so yourself."

Having delivered himself of these noble sentiments, to which he added a snort of amusement for good measure, Mr. Massey slipped from the room, leaving the old grandfather muttering to himself in what sounded like a foreign tongue and cracking his finger-joints.

.   .   .   .   .

Mr. Massey had already found the remains of a steak-and-kidney pie in something that looked like a hip-bath, together with some cold creamed potato and a dish of brussels sprouts, and was spooning large helpings of each on to a plate, when Sally entered the kitchen. She was in pyjamas and dressing-gown, with woolly slippers on her feet; and at sight of Mr. Massey she gave a little chuckle.

"I should have known I'd find you here," she said, carefully closing the door. "I'm so empty I had to come in search of a glass of milk."

"Why not stoke up on a plate of this pie?"

"*Cold?* No, thanks! Have you any conception of what that's going to do to your stomach?"

"It's going to fill it, and that's what I want. I'm as empty as a bass drum. A glass of milk might keep *you* ticking until breakfast; but my system calls for something solid, and calls for it at the pitch of its voice."

"You're not going to eat those brussels sprouts!"

"I'm going to eat most of them."

"An hour from now you'll feel as if you had a couple of bearcats fighting in your stomach."

"No, no!" Mr. Massey said confidently, reaching out for the salt. "Sometimes I think I should have been a sword-swallower. Could be I'm mistaken; but I get the impression that a fistful of old razor blades, a couple of pounds of iron nails, and a generous helping of broken bottles would satisfy my hunger any time without causing me the slightest inconvenience. Some day I'll put it to the test—but not until I've run out of steak-and-kidney pie."

He worked away steadily, while Sally looked on in wonder and misgiving. From time to time he washed down the dreadful mixture with a toothful of brandy, having had the forethought to bring a supply with him. His mind appeared to be occupied with reflections of a somewhat depressing nature, and until he had eaten most of the pie he attempted no small-talk whatever. Sally, sitting on the edge of the table, sipping her milk, waited patiently. She, too, had thoughts to keep her busy.

"Good pie," Mr. Massey remarked at length, pushing back his plate. "I feel a new man already."

"Give it time," said Sally. "You can't expect the sprouts to get down to their deadly work right away, you know."

Mr. Massey moved his chair a little, and slipped an arm around her waist.

"Beale was telling me the oddest thing," he went on,

giving her a squeeze. "You remember how Aunt Martha put John and his American friend in connecting rooms so they could talk all night if they wished without disturbing the household, and how there was widespread consternation when it transpired that John's friend was a most seductive young woman with a mysterious background and every curve in the right place."

"She may have every curve in the right place; but what's this mysterious background you mention?"

"To my way of thinking, any girl who carries a gun in her handbag among the powders and paints has a mysterious background, curves or no curves."

"Can't you leave her curves out of it?"

"They keep popping up."

"Anyway, the gun is a trick cigarette-case."

"It is?"

"Yes. I saw it in action the other day."

"I'm delighted to hear it. However, we're getting away from the point, which is the connecting door between the two rooms. Beale tells me he saved the day, and earned Aunt Martha's undying gratitude, if not John's, by locking the door and putting the key in a safe place. I wasn't there at the time, but I can well imagine the scene when he made the announcement. I can see the old aunt's face lighting up like a beacon as she takes in a great breath of relief and lets it out again—and what surprises me is that she didn't rush forward and kiss Beale on both cheeks. Or did she?"

"No, she didn't."

"I'm sure the urge was there. Of course, she had to fight it down. Apart altogether from its establishing a precedent, Nunk wouldn't like it. He's conservative that way. Hasn't moved with the times."

"Beale *did* tell you something, didn't he?"

"He did. He told me he hung the key in the pantry, but it's not there now."

"What's odd about that?"

"Nothing, I suppose," Mr. Massey admitted. "But Aunt Martha wouldn't like it."

"You think John took the key?"

"Well, it wouldn't be much use to anyone else. Of course,

there's a chance that Aunt Martha took it, just to be on the safe side."

"What's safe about it?" Sally wondered. "It would give John a little more trouble, that's all. I don't see that that's really important to anyone but John and Prue. What *is* important is the missing masterpiece. So long as it remains missing, and the thief hasn't been detected, we're all under suspicion."

"You feel like a toad under the harrow, what?"

"Not exactly. But I do wish we could get it cleared up before Christmas, and that gives us only three days. Do you know what I saw on my way down?"

"No. And even if I did, I'd like to hear about it from your own ruby lips."

"I saw Prue at one of the front windows," Sally went on, disregarding this remark. "She seemed to be in her nightie and dressing-gown, and was just standing there, staring out into the night."

"You didn't see what she was staring at?"

"There wasn't anything to stare at. It's as black outside as a bucket of soot."

"No lights flashing a signal in Morse code?"

"Not that I could see. But she must have been watching for something."

"Maybe she's a flying saucer fan," Mr. Massey suggested tolerantly. "We find them in all sections of the community. John wasn't around?"

"No, she was alone."

"Maybe he's not interested in flying saucers."

"She didn't hear me, either—I took good care of that." Sally wriggled clear of Mr. Massey's encircling arm. "Now I think it's time all honest folk were in bed."

"High time," Mr. Massey agreed. "But whose?"

CHAPTER ELEVEN

MR. MASSEY stared deep into Alison's clear blue eyes, which were as full of innocence as if it had been pumped in under pressure. The thought came to him, from some usually reliable source, that in a few years' time other men would stare deep into those eyes, and more than likely have cause to regret it.

"Please, Cousin Hugh!" she begged prettily, venturing to touch his arm. "You'll help me, won't you?"

"What's your problem?" Mr. Massey inquired, selecting a cigar and gripping it firmly between his teeth.

"I've lost my brooch—the one with my initials on it."

"A valuable piece of jewellery," Mr. Massey nodded. "Studded, I seem to recall, with pearls of great price, not to mention the odd ruby. But tell me, my little pigeon, what do you want me to do about it?"

"Would you help me look for it, please?"

Before replying, Mr. Massey lit his cigar, at the same time giving her another searching glance. Every instinct developed in hunting peevish grizzly bears warned him that there was something dashed odd about all this, and that the proper thing to do was turn down the proposition without a moment's delay.

"What gives you the impression I'm a wizard at finding lost brooches?" he asked on a note of reserve.

The child's lip trembled, and it seemed that any moment now her eyes would brim with tears.

"There isn't anyone else I can ask," she said unsteadily. "And Granny won't let me go out by myself. She's afraid I might slip and break my leg."

"Grannies are like that. They think of everything—everything unpleasant, and usually fatal, I mean. That's because they love their little grandchildren so much, bless their gentle hearts!"

"I know. But it can be a damn' nuisance."

"Pardon me if I seem a little slow to grasp the situation; but with the countryside deep in snow, how do you suggest we might set about locating the missing bauble?"

"It's not a bauble—it's a brooch. I dropped it out of my bedroom window, so it's bound to be somewhere below, isn't it?"

"Provided the law of gravity still functions," Mr. Massey nodded. "Very well—get your coat. We'll brave the elements."

"Oh, *thank* you!" Alison said happily. "Thank you *so* much, Cousin Hugh!"

"And don't call me 'Cousin Hugh'," Mr. Massey added. "Through some involved thought-process or other, it makes me feel as if I had side-whiskers and a yellow waistcoat."

Alison skipped off joyously, to return a few moments later garbed for the great outdoors. Mr. Massey considered it unnecessary to add anything to what he was already wearing. It seemed to him that this was a device to get him out of the house—possibly while Derek planted an infernal machine under his bed. It might be wise, he reflected, to take a look around before retiring for the night. The prospect of having a leg blown off by a home-made bomb was one he regarded with but little warmth.

"That's my window up there," Alison said, pointing. "I was leaning out, and the brooch slipped from my fingers."

"These things are happening all the time," Mr. Massey remarked philosophically, meanwhile running a keen glance over the surrounding snow. There had been a fresh fall during the night, and the surface was soft and yielding. Any small, comparatively heavy object, falling from two storeys up, would sink almost without trace. "Don't move around," he added. "We've got to spot where it went in."

He was standing quite still, peering at the snow, when from somewhere above came the oddest sort of sound, as of some large body rushing through the air. Without pausing even to look up, he whirled, snatched Alison up in his strong right arm, and leaped away from the wall. All this was instinctive, and he had already covered some few yards when the thought came to him that the house was falling. How Derek had accomplished this was not clear; but that the lad was responsible he did not doubt.

An earth-shaking thud from behind seemed to confirm the suspicion that at least one wall of the historic mansion had fallen flat on its face. The danger appeared to be over. Casually dropping Alison into the snow, Mr. Massey turned to look back.

At that very moment, uttering a succession of heart-rending cries, Derek came sliding down the roof, clutching vainly at the icy slates, and with a last despairing howl arched out into space. From three storeys up he fell like a stone, but with arms and legs thrown wide as if to check the speed of his descent. His mouth was open, though no sound now issued forth, and his eyes were shut. He struck with a heavy thud; and Mr. Massey, standing a few yards away, was convinced the ground trembled under the impact.

"*Oh!*" Alison quavered. "Oh, poor Derek!"

Mr. Massey felt this was playing it down a little too much. His impression was that the remains would have to be dug out of the ground with crowbars and pickaxes, for Derek had come down like some missile from outer space. With another storey or two to go, undoubtedly he would have been glowing all over before he struck.

It was at this juncture, as Mr. Massey moved forward to take a look at the body, that the old grandfather appeared as if shot from a gun like some breakfast cereal.

"What the deuce was that awful yell?" he inquired, peering suspiciously at the great mound of snow. "There was something inhuman about it."

"That was Derek," Alison explained before Mr. Massey could get in a word.

"I should have known it," the old coot nodded. "So it *was* something inhuman, what? Where did all this dashed snow come from?"

"It fell off the roof," Alison told him, trustingly taking him by one hand and looking up into his face.

"Haw! Fell off the roof, did it?"

"Yes. And so did Derek."

As this penetrated the outer crust, the old grandfather leaped a few inches off the ground and uttered a startled croak.

"Derek fell off the roof?" he squawked in consternation, his voice breaking in the oddest places. "God bless my soul! What will his mother say? I don't doubt for a moment she'll blame me for the whole thing. Where is he now?"

"He's in here," said Mr. Massey, peering into the hole that marked the spot where Derek had come to earth. "He fell smack on top of this mound of snow, so maybe his injuries aren't completely fatal."

"Is he moving or breathing?" the anxious grandparent

inquired, getting his voice under control. "Or even moaning, what?"

"He's certainly not moving, and I don't hear a sound."

"I'll bet a penny every bone in his body is broken," Alison remarked, without any display of emotion. "If he's not dead, he'll be a cripple for life. The best he can hope for is to have someone wheel him around in a chair—but it won't be me."

"Be quiet, you little monster!" the old coot snorted, bending on her his most terrible glance, though the sentiments she had expressed were almost precisely his own. "Have you no natural feelings whatever? Don't let me hear you speak like that again about your poor brother!"

Having delivered this stinging reprimand, to which Alison responded with a sweet and trusting smile, he turned to Mr. Massey, who was still peering down at Derek in his snowy bed.

"Can't let him lie there until he freezes solid," he said briskly. "He's not a dashed bear holed-up for the winter, living on his fat. Grab him by the leg, my boy, and haul him out. Life is too short to fritter precious hours away like this, standing around getting frostbite. Haul him out, and we'll put him to bed and have him looked over by the plumber— I mean, of course, the doctor."

Thus encouraged, Mr. Massey reached down and secured a firm grasp on the slack of Derek's jacket, and with a single heave lifted the lad clear, afterwards laying him tenderly on the snow. This was a poignant moment. The old grandfather ventured forward to peer at those pallid features; and though outwardly he appeared unmoved, a close observer might have caught the glint of a tear in his eye.

"Looks as dead as a leg of pork," he remarked without emotion. "Hard to tell, though—sometimes I fancy I see his stomach heaving up and down. Take his pulse, my boy, and tell us if the spark still lingers—because if not, I'll have to see about breaking the news to his parents in a cable at about five shillings a word, and at those rates you've got to make every syllable count."

"I seem to feel a feeble flutter."

"Heaven be praised!" the old grandfather said piously,

though normally he was by no means a religious type. "Lift him up tenderly, my boy, and carry him to his room. And if you can accomplish it without his grandmother seeing him, so much the better, because if she catches a glimpse of him in his present condition she'll blow a fuse. Meanwhile I'll get the local bonesetter on the 'phone. Then, should the worst happen, at any rate nobody can say we didn't do our best."

.   .   .   .   .   .

Mr. Massey was down a little early for dinner, and Sally found him alone in the drawing-room, wearing a preoccupied expression as he poured himself a brandy. Nor was his expression misleading, He was in fact so preoccupied that his glass was almost full before he recollected himself.

"You look as if you were trying to solve some problem that has all the electronic brains baffled," Sally commented.

"I was thinking about Derek."

"Everyone in the house has been thinking about him since he fell off the roof this morning. What's the latest bulletin?"

"No change."

"He's still unconscious?"

"In my opinion, he's still pretending to be unconscious. No doubt he was out cold at first, from fright if from nothing else; but I have a hunch he's been wide awake and ticking for the past few hours."

"Dr. Morton says he's suffering from shock."

"Dr. Morton doesn't know him. The lad has a shock-proof system. He's just lying up there with his eyes shut, wondering how much I suspect and how much I can prove, and convincing himself that the worse he seems to be the more readily we'll forgive and forget his boyish prank." Mr. Massey snorted into his glass. "I can read his mind like a railway poster."

"What boyish prank is this? You don't mean falling off the roof, do you? I'm sure he didn't do that for fun."

"His aim was to squash me as flat as a flounder," Mr. Massey said tolerantly, smiling at the very idea. "Whether or not he meant to include Alison in the purge, I can't be certain. I suspect he did. If I hadn't got off the mark like a kangaroo

121

prodded with a pin, I'd have been spread over the flags in a thin paste. And so would Alison, bless her black little heart!"

"Better give me a toothful of brandy or something to help get this down," Sally said, after a brief pause. "Are you hinting, in your own bashful way, that Derek tried to murder you and Alison?"

"More likely his idea was to cripple us for life. Or possibly it didn't occur to him that five or ten tons of snow, falling from a height of sixty-odd feet, would be apt to cause more than minor shock and abrasions."

"He was responsible for the snow falling off the roof?"

"Yep. Also he was responsible for my being directly underneath it when it fell. When he sent it on its way, he had me in his sights. He must have had a good quantity piled up and ready on the roof. When his unsuspecting victim stepped into the target area, he started his little avalanche, sending up a silent prayer it would ring the bell."

"Only you weren't unsuspecting?"

"I'm never unsuspecting when dealing with Derek or Alison." Mr. Massey poured himself a little more brandy, for he felt it was doing him good. "It's like stalking a man-eating tiger. One has to keep on the alert. If I hadn't been keyed-up a little tighter than usual, I shudder to think of what might have happened."

"Better pour me another before your hand shakes too much. It sounds rather far-fetched, you know. For instance, how could he possibly see you from where he was? He was at the attic skylight, halfway up the roof, and you were right in against the wall of the house. He couldn't have seen you unless he had a periscope."

"He had a mirror on the end of an old salmon-rod, which was just as good. I found it in the attic shortly after my miraculous escape from assassination."

"Oh!" Sally murmured. "That *is* rather a black mark, isn't it?" She looked at Mr. Massey, her eyes widening. "If you hadn't got out from under, that lorryload of snow *would* have put a crimp in your hair, right enough. It didn't miss you by much?"

" 'A matter of inches', our hero replied nonchalantly.

I must have bust all records for the standing jump, snatching up Alison on my way."

"Then she didn't know what was coming? If she was in on the plot she'd have stood well clear."

Mr. Massey shook his head.

"She didn't know what was coming," he agreed. "As a matter of fact, she thought Derek wanted me out of the house so he could plant an infernal machine under my bed and blow me to pieces. He gave her ten shillings to get me outside for ten minutes, and told her exactly what to do and how to do it."

"How did you learn all this?"

"She told me. We had a heart-to-heart talk shortly after the incident occurred, and I convinced her that in the public interest it was her duty to tell the whole truth."

"You mean to say she was ready to stand around twiddling her thumbs while Derek blew you to pieces?"

"No, no! You underestimate the little angel. It wouldn't have done her a bit of good to see me blown to pieces. Her idea was to double-cross Derek by waiting until the bomb was planted, then inform on him in the hope of a substantial reward. And if Derek was skinned alive, as seemed likely, that would make it perfect."

"Oh!" Sally said. "I'm afraid I'm out of my depth in these criminal circles."

"You've got to keep on your toes. Unfortunately for Alison, Derek was one jump ahead of her. The only mistake he made was in getting out on the roof to start his avalanche going. He should have had a rope around his waist. But there you are. A boy has to learn." Mr. Massey glanced towards the door as Claude entered. "By the way, treat all that as confidential."

"Of course!" Sally nodded. "Nobody will know a thing about it until you're blown through the roof."

.   .   .   .   .

John knocked quietly at the connecting door, then without further shilly-shallying turned the handle and walked in.

He had chosen what looked like a most embarrassing

moment. The glamorous Miss Goodrich was half into her nightie and half out of it, and even the half that was in could scarcely be regarded as modestly tucked away, the nightie itself being of such gossamer material that it looked as if it had come straight off a fairy loom. Nevertheless Prue showed no embarrassment whatever, and with a most entrancing wriggle shook the filmy garment into place. Nor was John the type to waste time on insincere protestations of regret. Stepping forward briskly, he folded her in his arms, and for some moments they clung together, lip to lip in a passionate kiss.

"My sweet!" John whispered at length, first taking in a deep breath and letting it out again.

"Honey!" Prue replied, on an equally tender note. Then she held him at bay, though not very far, meanwhile staring deep into his eyes. "Honey-pie, it's got to be tonight!"

"Oh!" John said, on a rather flat note. "It's got to be tonight, what?"

"Yes. It's got to be tonight."

"Oh! Right-o!"

"Everything's set," the beautiful young woman continued, as if trying to convince herself rather than her honey-pie. "I guess we'll never get a better chance, so why put it off any longer?"

"Conditions pretty favourable tonight, what?"

"I mean, with Derek lying unconscious, nobody's going to think about *us*, or wonder what we're doing. And if we put it off, anything could happen."

"What, for instance?"

"For instance, I could hand your fat brother a poke in the eye!" Prue replied, and much of the tenderness was gone from her voice.

"Claude, what?"

"That's right. Claude."

John's strong right hand, which had been caressing Prue's flank, bunched into a fist.

"Been annoying you, has he?"

"He hasn't made a pass at me, if that's what you're thinking. I don't believe he'd know how."

"He could look it up in a book."

"It's what he says about *you*, honey."

John's hand relaxed, and once again he fell to stroking his beloved's flank, which felt warm and wonderfully smooth to the touch. The routine appeared to soothe him, for his voice was tender and filled with love when he spoke.

"What does he say about me, sweetheart?"

"He says you're a no-good bum."

"He doesn't!"

"That's it boiled down, with the fat skimmed off. He wrapped it up nicely; but the message was there. He said you were a shining example of wasted talents, and what a pity it was you'd never found anything to hold your interest."

"But I *have!*"

"He meant in the line of work, honey," Prue answered, with a delicious little shiver, and snuggling closer into his enveloping arms. "The way he tells it, you're going to live on your father's charity all your life."

"That's better than skinning the populace, like a politician. And besides, it's not true. The old man won't last that long."

"I know it's not true—but that doesn't make it any easier to take. What I'm afraid of is that I'll lose control and hand him a poke in the eye."

"Everyone would think very highly of you if you did," John said soothingly. "There's nothing you could do would get you faster into the family's good graces. Don't worry about Claude. He's just a stuffed shirt, and badly stuffed at that. But if you think the time has come to burn our boats, that's all right with me. Just put me down as your slave, waiting on you hand and foot."

"You say the cutest things!" Prue murmured; but it was obvious she was thinking of something else. "You don't feel bad about it, do you, sugar?" She gazed appealingly into his eyes. "You don't feel real bad about it, huh? I wouldn't ask you to go through with it if I thought you were going to have it on your conscience maybe for years."

"No, no!" John whispered, on a throaty note, pressing her all the more strongly to his bosom. "I'll go through with it to the bitter end. My conscience won't bother me a bit— I'm not sure if I was issued one, anyway. If I was, it doesn't seem to work too well. You say the time is ripe, and that's good enough for me. Nothing will stand in my way—I hope."

"The longer we wait, the more risk we run. I think your father sort of suspects us."

"You do, what? How do you get that impression?"

"It's something in the way he looks at me when he doesn't know I'm watching him."

"I've noticed it myself," John nodded. "But in my opinion it has nothing to do with what you're thinking about." He held her at arms' length and stared deep into her eyes. "Well, let's decide, sweet! Do we or don't we?"

"We do!" the beautiful girl said firmly.

"Right-o! We do. Here and now?"

"Here and now. Why wait?"

"Right-o!" John said again, releasing her. He moved quietly to the door, and switched off the light. "Just stay put a moment, poppet, while I make sure the coast is clear."

Quietly opening the door a quarter of an inch, he put one ear to the crack and waited patiently for results. No sound that seemed suspicious impinged on the quivering ear-drum, and after a few moments he took his ear away and replaced it with his eye. Peer as he might, he saw only lurking shadows. He opened the door a little wider, and thrust out his head— and the certainty that anyone who saw him thus peering forth from his beloved's room like a turtle from its shell would put a wrong construction on the matter made him as wary as a rat in a cats' home.

"All clear!" he whispered, pulling in again. "Better throw on your dressing-gown, sweetheart—it's cold outside. Meanwhile, I'll collect the goods."

With these terse words (he was beginning to feel a little strung-up), he stole out, moving almost without a sound, for he had had the foresight to remove his shoes before entering Prue's room.

Left alone, that glamorous young woman threw on her dressing-gown and wiggled her feet into slippers. Groping on the bedside table, she found her torch. This completed her simple preparations, and without pausing however briefly to examine her conscience she left the room, laying a course for the gallery overlooking the hall. A few moments later, with nothing to report, she stood at one of the tall windows commanding the avenue and the distant road.

It was a dark night, with layer upon layer of heavy cloud hiding the stars; and Prue, staring out, might as well have been peering up a chimney. Raising her torch, she pressed the button twice, and waited.

Three times a light winked at her from somewhere near the road.

She drew in a quick breath, and a little shiver ran through her shapely figure. Once again she pressed the button, and once the light outside answered her right back.

That was all. The message had been received and understood.

As she turned back towards her room the gallery lights were switched on, and she found Claude, in pyjamas and dressing-gown, staring at her in a very significant manner at a range of a few yards.

CHAPTER TWELVE

As BEFITTED a rising young politician who hoped one day to shape his country's destiny—and his own at the same time—Claude was seldom caught on the wrong foot. Even this present situation, delicate as it was, found him at his ease, though the brief glimpse he got of Prue's nightie, before she could draw her dressing-gown about her, resulted in an immediate acceleration of his pulse. Furthermore, as he moved closer to her, he had a suspicion that the *bumpetty-bump* of his heart could have been picked up on a tape-recorder a hundred yards away, and when played back would be indistinguishable from the beating of a tom-tom in the depths of the jungle.

"Come, Miss Goodrich!" he said in a low voice—for he had no wish to rouse anyone from well-earned slumber. He took Prue by one wrist, and attempted to steer her towards his room. "This way, please."

"Just a moment, brother!" Prue begged, hanging back. "Which way do you mean?"

"Will you step into my room for a few moments, please?" Claude thought that over, and decided it could be taken in more ways than one. "I feel you owe us an explanation."

"I don't owe you a thing. And even if I did I wouldn't step into your room, either. If you want me in your room you'll have to drag me in by the hair, and the betting is I'll beat your brains out with this torch before you get me there. What's *eating* you, anyway?"

"Nothing is eating me," Claude replied stiffly, abandoning for the time being all hopes of a conference in his room. "The fact of the matter is, I caught you red-handed."

"What did you catch me *at*?" Prue asked, opening her eyes wide. "What was this awful thing I was *doing*?"

"You were signalling with your torch to someone on the road."

"In Morse code, huh?"

"I don't know what code you used. Doubtless you had some signal prearranged. The important thing is, who was your accomplice?"

"That was Santa Claus out there," Prue replied nonchalantly. "I was letting him know what I wanted in my stocking for Christmas."

Had Mr. Massey been present, he would have jumped at this opportunity to assure Prue that she already had in her stocking everything a girl could want; but Claude was a more serious-minded type, with no time for such frivolity. Furthermore, behind his icy exterior he was boiling with rage inside. It drove him to the verge of hooting like a factory siren to think that this beautiful young woman, with whom he had come dangerously close to falling in love, had turned out to be a crook. That sort of thing might very well happen to people like John, who had no intelligence, anyway. It had no right to happen to a rising young politician.

"Do you deny that you were signalling?" he asked coldly.

"I deny nothing, and I admit nothing," Prue replied, on an equally aloof note. "If there are any explanations to be made, I'll make them to your pop. Meanwhile, brother, my advice to you is to go throw yourself in a ditch."

It was at this point, as Claude speculated on his blood-pressure with one half of his mind, and sought with the other words that would burn and sting like a swarm of hornets, that John appeared in the shadowy corridor at his back. In his right hand he held at shoulder level what looked like a cricket-stump; and no crystal ball was needed to foretell that in another moment or two, barring accidents, Claude was fated to meet with an unpleasant surprise.

"No!" Prue said sharply; and John paused, looking annoyed.

"No what?" Claude inquired, unconscious of the danger of having his head broken.

"No, I won't go to your room!"

"You said that before," Claude pointed out, while John, with a glint in his eye, crept forward a few more inches. "Besides, since it would appear you mean to adopt a defiant attitude, the obvious solution is to hand you over to the police. One cannot afford to be chivalrous where a painting worth many thousands of pounds is concerned." He paused a moment to clear his throat, then added: "Nor will your beauty sway them, my dear Miss Goodrich."

"No!" Prue said, seeing the cricket-stump rise slowly. She relaxed as it sank again. "No, of course my beauty won't sway them." She took in a deep breath. "I think you'd better go," she went on, her glance just grazing Claude's left ear. "Go now, while you can." She nodded slightly as John's eyebrows rose another notch. "Go at once."

"I don't know what the devil you're talking about!" Claude snorted. "Why should I go at once?"

"Because I might bust this torch over your head if you don't. And I'd be sorry to do that. It's a good torch."

The message had got through. John turned, though not without reluctance, and withdrew into the dark corridor. Prue's fingers beat a quick tattoo on the panelling to cover any sounds he might make in his retreat.

"I must ask you to return to your room," Claude said at length, having turned the problem over and over in his mind and studied it from every angle. "If you refuse, I shall be compelled, most reluctantly, to use force."

"You don't need to use any force, brother," Prue assured him. "Just move aside and I'll return to my room like a tired bird to its nest. We can pick up the threads come morning."

"I shall then lock you in," Claude added, courteously stepping aside to let her pass.

"Huh? You'll lock me in?"

"Certainly. So that you cannot signal to your accomplice, whoever he may be."

"You've got some idea of going after him?" Prue asked curiously.

"Yes. I intend to go after him and take him into custody."

"He'll eat you alive, whether or not he likes the rank flavour."

"I shall carry a weapon of some sort—probably a shotgun. Should your friend become at all aggressive, I shall consider it my unpleasant duty to shoot him in some not necessarily vital spot, such as the leg. Move along, please."

Prue moved along, but at her leisure. She reckoned that by now John had left the house and was within sight of the successful accomplishment of his mission. Claude might go poking around with a shotgun, pining for an opportunity to shoot someone in the leg; but the odds were against his arriving on the scene in time to bag a victim. Yet it might be as well, she thought, halting at her door, to delay him a little longer.

"Look," she said, searching his face in the gloom, but finding nothing of value. "Is this the way you treat your guests in Scumton Hall? Is this the boasted hospitality of the Leighs? Just because I stand at a window with a torch in my hand I'm locked in my room and treated like I'd been caught spreading the plague. What's it all *about*?"

"You know perfectly well what it's all about," Claude replied stiffly. "It's all about the Rembrandt, and damn' well you know it!"

"What about the Rembrandt?"

"You've stolen it—that's what!"

"That statement verges closely on the slanderous," Prue commented critically. "I'll bet you wouldn't make it with a few witnesses standing around with notebooks. Can you *prove* I stole the Rembrandt? Maybe I flashed a message to someone outside; but what makes you think it had any connection with your darn old picture? I could have been making a date with a boy friend, couldn't I?"

"Bah!" the young politician snorted scornfully, raising one hand to push her into the room, but pulling it back in the nick of time to save himself a nasty knock on the head with

Prue's torch. "You're trying to delay me in the hope that your accomplice will take alarm and make his escape. Oblige me by stepping into your room without any further nonsense. Or would you prefer me to rouse John and have him stand guard over you until I return?"

He was gratified to note that this suggestion had had the desired effect. Apparently this beautiful young woman, though abandoned to a criminal career, could still feel the pangs of shame. At mention of John she hung her head; and although it was much too dark for him actually to witness the phenomenon, Claude had no trouble in imagining her blushing all over. In fact, he found it quite a pleasant mental exercise.

"You'd like that?" he asked, turning the knife in the wound—purely for her own good, of course. "I'll call him now, shall I?"

"Oh, no!" she whispered. "Please don't! I . . . I couldn't face him."

"You should have thought of that before embarking on a career of crime," Claude said sternly. "Perhaps only now you begin to realize into what desolate surroundings, what blighted wastes, the primrose path has led you." His voice softened a little, for after all he was only human. "But do not despair!" he went on, laying a fatherly hand on her shoulder. "Be of good cheer! You are young. It is not yet too late to turn back. It is not too late to make amends. The day may come when once again you can raise your head and stare society in the face, proud and strong in the knowledge that you have atoned. Look up! The future lies before you!"

Deeply moved by this powerful peroration, Prue turned away, hiding her face in her hands, and with a muffled sob as her only reply crept into her room. The door closed quietly. A moment later it opened again, and she passed out the key. This simple act warmed Claude through and through like a noggin of rum toddy. Here, he told himself, was a reformed character, a brand plucked from the burning—and he was the one who had done the plucking. Doubtless a good mark would go down to him for that.

Carefully locking the door, he pocketed the key and moved off to his own room; for it had occurred to him that if he was to dash forth into the night in pursuit of a desperate criminal more than likely armed to the teeth, it would be as well to put on his trousers.

. . . . . .

While all this was going on, John had left the house by a dining-room window and hurried into the night. For the first few yards he maintained a steady progress through the snow; then a thought seemed to strike him, and he paused, looking down at his feet. In the press of events, his mind being occupied almost entirely with visions of a cricket-stump splintering over Claude's head, he had forgotten to put on his shoes. The question was, should he go back and get them now, or should he push on, laughing scornfully at the danger of frost-bite?

He pressed on. The prospect of losing a few toes, and perhaps hobbling on a stick for the rest of his life, filled him with gloom; but now that Claude was hot on the trail, details such as the loss of a toe or two could not be allowed to weigh in the balance. More important issues than toes were at stake.

He was nearing the massive ironwork gates, the pride of Scumton Hall (they had been rusted solid for the past seventy-nine years), when without warning a figure appeared from underneath the immemorial elms, blocking his path. John's first thought, as he pulled up, was that this was a bear; and had it dropped on all-fours, and growled, he would have been convinced he was right. Next moment, however, taking a closer look, he saw a cigar projecting from among the fur, and knew he had to deal with a man like himself, though better dressed to withstand the cold.

"Ahuh!" said this person, first removing the cigar. He advanced a few paces, looking John over as best he could in the unearthly twilight reflected from the snow. "You're young Leigh, huh? Huh?"

"That's right," John admitted frankly. "And you're Pop, what?"

"I'm not *your* pop!" the gentleman in the fur coat grunted; and it seemed to John that for some obscure reason he had taken umbrage. For a moment he was silent, chewing his cigar. (He had a loose denture either above or below, John thought.)

Then once again he went on the air. "You got the picture, huh? Huh?"

"Right here!" said John, tapping the rolled canvas he carried under his left arm. "By the way, I think it might be as well if we didn't linger here too long in pleasant prittle-prattle, and so forth. My brother saw Prue flashing the message to you, and I shouldn't be at all surprised if he suspects something."

"The hell with him! Let him suspect until he's black in the face!"

"I know. But he's liable to come out with a shotgun, popping at every shadow, and personally I'm not keen on spending my Christmas in bed, with some medical type going over me with a mine-detector, picking out the buckshot. My opinion, for what it's worth, is that we should part without any unnecessary delay, because Claude—my brother, you know—took a very poor view of Operation Rembrandt, and I have a theory he'd welcome a chance to blow off a head or two by way of squaring the account."

"Zat so?" said the befurred one, curling a contemptuous lip around his cigar. "If he comes near me with his darn shotgun I'll ram it down his throat."

"And I'd love to watch you do it," John admitted courteously. "But apart from that aspect of the matter, my feet are getting cold."

"Yeah? I thought they were."

"I find socks by themselves aren't enough."

Still chewing his cigar, the character in the fur coat looked down at John's feet, and for some moments was content to stare without saying a word.

"Yeah," he said at length, on a rather quieter note. "Socks by themselves aren't so good in snow. Boots are better, huh?"

"Much better," John agreed. "So, knowing my feet feel like a couple of ducks in the deep freeze, you won't take it amiss if I head back to the old hay-bag, what? They tell me frostbite can be a very painful affliction, and it's remarkable how attached to one's toes one becomes when in danger of losing them. Normally, of course, we never spare them a thought. Only when we have visions of them falling off like apples do we realize they're an essential part of our equipment."

"Yeah, yeah! Every word you say is true." The citizen in the fur coat reached out a gloved hand. "I'll take a look at the picture before you go."

"Think you can spare the time? Every moment I expect to see Claude pounding up the trail with a gun in each hand and fire in his eye."

"It's okay with me if he has fire in his——" The befurred one checked himself abruptly, peering towards the shadowy bulk of the house. "Maybe we better not waste any time," he admitted, seeing it from John's angle for the first time. "A nut with a shotgun can be a danger to all, at that. But I don't move from here until I get a look at that picture, see?"

"Better take a look at it, then," John said, obligingly untying the ribbon that held the canvas. At the same time, it occurred to him that this old bird had a suspicious sort of mind. He held the canvas open as best he could—it showed a tendency to curl up again if he relaxed for a moment. "You won't see it at its best. The light is bad. But at least you'll be able to satisfy yourself it's the Rembrandt, if you have any doubt."

"That's the Rembrandt?" the old bird muttered in a choking sort of voice. *"That's* the Rembrandt!"

"It is, isn't it?"

John held the picture off to one side, and took a look at it himself. Almost at once he realized that somewhere a cog had slipped. In place of the rather florid features of the burgher, he found himself confronted by the portrait of his great-grandmother—and though the light was bad, and the portrait was a gloomy piece of work at any time, her glance went through him like both barrels of a ray-gun. He could understand why his father, who had known the old battle-axe personally, shied like a nervous filly every time the picture caught his eye.

"Whew!" he said, recovering his poise, or some of it. "It's the old great-granny in person. Comes as a bit of a shock, what? Makes you wonder how the winkle feels, impaled on the pin. If she's like that in oils, what must she have been in real life,

with the eyeballs revolving in their sockets? The mind boggles, what?"

The citizen in the furs was still making animal noises to himself, and appeared to be more or less rooted to the ground; but suddenly something snapped. Uttering an inarticulate growl, he snatched the canvas from John, rolled it into as tight a tube as possible, and began to beat him over the head with it, using both hands to get a more telling blow.

"The devil take you and your darn old great-granny!" he panted, tossing aside the family portrait, which had buckled almost at the first blow, and using his fists instead. "A pox on the whole crooked bunch of you, great-granny and all!" He launched a murderous uppercut at John, and came close to falling flat on his face when it failed to connect. "Stand up and fight!" he snorted. "Stand up and fight, you yellow young skunk! You and your darn old great-granny!"

"Something dashed odd about it," John admitted, warding off a couple of haymakers. "Take it easy, old trout—you'll rupture something. It was the Rembrandt we cut out and hid away—no doubt about that. I mean to say, on the one hand you've got this bluff, hearty citizen with a twinkle in his eye, a roystering blade and a devil with the ladies; and on the other we have old squaw Eagle-nose, the scourge of the nineteenth century. Couldn't possibly be confused, what? Even in a hurry, you couldn't mistake one for the other. And we weren't in a hurry. So it looks as if someone did a quick switch, what? Sabotage, that's what it is, no less."

It was obvious from the tone of his answering snort that the old bird had nothing but contempt for this theory, and more than likely he would have said so the moment he got his breath back but that Claude, just then drawing within range, took a sporting shot at the two figures struggling in the snow. Claude did this not so much because he was eager to shed blood, but because he wished it to be clearly understood by these desperate characters that he was armed and ready to shoot. Now that he had actually made contact with them, he was anxious to see them withdraw hurriedly— and if they withdrew so rapidly as to obviate all chance of pursuit, that was fine with him, too.

Luckily, having been terrified of firearms since his

boyhood, when his brother Alfred had lodged an airgun pellet in his stern with malice aforethought, Claude was an indifferent marksman. The charge of duckshot that went whistling through the night passed well to the left of John and his accomplice, and a good ten feet high. Nevertheless it became plain that Claude meant business, for without waiting a moment to see if he had drawn blood, he loosed off another broadside, this time blowing a hole in the snow halfway to the target.

"Run for your life!" John bawled.

Whether he intended this as advice for his accomplice, or to spur himself to superhuman efforts, was not clear, for the citizen in the furs was already running for his life, and running good. Purists might have found much to cavil at in his style, and after the first twenty yards it was evident that he was out of training; but he was covering the ground, snow flying in all directions as, arms flailing and head well back, he hurled himself towards the road.

"Halt!" Claude roared, fumbling with the shotgun. "Halt, or I'll fire!"

He raised the gun close to his face for a better look, and at that moment his questing thumb found the lever, and the case ejected from the left barrel caught him a smart crack between the eyes. He staggered back with a sharp yelp of pain; but by now his fighting blood was roused, and a berserk fury filled his bosom like a bad attack of heartburn. Muttering coarse oaths, he slipped two cartridges into the breech and charged forward, resolved to come to closer quarters this time before loosing off. Every shot must tell. Every pellet must strike home. Who was it had told his men to hold their fire until they could see the whites of the other fellows' eyes? No doubt the advice had been sound on that occasion; but it could not be applied to the present situation, since these two underworld characters seemed resolved to retire from the field without affording him an opportunity of seeing the whites of their eyes or anything else. And besides, Claude reflected—thoughts were scurrying around in his head like caged mice—more than likely the whites of their eyes were yellow from evil living, anyway.

John had lost no time in following the example of his

partner in crime, who had left a trail like a runaway grizzly. It did not occur to him to make his identity known to Claude. For that matter, he felt that it would be most unwise to loiter around, treating the whole matter as a joke, until Claude came dashing up. That would involve too much danger of being bowled over like a rabbit. Claude seemed to be in the mood to shoot first and listen to explanations afterwards —and though he was a poor shot, nasty accidents could happen.

By now the citizen in the fur coat had reached the road, wheezing hoarsely. His stride had lost much of its spring, and there seemed a good chance that he might founder at any moment; but with dogged courage he kept going until some hidden obstacle caught his foot and brought him down. He lay flat on his face in the snow, a spent force.

John grasped him by the slack of the coat and heaved him to his feet.

"Keep going, pardner!" he said encouragingly. "Unless you want to spend Christmas in the can. The sheriff and his posse are coming up behind."

"The hell with them!" the fugitive gasped, shaking off John's helpful grasp. "The hell with you, too! I hope that nut blows the pants offa you, you bum!"

"He's liable to blow the pants off us both if you don't get a wiggle on."

This reminder that Claude played no favourites had the desired effect. John's pardner lurched forward, and in a few moments was at the door of a large and powerful limousine parked well in underneath the trees. He opened the door, and hauled himself in behind the wheel. At the same time, John opened the other door, and was about to climb in when his pardner placed a foot against his chest and with brutal violence thrust him out.

"You get the hell outa here, you bum!" he snorted.

Taken by surprise, John stumbled back, tripped, and sat down in the snow. The door slammed, the engine started, and the car leaped forward.

Claude, plodding doggedly on like some intrepid explorer with his sights set on the South Pole, reached the gates in time to see the car accelerate up the road. Throwing the gun to his shoulder with careless abandon, he fired both barrels. The range was extreme; but he had the satisfaction of hearing the pellets rattle on the body, and the thought that a paint job might be called for warmed him up.

He did not see John. That young man, lying quite still in the shadow of the trees, did his best to look like a Yule log dragged from the woods by the local peasants.

Claude, turning back towards the house, was not dissatisfied. He felt he deserved the greatest credit—and had no doubt he would get it—for what he had achieved. True, the crooks had got away, though more than likely they were wounded, and might possibly die on the way; but the important thing was that in their terror and confusion they had left the Rembrandt behind.

CHAPTER THIRTEEN

"PROWLING around, what?" said the old grandfather, looking Mr. Massey over inch by inch, but not with active suspicion. "There are times, my boy, when you put me in mind of a young leopard in its strength." He brooded a moment, and then added, on a rather poignant note: "I was like that myself, once. It doesn't last."

"Prowling around," Mr. Massey nodded. "There was a certain amount of coming and going, Nunk, before you showed up. Sounded like quite a heavy traffic. Things have quietened down now, though."

"Hasn't been the same since Claude locked Prue in her room," the old coot nodded. "It seems he caught her signalling to some low character outside, and took it on himself to shut her up for the night. That's the trouble with the dashed political mentality—if you have it, you've got to interfere in everything, whether it concerns you or not. Pot-bellied bean-brain! Why the devil can't he keep his big snout out of this business? It's difficult enough without him floundering around like a drunken elephant."

Gloomily, his hands in the pockets of his dressing-gown, he stared out into the night, where at that very moment

Claude was pushing resolutely forward on the trail of the missing masterpiece.

"Always mucking things up!" he muttered. "Been like that all his wretched life. Charges in, no doubt with the best intentions, and lays a double-barrelled hex on everything in sight. By the time he was in his 'teens I knew he was cut out to be a successful politician, because he never could keep his paws off other people's business. Damned politicians—there should be an open season for them!"

The sound of Claude's first broadside came tapping at the window-pane. At this evidence that his son was involved in a shooting war with the desperadoes he had set out to trail, the old grandfather became more dejected than ever.

"There he goes!" he said heavily. "Both barrels. Duckshot whistling all over the place, and every man's life in jeopardy. Especially his own. He's more likely to shoot himself than whatever he aims at. Just as well all the animals are shut up in this weather, or the odds are he'd bag himself a horse. Think of a fool like that helping to shape the destinies of the country!"

"Should I push out and see what's going on?" Mr. Massey asked.

"No, no, my boy! Be wise, and stay where you are. If he saw you coming he'd do his best to blow you to pieces, working on the theory that prevention is better than cure and it's better to be sure than sorry, and, possibly, that a stitch in time saves nine. Certainly he'd have some cliché to fit the situation. He's never been without one yet. What a miserable creature he is! What pleasure does he get out of life?" The old grandfather threw off a snort of amusement. "The first time he looks like falling in love with a girl—or possibly with her father's automobile factories and oil-wells and paper mills and so forth—she turns out to be a crook! Ironic, what?"

"You mean Prue?"

"Prue, of course. Had you not remarked the slight gleam in his eye when his glance rested on her? That was something new, my boy. It had never been there before. There were moments—though you'll find this hard to believe—when he looked almost human. Normally his eye is detached, cold, impersonal. It could be grafted on to a dead codfish on a

139

slab, and no questions asked. Only an expert could tell the difference. But since Prue arrived, a little warmth has crept in. Not with confidence, mark you! Not boldly, sure of its welcome. No. There was about it something of the air of a dog in a strange neighbourhood, knowing that at any moment it is liable to receive a well-aimed stone in the short ribs. Nevertheless it was there; and that, for Claude, was something new and full of wonder. Ah! There the damn' fool goes again! I was beginning to suspect he had shot himself between wind and water—and he's practically nothing else—with the first salvo."

"Those shots were farther away," Mr. Massey remarked. "On the road, or thereabouts."

"No doubt he has trailed the criminals to their car," the old grandfather nodded, though without any trace of pride in his tone. "He doesn't know what fear is—he hasn't enough intelligence. We may shortly expect his triumphant return, provided these criminal types he has been annoying haven't lost patience with him and beaten him into a state of insensibility."

"What makes you think there's more than one, Nunk?"

"I have no idea how many there are, my boy; but I am confident that Claude will assert there were seven or eight, all very large and powerful characters, and ferocious to a degree. However, as I was saying, is it not sad indeed that the one young woman abundantly equipped with that indefinable something needed to stir Claude's sluggish senses should turn out to be the accomplice of thieves and gangsters of the lowest type? No fit consort, you will agree, for an ambitious young politician who hopes one day to move into No. 10 Downing Street while thousands cheer."

All this was delivered in a calm, judicial tone, as if the old grandfather entertained no doubts whatever on the question; but nevertheless it was accompanied by a slight elevation of one eyebrow and a searching glance, and Mr. Massey felt that the old uncle would welcome an outside opinion, though it might not necessarily dispose him to change his own.

"You're satisfied she *is* a crook, Nunk?"

"I am not satisfied about anything," the old coot replied frankly, if without giving a direct answer to the question. "It would appear that she at least had a hand in swiping the Rembrandt; but who knows what her motive may have been? Would it not strike you as possible, my boy, that she is in the power of some unscrupulous hound who forces her to do these things?"

"It hadn't occurred to me. Did you get that idea from a film or a book?"

"It's all my own," the old coot said shortly. "Almost certainly the girl is the accomplice of some very depraved characters; and yet one balks at the notion that she is a crook, so to speak, in her own right. She looks one in the eye so frankly, so honestly, with such childlike candour, that one finds it difficult to believe she is, behind that winsome smile, plotting a raid on the family valuables."

"There's one aspect of the matter you seem to have overlooked, Nunk."

"Indeed?" said the old grandfather, raising his eyebrows in polite inquiry. "What might that be, pray? I did think I had studied it from every angle—and believe me, my boy, crook or no crook, there's one young woman for you who amply repays study from every angle! My own interest, of course, is purely academic."

"Leaving that aside for the moment, what you seem to overlook is her relationship with John."

"Her relationship with John? Tut-tut! My boy, what are you suggesting?" The old coot raised one hand. "No, no! Best leave it unsaid! I'm quite satisfied that her relationship with John is absolutely straightforward and above-board and all that sort of tosh." He paused a moment to clear his throat, which had become a little clogged through the intensity of his feelings. "My boy," he went on then, the job completed to his satisfaction, "they are simply friends. Good friends. Even very close friends. No doubt John has given her his heart for the time being. Can we blame him for that? She is an unusually lovely, seductive and charming young poppet, and if I were in John's shoes I can assure you the affair would be on an entirely different footing—and, I might add, one much more satisfactory for all concerned."

The old grandfather checked himself, cleared his throat again, and continued on a more sober note.

"It seems to me that this young woman may have been planted at Oxford as a type of lure—and you would go a long way, my boy, before finding a more effective lure, so far as the average undergraduate is concerned, than a beautiful young woman with every curve in the right place and a large helping of that mysterious quality currently known as 'oomph'. It is really amazing how undergraduates will cluster around a poppet like that. Prue, as you may have noticed for yourself, is an outstanding example of the species. No doubt her accomplices would brief her fully on which subjects to cultivate. I mean, of course, students of wealthy families, in whose homes one could confidently expect to find articles of great value lying around on every hand. It would then be her function to organize an invitation to the selected home—no very difficult task with an impressionable young bean-brain already eating out of her hand. Finally, either she would swipe the chosen article herself, or admit one of her partners in crime to do the trick."

Here the old grandfather paused again, peering forth into the night, though not because he was at all anxious for Claude's safety.

"That's my theory," he added after a few moments. "If you have a better one, tell me about it some time I'm not too busy."

Raising one corner of his dressing-gown, he rubbed a section of the window-pane, and peered out.

"My boy, do you see something stirring down there, what? Something like a large animal—and Claude *is* a dashed large animal, especially around the stomach. It *is* some person or animal approaching slowly, as if leaving a trail of blood in the snow, is it not?"

"It's Claude," Mr. Massey nodded. "I don't see any trail of blood in the snow; but he's not bouncing along like a rubber ball, either."

"No doubt the long chase exhausted him. Let us go down and give him the greeting he deserves. It's not every day a hero returns to Scumton Hall."

Claude was indeed exhausted. The brisk gallop through the snow had left his legs like a couple of yards of jellied eel; and only now did he realize that the danger, too, had thrown a severe strain on his nervous system. Though he had not actually shed any blood for the honour of the family, he felt as if his sump had been drained to the last fluid ounce. The gun in one hand, and the rolled canvas in the other, he staggered into the hall, staring with dull eyes at the old grandfather and Mr. Massey, but unable, for once in his life, to say a word.

"My dear boy!" the old coot exclaimed, taking him by one elbow. "You look as if you'd been run over by a couple of charabancs loaded with beer-swilling members of the proletariat waving flags." He steered him towards the dining-room. "Drag yourself in here before you collapse, and we'll see if we can't find something to put the sparkle back in your eye."

Mr. Massey switched on the lights, and the old grandfather noticed at once that one of the windows stood wide open at the bottom.

"Dashed thoughtless of Beale!" he commented. "Must tear strips off him in the morning about that." Dismissing the matter from his mind, he settled Claude in an armchair, where the hero sat staring at nothing like a startled gurnard. "A toothful of brandy will bring back that healthy lemon shade into those cheeks," he promised, carefully relieving him of the gun and passing it to Mr. Massey for inspection. "Just make sure that dashed thing isn't loaded, my boy. We don't want anyone's head blown off if we can avoid it."

Leaving Claude still staring, he pushed off briskly, returning in a few moments with a decanter and three glasses on a tray. The tinkle of the glasses, and the gurgle of the brandy flowing out, seemed to rouse Claude from his coma. He sat up a little; his glance focused nicely; and his right hand came up to clutch the glass the old grandfather was about to hold to his lips. In his left hand, pressed tight against his side, he still held the canvas for which he had risked his life. It was a little the worse for wear, buckled in parts, squashed flat in others, and wet all over.

"*Aaaah!*" Claude murmured, smacking his lips.

A generous snort of brandy had gone down the scuttle, and already he was conscious of a warm glow spreading out in all directions, as if through some mishap he had swallowed a shovelful of glowing coke. A little of the lemon shade referred to by his noble sire stole back into his cheeks, and his eyes regained their normal keen, intelligent and piercing gleam as he fixed his glance on the decanter. There was, he was pleased to note, an ample supply on hand for all immediate requirements.

"Feeling better, what?" the old grandfather inquired, having taken a little medicine himself simply as a precaution against catching a chill on the liver. "You certainly look better. You look as if you had a fifty-fifty chance of pulling through. Five minutes ago you were ready for the embalmer."

"I feel much better, thank you," Claude replied, first emptying his glass. "Very much better. I was exhausted when I got back. It was a stern chase."

"What were you chasing?"

"A brace of criminals." Claude held out his glass to be topped up. "Better let me begin at the beginning. For some time I have had my suspicions of Miss Goodrich."

"You have?" said the old grandfather, looking politely surprised. "What did you suspect her of, may I ask?"

"I suspected her of complicity in the theft of the Rembrandt."

"God bless my soul! No doubt that explains why you watched her so closely, what?"

Claude chose to ignore this question, which struck him as being far from sincere.

"Tonight I caught her in the act of signalling with a torch from one of the gallery windows," he continued heavily, knocking off a moment to sink another toothful of the old painkiller. "I had anticipated something of the sort," he went on then, after smacking his lips several times in quick succession. "She refused to explain her behaviour, so I took the liberty of locking her in her room."

"Haw!" the old grandfather snorted, looking completely taken aback. "You don't mean it!"

"Certainly I mean it!"

"You have the crust to sit there like a brazen image and tell me you've locked an honoured guest in her room?"

"She's not an honoured guest," Claude pointed out. "She's a crook."

"You have proof of that, what?"

"I am unlikely to go to such lengths merely on suspicion."

"As a politician, you'll find yourself going to any lengths on nothing at all," the old grandfather replied crisply. "Nevertheless this locking of beautiful young ladies in their rooms is scarcely in the best family tradition, and I take a poor view of it. Admittedly there was a time when I thought nothing of locking a young lady in her room myself; but I was always most careful to lock myself in with her, which took the harm out of it, and they never took offence. But do go on! Let us hear the rest of your sordid tale."

"There's nothing sordid about it!"

"There's nothing particularly chivalrous about it, either. Locking a helpless maiden in her room! Haw! Wouldn't go down too well with King Arthur and the boys."

"I feel I was fully justified," Claude said coldly. "If I hadn't locked her in, she'd have given the alarm."

"What alarm? What the deuce are you yammering about?"

"She'd have given the alarm to her accomplice—the scoundrel she'd been signalling to."

"You mean, she'd have let him know you were taking up the trail?"

"Precisely."

"This knowledge would have filled him with alarm?"

"Whether filled with alarm or not, he would certainly have skipped without a moment's delay," Claude replied, with the air of one explaining something to the village idiot. "As it happened, thanks to my locking Miss Goodrich up, I took the scoundrels by surprise."

"How many of 'em?"

"Two."

"Only two?"

"That's all. How many did you expect?"

"These two were heavily armed, what? Bristling with bombs and sub-machine guns and brass knuckles and so forth?"

"I have no doubt they were armed, though it seems unlikely they would carry bombs. But I allowed them no chance to use their weapons."

"You kept out of range, what?" The old grandfather nodded approvingly. "And very wise, too!"

"As a matter of fact, they were fighting when I came on the scene."

"Fighting? What were they fighting about?"

"Probably over the division of the loot."

"You mean the Rembrandt? You can't cut an Old Master down the middle and each take half, my boy. Doesn't make sense."

"At any rate they had come to blows, whatever it was about," Claude continued doggedly. "One appeared to be attacking the other with the utmost savagery, beating him about the head with a club. They hadn't seen me, so I raised my gun and took a shot at them."

"It's *my* gun," the old grandfather pointed out, sourly. "And you've got the barrels full of snow, what's more. So you took a shot at these gangsters? You mowed them down, what?"

"The range was too great for the shot to take any serious effect. It may have stung them a little; but that would be all."

"A few pellets in the ear could be a very painful business. What did they do after you'd fired your broadside?"

"They ran," Claude replied simply. "They ran like rats. That was no more than I had expected. I had bargained for it. They were so taken by surprise, so shaken, they could think of nothing but saving their miserable hides. So they turned and ran, leaving the Rembrandt where it lay. I fired the second barrel to hurry them up, then reloaded and followed them to the road. But their car was already moving off when I reached the gates. I fired at it, and heard the pellets rattle on the back. Any damage done, however, was to the paint."

"Could you describe these birds at all?" the old grandfather asked on a nonchalant note.

"Not very well, I'm afraid. One was short and broad, and appeared to be muffled in a fur coat reaching almost to the heels. The other was much taller and slimmer, and, so far as I could see, was wearing neither coat nor hat. That's all I can say. It was quite dark under the trees, you know. But for the snow I shouldn't have seen them at all."

"You said one was beating the other over the head with a club?"

"That was when I saw them first. But then he threw the club aside and closed in, probably with a knife."

"Ha! What makes you think he had a knife?"

"I'm almost certain I saw something flash in his hand."

"More than likely a diamond ring," the old coot mused. "These aristocrats of the underworld seem to go in for jewellery in a big way, possibly as a means of expressing their personality." He poured himself another drink, but in an absent-minded way, as if his thoughts were on something more important. "The whole business seems dashed odd to me," he confessed at length. "Frankly, my boy, I don't see what Prue could have had to do with it."

"She was signalling to the two scoundrels outside."

"If they already had the picture, what was there to signal about? That's it you've got under your arm, what?"

"Of course!" Claude said, offering him the roll of canvas. "I'm afraid it got a little damaged in the struggle; but to have recovered it at all is nothing short of a miracle."

"Miracles happen all the time around here," the old coot agreed, though not on a genuinely reverent note. "Let's have a look at what's left of it, anyway."

He spread it out as best he could on the floor; and the long-lost glance of his grandmother, caught and preserved for ever by the artist's skill, went into him like a butcher's skewer, detouring only for the larger bones.

"God bless my soul!" he snorted, scrambling to his feet while the canvas rolled itself up again and the painted eye-balls vanished as by some conjuring trick. "Where the blazes did that old besom come from? Is *this* the masterpiece those two dirty dogs were fighting over?" He turned to Claude, raising one hand above his head as if taking his stance to call down some awful judgment on the rising young politician. "Why the devil did you have to interfere?" he snarled, clicking his teeth almost in Claude's face. "How is it that you can't mind your own damned business? Will you forever remain a thorn in my flesh? Why, you great pot-bellied clot, if you'd stayed in your bed tonight, instead of slinking around on Prue's heels, I'd have been rid of this blasted nightmare once and for all!"

"I can't understand it!" Claude muttered, staring bug-eyed

147

at the canvas. "Naturally, I thought it was the Rembrandt. I didn't even know this portrait had been taken from its frame." He raised his head, and bent on his old man a glance that began by being dull but rapidly became piercing. "When *was* it taken from its frame? The gallery has been locked ever since the Rembrandt was stolen, and you've had the key."

"Must have been taken earlier tonight, what?" The old grandfather rubbed his chin. "I believe I was in there today. Seem to recall flinching as usual as I met that steely glance. Always makes me feel as if I'd been caught with my pants down."

"Then it was taken tonight," Claude agreed. "But how did the thief get into the gallery?"

"Could be a duplicate key, I suppose. The question is not *how* it was done, but *why* it was done. Why should anyone steal a portrait, by a second-rate artist, of a dashed old battle-axe looking like something straight out of your dreams after a supper of Welsh rarebit? The thing has no value whatever—except, perhaps, for scaring little children into doing what they're told." He added, raising the decanter: "It's all damned mysterious and unsettling, and I've had about enough of it. Worst dashed Christmas I've ever known! One moment we have the Rembrandt stolen; the next, Derek falls off the roof and comes close to breaking every bone in his bulgy body; and now some nut swipes this horrible heirloom and you have to poke your nose in and recover same for the generations to come! It's hard!"

"Why not toss it on the fire?" Mr. Massey asked casually. (He had been sitting quietly to one side, cleaning the gun.) "Or take it out and bury it in the woods? A man of courage wouldn't hesitate a moment. Wipe this horror right out of your life."

"No, no!" the old coot protested, though on a vaguely regretful note. "One cannot treat one's dashed grandmother in so cavalier a manner, my boy. After all, but for her lending an ear to my grandfather's pleading, you, and I, and all of us, would not be here today. A solemn thought, what? If she had turned the old boy down, where would we be now?"

"The question does not arise," Claude said coldly. "She

lent him her ear, and here we are. Personally, having received no thanks for what I've done, I'm going to bed."

"At what time, my boy, were you thinking of letting Prue out of her room?"

Claude's only reply to this polite inquiry was a scornful snort.

CHAPTER FOURTEEN

SINCE some time before lunch that day, Derek had lain in bed, as Mr. Massey expressed it, like a dead porpoise washed up on a beach. He lay relaxed and still, more especially when anxious members of the family crowded around; and if he breathed at all, it was so lightly, and at such extended intervals, that it was necessary to watch him closely, for minutes at a time, before shaking off the conviction that the lad had handed in his spade and bucket.

Nevertheless efforts had from time to time been made to feed him with a spoon; and by dint of patience and perseverance, and at the cost of a few stains on the bedclothes, a little thin broth had been introduced into his pipeline, though without bringing about any miraculous improvement in his condition. This was very poor faré for a lad who boasted he could sink his own weight of food in a week and look around for more; but Dr. Morton was of the opinion that solids at this stage might have a most undesirable effect on his patient's health, and could, indeed, result in his blowing his top.

"Something to do with sending the blood rushing to the brain like a tidal bore, sweeping all before it," the old grandfather explained casually. "Frankly it's news to me that he *has* a brain; but I suppose we have to take old Morton's word for that."

So from time to time the old grandmother slipped a spoonful of broth between the patient's lips, and with gentle fingers stroked his throat until she could feel reasonably confident that the appetizer had gone down past the bottleneck, and was not merely being retained under the tongue, to be dribbled out at one corner of the mouth on the first opportunity. It was slow work, and there was nothing to show it was helping to save a life.

"He must be as empty as a drum," the old grandfather commented, watching this performance some time after dinner. "He's had nothing since breakfast—and they tell me he lost *that*, too."

"Yes. He was very sick."

"Easy come, easy go!" the old coot mused, more to himself than for his wife's benefit. "What you should do, my dear, is stick a funnel in the end of a few feet of garden hose, and feed him through that. I mean, it's obvious that if you push the hose far enough down his gullet, nothing can go wrong."

"Unless, of course, it happens to choke him."

"One could lubricate it with something, what? A little lard, or possibly butter, should enable it to slip down without a hitch. By tipping the contents of the bowl into the funnel, you would then ensure that at least the boy would not suffer from malnutrition. Though frankly, my dear, in my opinion he has enough fat laid by to keep him going for a month."

"While he is in this condition, a few spoonfuls of broth is all he needs. Otherwise I should certainly get a length of garden hose, as you suggest."

"One with earwigs in it."

"Or perhaps, better still, a stirrup-pump. Now please be good enough to take yourself off and let me get on with the work."

"Consider me as already on my way," the old coot replied courteously, moving towards the door. "Believe me, my dear, the performance is one that gives me little real pleasure to watch, and it is only because of my deep-rooted sense of duty that I am here at all."

The grandmother's only reply to this was to slip another spoonful into Derek's system, at the same time going into the throat-stroking routine as before. It seemed to her that the patient was getting the stuff down a little better, though he showed no sign of coming to his senses.

Derek was indeed getting it down a little better. Iron self-control was needed on his part to refrain from snatching the bowl from his doting granny's hands and knocking back the contents with one resounding slurp—and if in the flurry the doting granny's thumb happened to get between his teeth, that would go down, too. His stomach roared for something solid. Due to shock, or possibly reaction, he had parted with his breakfast, and now the very thought of food made him water at the mouth. This broth that was spooned into him every few hours did nothing to relieve the pangs. Unbidden into his mind came visions of great steaming roasts of beef, and hams, and legs of mutton, and steak-and-kidney pies—and once, when a picture of three or four roast chickens showed up on the screen, a tear forced itself between his eyelids and trickled down his nose. To lie motionless for hours, pretending to be unconscious, was difficult enough; but to lie without sound or movement, while starving to death, called for almost superhuman resolution.

Nevertheless the lad persevered, though by the time he was given his last spoonful for the day he felt as if his insides had been scooped out with a shovel. He was in a very delicate position, and knew it. His attempt to launch a few tons of snow on the heads of Mr. Massey and Alison had misfired badly; and he was aware, from a few words he overheard, that but for his fall off the roof, and the fact that the old fool of a doctor thought his head was damaged, Mr. Massey would long since have come down on him like a devouring flame.

Time was what he needed—time to study the problem from every angle. There must be a solution. Two more days, and Christmas, season of peace on earth, goodwill to men and all that boloney, would be with them. Two short days, and Mr. Massey, who normally appeared to have little or no loving-kindness in his constitution, might confidently be expected to forgive and forget a schoolboy's innocent prank. Even should Mr. Massey himself remain unconscious of any change, still drooling a little in anticipation of the wrath to come, then the old granny, whose heart surely swelled with love until it was fit to burst every time she looked at her grandson, could be relied on to restrain his unnatural ferocity. Yes, Granny would see to it that no unseemly incident marred the festive season; and by the time the feasting and drinking and general debauchery was over, more than likely Mr.

Massey would have forgotten he had a crow to pluck with his young cousin, a weakly lad just out of bed after an accident that might well have ended a promising career.

This was the thought that gave Derek strength to lie all day like a dead dog, though for a moment his faith weakened when Mr. Massey spoke of prodding him with a pin to see what would happen. Mr. Massey seemed keen on carrying out this cruel test, reverting to it several times; and Derek was convinced that but for Sally's opposition a pin would indeed have been buried to the hilt in some sensitive part of his person. Nor, brooding about it later, did he try to convince himself he could have passed the trial with an inward sneer at such childish methods. Men of iron there might be, and he had no doubt that in due course he would develop into one of them; but the man who could lie relaxed, breathing lightly, while without warning pins were jabbed into his flesh, had yet to be born.

But now, even before the household had settled for the night, Derek knew he could not stick it out. Nothing that Mr. Massey might do to him could be as bad as another day on the old grandmother's broth, which filled his mind with thoughts of mutton bones dipped in bathwater. With un-flinching courage he faced the fact that unless within the next few hours he got his teeth into something solid, and plenty of it, his plan was doomed to failure. He could not carry on through the night on an empty stomach. A few more hours of starvation, and he would be ready to eat his shoes.

He waited. His stomach rumbled and grumbled, and visions of rich food came to him like scenes from Paradise to some anchorite in his cave; but he waited. To move too soon could lead only to exposure and the threatened doom. Mr. Massey would be slow to believe that the patient, when found with his head inside the refrigerator, was moving around in a coma.

It seemed hours since the old grandmother had planted a light kiss on his brow and pushed off for the night, yet still to the lad's straining ears, between the rumbles of protest from his stomach, came the sounds of people moving about. The possibility that someone might quietly open the door at any moment, and peer in at him in vulgar curiosity, made him cautious. The impression he wished to convey was that he had not moved a muscle. Nor would it be safe to move a muscle until all and sundry were sound asleep.

Midnight went by, and still he caught the sound of voices, faint and far away, but enough to warn him that prowlers were afoot. Not for the first time, he brooded briefly on his misfortune in being born into so odd a family. Other people might go to bed, and in fact seemed to like it; but apparently the Leighs considered that the proper way to spend the night was in skulking around like hungry beasts of prey.

Eventually, however, it seemed that the family had retired for the night. For upwards of half an hour no menacing sound had vibrated on his ear-pans. He could wait no longer. His stomach was roaring like a couple of lions in an underground cavern, and he was convinced he could feel his strength ebbing away by the moment. Dragging himself out of bed, at the cost of a pang that went through his skull like a red-hot skewer, he pulled on his dressing-gown and wriggled his feet into his slippers. It had occurred to him to construct some sort of dummy in the bed, in case the old granny awoke and decided to take a look at him; but now he decided to take a chance. The old hen-brain, he reflected, would almost certainly bend down to kiss her little darling; and he had a hunch he might lose much of her sympathy should she find herself kissing a rolled-up shirt.

As he saw it, this was a venture that called for boldness. The sooner he got to the refrigerator, and back again, the better his chances of success. Peering around in the soothing illumination of the night-light, he found his pocket torch and satisfied himself that at least a few of its nine lives still remained in the battery. Then, drawing a deep breath, he opened the door and set forth on his perilous mission, his heart high and his stomach gurgling to itself on a note of anticipation.

Reaching the kitchen door without mishap, he stooped to clap one eye to the keyhole. All was in darkness; but in Scumton Hall that meant little or nothing, the natives being largely nocturnal in their habits, and for some moments Derek listened intently, for it would not have surprised him to walk into an ambush at this very spot. The thought that

Mr. Massey might be sitting just inside the door, waiting with the patience of a leopard at a water-hole, sent a cold shiver through his system; but the pangs of hunger, worse than ever now that food was almost within reach, drove him forward as with goads.

There was no ambush. He took in another deep breath, and his heart slowed down to something like normal. He did not switch on the light, but groped his way forward, drooling slightly. His fingers were already on the handle when it occurred to him that Mr. Massey, with fiendish cunning, might have fixed some sort of booby-trap to the refrigerator door. It was possible that when he opened the door something would blow up in his face, removing not only his eyebrows, but possibly the very hair of his head and the scalp along with it.

This thought gave him pause, and plenty of it, for he had no wish to have his scalp seared bare to the bone.

While he hesitated, the gastric juices bubbling audibly in his stomach, he heard a sound. It was not a sound that caused him any immediate anxiety, for it came from somewhere outside the house, and at the moment his mind was busy with a far more vital problem; but then he heard it again, and in an instant all thought of booby-traps, and even food, was forgotten.

Someone, or something, was scratching at the door that opened from the kitchen into the coach-yard.

Derek was neither a nervous nor a superstitious lad; but he had often heard it stated, by those who claimed to know, that Christmas was as good a time as any to see ghosts. It occurred to him, while he stood as if glued to the floor, that it was his turn to see one now. His surface became covered with goose-bumps, and but for his iron self-control he would have howled like a dog.

This phase, painful while it lasted, soon passed. In a matter of moments the lad had himself in hand, and a scornful smile curved his lips at the very thought of ghosts. Calm, scientific reason was back in the saddle. More than likely some stray animal, such as a cat, was at the door, trying to get in to the warmth. Not that Derek found the kitchen particularly warm; but no doubt it was positively tropical compared to the sub-zero temperatures outside.

Then, just as he had that all figured out, Derek almost leaped out of his skin. It was all very well to put everything down to cats; but cats had paws, not large, man-sized hands to grope at windows with. It was a hand that Derek saw against the pale square of the uncurtained window—and a moment later he saw the head that went with it, a blob just a little darker than the sky serving as a backdrop to the scene.

What had started off as a ghost, and then switched to a cat, was now again transformed, this time into a burglar trying to break into the house, doubtless with some thought of swiping the family silver.

A murderous fury began to burn in Derek's bosom as if blown with a bellows. For burglars as a class he had nothing but contempt, being of the opinion that the risks they ran were far too great for the meagre rewards obtained; but for this particular bird, who had chosen this time and place to operate, he felt a surge of terrible repugnance. This low-life— this common, ugly, boneheaded, petty larcenist—threatened to come between him and the food he needed to keep body and soul together in the accepted relationship. At any other time Derek would scarcely have raised a finger to prevent this brutish character from tossing the silver in a sack and pressing forth into the night. Now it was different.

These thoughts had gone through the lad's mind like a bolt from a ray-gun, spurred on by an ever-mounting rage. Nor had the bird outside in the snow been idle. Somewhere or other he had found a large stone, and with this, in the most casual manner imaginable, he now broke the lower pane of the window. The glass caved in with a crash that brought Derek out in a cold sweat, for he was convinced it had been heard all over the house and that every able-bodied member of the family would arrive on the scene as if jet-propelled. He could have screamed with rage and hate. Already he was cut off from his base—and without getting a bite to eat, at that.

Now the character outside had knocked out all the jagged peaks of glass sticking up from the frame, obviously with the intention of clambering through. Meanwhile he whistled unmusically between his teeth, like one without a care in the world. But for this, more than likely he would have heard

Derek's pipes rumbling, and taken warning. Satisfied at length that there was little danger of being slit up the middle like a herring, he got his elbows on the inside sill and thrust upward strongly with his legs.

At the same moment, Derek bounded forward like some savage beast leaping on its victim, and brought a chair down on his head with all his strength. It was a light chair, of inferior construction, incapable of standing up to so rigorous a test. One or two legs came off, and Derek found himself with little better than a remnant in his hands. Nevertheless he got in another lick, his victim having tumbled forward into the kitchen with a grunt of surprise and pain. The rest of the legs came off, and the seat splintered to matchwood. Derek tossed aside what was left, and prepared to run for his life. His only regret was that he hadn't picked the old oak carver as his weapon. *That* wouldn't have come to pieces in his hands.

There was an ominous silence from the vicinity of the window. Derek waited a few moments, listening for stealthy movements, wondering if this duck carried lethal weapons about his person. He heard no sound of movement, no muffled click as of a gun being cocked. Nothing registered on his ears but a sort of snoring sound that made him suspect this dirty dog suffered from adenoids. Finally, holding it well off to one side, he switched on his torch.

It immediately became plain that there had been an unfortunate mistake—and the bird it was most unfortunate for was Uncle John. There he lay, face down on the floor, spreadeagled among the broken glass—and it seemed to Derek that the only reason he wasn't spreadeagled in a pool of his own blood was that the chair had disintegrated at the first blow. Nevertheless, blood or no blood, he gave a very good imitation of an innocent bystander struck by a thunderbolt, and Derek had an uneasy premonition it would be some time before he got around again under his own power, if ever.

What struck Derek as the oddest feature of all was that this uncle, who had impressed him as being a moderately normal sort of bird though with a lot of bone from the ears up, had been paddling around 'mid snow and ice with nothing on his feet but his socks, which now were worn so badly as a result that they were up on his ankles like spats.

Derek may have been uneasy, but no repentant tear gleamed in his eye. It did not bother him at all that he had laid his uncle out as cold as a cockle. As he saw it, the uncle had asked for shock and abrasions by prowling around breaking windows at this hour of night. That sort of behaviour was bound to get him into trouble. What bothered Derek was that someone might have heard the hullabaloo and come down to investigate.

Leaving the uncle where he lay, he went back to the refrigerator and by the light of his torch went over it closely for booby-traps. Finding nothing suspicious, he opened the door and peered inside; and a feeling of bitterness welled up in him when he saw that, regardless of the fact that the only grandson was hovering between life and death for most of the day, the family had done itself unusually well in the line of eats. Everywhere his eye rested—and it never rested for long— was something solid and satisfying for the inner man, in quantity enough to slake the most voracious appetite. Forgotten was his resolution to return to bed without wasting a moment. Ignored was the limp body on the floor. All thought of danger was brushed aside. He made a quick selection, helped himself to a knife and fork, and sat down to eat by the light of the bulb in the refrigerator, having propped the door open with a chair.

He was a steady eater. There was nothing brilliant about his work, but neither was there any wasted energy, and a high standard was maintained. The food was sliced into convenient portions, stuffed into his maw, and masticated until in a fit condition to slip down the gullet without undue strain. Meanwhile another forkful had been readied for the mill, and so the work went on until a condition of satiety had been attained and a gentle perspiration moistened the brow. The only sounds to be heard were the clatter of knife and fork, the steady champ of jaws, and the odd animal grunt.

On this occasion Derek had not only to make up for lost time, but to lay in provision for the future as well; and there was a rather glassy look about his eye, and a higher sheen to his brow than would normally have seemed desirable, when at length he pushed away his plate and sat back, uttering what may or may not have been a hiccup.

For some moments he sat like one entranced, staring at the opposite wall; then, slowly turning his head, he bent a thoughtful glance on his uncle, who had stirred a little, but not enough to make any difference. It would not do, Derek thought, to push off to bed and leave the uncle lying there like a dead dog. Not only would it be an unchristian act, but in no way would it redound to his credit should his part in the drama be discovered—and that his part would be discovered he scarcely dared to doubt. Here was his chance to chalk up a cross on the other side of the ledger, for it was widely held that nothing rated higher than tending the sick and wounded, and to his critical eye Uncle John looked both.

Rising heavily, he moved over to the uncle and turned him over on his back a little at a time. He was glad to note that the patient was still breathing, though how long this happy state of affairs might continue was anyone's bet. After resting a few moments, he dragged the body across the floor, the bare feet trailing. While so engaged, as he came closer to the refrigerator, he noticed with interest that the victim's feet had turned blue, and it warmed him up to think that at least he could not be blamed for this development. Moreover it was a very sinister shade of blue, and it seemed to Derek an odds-on chance that the uncle was fated to lose a few of his toes through frostbite.

Something stirred in his mind like a worm in an apple. For some moments it eluded him; then he pinned it down. Somewhere or other he had read—or so he thought—that spirits rubbed into the affected part frequently averted serious consequences by steaming-up the circulation and inducing a gentle glow on all sides. It could be something entirely different he had in mind, such as the bite of a mad dog; but since the toes belonged to his uncle, and not to himself, he was ready to take a chance, provided he could run down a bottle of spirits. Brandy, rum, gin, whisky—he wasn't fussy.

He located a bottle of brandy in the pantry. By way of satisfying himself that it *was* brandy, and not turpentine or paint-remover, he took a snort. With a cunning old coot like Beale, it was best to be on the safe side. Beale, he reflected, smacking his lips, was capable of putting rat-poison in a brandy bottle and leaving it to be found by some thirsty soul to whom he had taken a dislike. But this was the genuine article. Either that, or it was very good turpentine.

For some minutes he had been rubbing the brandy into John's feet, from time to time taking a quick snort to keep up his strength, when one of those instincts that have been handed down from caveman days warned him he was under observation. Turning his head, he found the uncle he had written off as certainly unconscious and possibly dead watching him in a peculiarly piercing and malevolent manner.

CHAPTER FIFTEEN

THERE was no immediate exchange of notes. Derek squatted on the floor, with John's left foot in his lap, staring at the patient; and John lay flat on his back, staring at Derek as already described. The lighting, still supplied by the refrigerator bulb, added a theatrical touch to the scene.

"What's that stuff you're putting on my foot?" John inquired at length, wiggling his toes a little, cautiously at first, because he had a notion they might fall off.

"Brandy."

"Brandy? I thought it was sulphuric acid. It burns like fire."

"Maybe it does; but it's good for frostbite."

"Have I got frostbite?"

"I wouldn't know," Derek replied frankly. "I've never had it myself. But before I started work your tootsies were a sort of royal blue, turning black, and now they're red all over. That's an improvement, to my way of thinking."

"The treatment has certainly warmed them up," John admitted. "In fact, they couldn't be much warmer if you'd put a match to them and set them burning like the Christmas pudding. But I have a theory that the brandy should be applied internally, rather than rubbed into the soles of the feet. Pass the bottle."

Derek passed the bottle; and the patient sat up and took a hearty slug. Pausing only briefly to get his breath, he took another.

"The beauty of my method," he explained to Derek, "is that the effect is general rather than local. And besides, it goes in better this way. I'm not belittling your performance, laddie, because more than likely you've saved me a couple of toes, and toes are things that don't grow again; but to my mind this brandy is too rare a tipple for use as an embrocation, lotion, or rub."

Here he paused to take another toothful, after which he wiggled his toes again. Satisfied that they were in good working order, he raised his glance to the lad's open features.

"Shouldn't you be in bed?" he asked politely. "Don't take it that I have any wish to pry into your affairs; but up to an hour ago you were regarded as hovering like a whirly-bird between life and death."

"I recovered," Derek said briefly.

"You recovered?"

"Yep. I woke up."

"Feeling youthful and invigorated, no doubt?"

"Feeling damn' hungry."

"So you snuck down to stuff something solid under your belt, and stuff it good?"

Derek nodded, brooding over the injustice of things in general.

"I was ready to eat the cat, fur and all," he stated. "And you'd be the same, too, if you'd had nothing in your craw all day but a few spoonfuls of dirty dishwater."

"I hesitate to believe you were fed on dirty dishwater."

"That's what it tasted like."

"How do you know what it tasted like? You were supposed to be unconscious."

"I could still taste that muck. It had a flavour all its own."

"I've been fed on broth myself," John nodded understandingly. "It becomes a little monotonous after the first spoonful, but is always pressed on invalids—and almost everyone who falls from the roof of a house three storeys high can be regarded as an invalid for the time being. You've had a miraculous escape, my boy."

"Yeah," Derek agreed. "So far, anyway."

"You feel you may have a relapse?"

"Could happen."

"We can only hope and pray," John pointed out. "So then you came down looking for a snack, what?"

"I didn't want to trouble anyone."

"Always thinking of others! What was it you belted me with?"

"A chair," Derek replied moodily. "It was the first thing that came to hand."

"I suppose I should be thankful it wasn't a battle-axe."

"If it hadn't come apart, you wouldn't have known the difference. It must have been worm-eaten, or something. It practically turned to powder in my hands."

"Otherwise I'd have no back to my skull," John nodded, tenderly massaging the area. "As it is, I have a bump the size of an orange—a Jaffa orange. You'll have to break yourself of this habit of laying people low with chairs. It's no way to win friends and influence people."

"I thought you were a burglar."

"If I hadn't guessed so much, I'd have eaten you alive by now." John rose to his feet and steadied himself against the table. "You're an odd mixture. First you do your best to knock my brains out with a kitchen chair, then you rub brandy on my feet in case I might lose a toe from frostbite. You're not consistent."

"Maybe I'm not consistent," Derek admitted coldly. "But I'm not crazy enough to go running around in the snow in my bare feet, either."

"I wasn't barefoot when I started out. I was in my socks."

"I'm not asking why you had to break a window to get in," the lad went on, still on that impersonal note. "That's your affair, and it wasn't my window, so what the hell? But the fact remains that through loitering around to thaw out your tootsies I'm liable to get myself boiled alive, and that's the aspect of the matter that strikes me as unjust."

"Who's likely to boil you alive?" John inquired with genuine interest, as if he meant to be there to watch the performance, and possibly to lend a hand stoking the fire.

"Hugh Massey is likely to boil me alive—curse him!"

"Why should he go to those extremes?"

"He has his reasons. But if I could have stalled it off until Christmas Day there'd have been so much peace on earth and goodwill to men floating around like smog he wouldn't dare raise a finger."

"How did you mean to stall it off?"

"By lying in bed, unconscious. It would have meant another day on broth; but even that's better than being skinned alive and dipped in salt like a picnic egg."

"Why can't you go through with the programme?"

"Because I hung around here to rub brandy on your feet." Derek cleared his throat in a very significant manner, at the same time looking his uncle plumb in the eye. "I'm taking it, of course, that you have no objection to all and sundry knowing you were running around barefoot in the snow like some old cluck doing penance for his sins?"

"I'd prefer that the news wasn't bruited about," John confessed. "I had my reasons, which seemed good and sufficient at the time; but more than likely the way you'd put it would give the congregation a hearty laugh at my expense. So I feel we can reach an amicable settlement here, what?"

"I think so," Derek said soberly. He raised the bottle, which John had stood on the table, and rinsed the dust from his throat. "I wasn't out of bed, and you weren't doing penance in the snow. You didn't see me and I didn't see you. That's what's known as a *quid pro quo*—or is it?"

"Never mind the *quid pro quo* part of it. How are you going to explain all the stuff missing from the 'frige? You've left nothing but a few crumbs for the cockroaches."

"The same way as you explain the broken window. Some tramp came along looking for a feed. He bust the window, climbed in, opened the 'frige, and stuffed himself to tonsil level, washing it down with brandy. Then he pushed off, a new man, his childhood faith in Santa Claus once more established on a firm footing. Right?"

"Right!" John agreed. "It might seem a little odd, of course, that he got away again without leaving any tracks in the snow; but these petty details needn't concern us."

"The hell with them! The bird who thinks of that can figure it out for himself." Derek took another quick bracer for the road, and hiccupped on a refined note. "Pardon me!" he murmured. "I think perhaps I had better be returning to my lonely couch. Dear old Granny—bless her loving heart!—

would certainly come over queer if she found it empty. And if she came any queerer than she is already, that would be a damn' fine how-d'ye-do, don't you think?"

With this jocular observation, to which he added a throaty chuckle, he set off on his dangerous journey, leaving John staring moodily at the bottle, which appeared to be as dry as the sands of the desert, or even drier.

.   .   .   .   .

Scarcely had John returned to his room, still in a depressed and brooding frame of mind, when the door leading to Miss Goodrich's holy of holies opened wide, and the beautiful young woman herself stood on the threshold, but not for long. Apparently overlooking the fact that she wore only a nightie of the most delicate texture, which did little or nothing to conceal her charms, she moved forward briskly, and in a moment, as was only to be expected, was folded in John's arms. For some little time they clung together as if spot-welded, then gently she disengaged herself, looking him over with anxious eyes.

"Are you all right, honey?" she murmured, pressing his right hand against her bosom to let him feel how her heart was going bumpetty-bump. "You're not wounded, or anything?"

"No, I'm not wounded. I may have a touch of frostbite in my tootsies; but otherwise I'm as sound as a bell."

"I thought I heard shots."

"You did. That was Claude. He loosed off a couple of broadsides, but without doing any damage. He always was a rotten shot. I'm surprised he didn't blow his own ear off in the excitement."

"He fired at you!" Prue whispered, opening her eyes until they looked as if they'd been drawn in with a compass for some problem in geometry. "He might have killed you!"

"Not unless he got someone else to lay the gun," John said soothingly. "But he certainly did give your old man a fright. For an elderly bird muffled to the ears in a fur coat, he covered the ground like an antelope. The way he went across the snow put me in mind of swallows skimming over a pond. He seems to be the athletic type, what? Or is it only when

163

some nut is pooping off at him with a scatter-gun that he can run like a hare?"

"I don't know," Prue admitted. "I can't remember anyone ever shooting at him with a gun before." She stared closely at her beloved, for it had just occurred to her that he was being rather uncommunicative. "Everything went off okay, honey?"

"Oh, yes!" John nodded. "Apart from a couple of trifling hitches, everything went off fine—especially your old man. He went off like a rocket, except he didn't wait to fizz."

"He wasn't shot, or anything?"

"No. He got clean away."

"He must have been delighted to get the picture."

"He was tickled pink. His joy knew no bounds. Until he took a look at it, that is. When he discovered it was a portrait of my great-grandmother, and not the Rembrandt, he lost a lot of his bounce."

"Old Needle-nose?" Prue whispered. "Now how the hell did that happen?"

"The ancient scourge in person," John said, on a brooding note. "The portrait we always passed by with gaze averted and quickened step, because there was a belief among us children that if we let it look at us too long we'd come out in boils. Your old man didn't like it, either. He took one peep and went up in the air."

"I know. He spends half his time airborne." Prue eyed her beloved in growing dismay—and the more she eyed him, the more it grew. "What happened when he came down again?"

"He tried to murder me. I'll bet it's the first time ever a man has been beaten over the head with a portrait of his great-grandmother. Just as well it wasn't in the frame, or I'd be lying out in the snow this very moment, as blue as if I'd been dipped in woad."

"You don't seem to have made an excellent first impression."

"I'm afraid he didn't take to me," John admitted, on a gloomy note. "Wouldn't give me a chance to explain—not that I had any explanation to offer, of course. The whole thing is a mystery to me. But your old man took it as a plot to do him down."

"After what happened before, you can't exactly blame him."

"No. But he might at least have listened, instead of trying to knock my teeth out. Then Claude showed up, and hot lead began to fly; so your old man broke off the engagement and ran for his life. I was getting into the car, too, with some idea of accompanying him down the road a mile or so and pouring oil in his wounds; but he kicked me out. He's like that. The hasty type. More than likely he's sorry already."

"Sorry he didn't kick you harder," Prue nodded. She had drawn back a little, and was looking her beloved over in a very searching manner indeed. "What was all this oil you were going to pour in his wounds—banana oil?"

"I'd have tried to offer some sort of explanation." John sat down, and absentmindedly began to massage his right foot, which had gone a little blue again. "Not that I have a clue," he admitted frankly. "I'm not one of these ducks who can solve a mystery by studying a pinch of cigar-ash. This thing has me baffled. I mean to say, we swipe the genuine article, tie it up nicely with ribbon, and hide it where you'd imagine not even a dashed bloodhound could smell it out, awaiting an opportunity to pass it on to the revered parent; but when the time seems ripe, and I hand over the goods as arranged, it turns out that what I've got is actually old Needle-nose in person, the bane of Scumton parish. Smacks of witchcraft, what?"

"Or maybe a shining example of the old double-cross, Leigh style."

"What?" John stared incredulously at his sugar-pie. "You don't mean you suspect *me*?"

This was exactly what the glamorous young woman had had in mind, and in another moment or two she would have put it into words; but just then, seeing his bewilderment and hurt, her heart gave the old familiar lurch as it flowed over with love and trust and a complex of similar emotions. Moving forward quickly, she went on her knees before him, drawing his head down so that she could kiss his ear.

"Oh, no!" she whispered, caressing the back of his neck. "Not *you*, honey! You wouldn't deceive me ever. It must have been someone else. Someone else found the Rembrandt and made the switch. Someone's been playing with us the way a cat plays with a mouse, getting a laugh out of us before he swats us down. Oh, who could it be?"

"Who could it be?" John echoed, holding her tenderly in his arms as best he could under the circumstances, for somehow or other his right foot had got in the way. "Well, I'm no Sherlock Holmes; but the fact that the picture selected for passing on to your old man, and therefore regarded as expendable, was the portrait of my sainted great-grandmother, seems to give us a clue, what?"

"It does?"

"I'm afraid so. My noble sire never liked that portrait. More than once he's confessed in public that even now it gives him nightmares. Admittedly the nightmares weren't about the old granny—they were about tiger-sharks. But he always blamed them on that portrait. It was just that he got a little confused while asleep, and found it impossible to tell the old dame from the finny monster, and *vice versa*."

"That's a clue?"

"To me, it looks like a clue. To the noble sire, it must have seemed a golden opportunity to get rid of his granny once and for all, never again to be pierced like a periwinkle by that needle eye, or to dream about sharks. And there's another angle. More than likely it gave him many a hearty guffaw to picture your pop's reaction on finding himself confronted by the scourge in person."

"Then you believe he knew the picture was going to my pop?" Prue whispered in consternation. "Oh, honey, do you think he's been wise to me right along?"

"I'm afraid that's how it looks as of above date," John replied gloomily. "The old duck may give the impression of being a sort of genial halfwit, but as a matter of fact he can be quite bright at times. Deep as a well, you know. Maybe it was foolish of us not to change your name before coming, and mention Philadelphia as your home town. We were a bit careless there. 'Miss Goodrich, of Detroit', must have made him think. 'Miss Clutterbuck, of Chicago', wouldn't have raised a ripple on the surface."

"I'd have got all tangled up!" Prue insisted. "I *know* I

would! And besides, there must be hundreds of Goodriches in Detroit."

"I know, my sweet. Only thing is, it started a train of thought, and the train kept rolling."

"You mean, he expected something to happen?"

"Must have," John nodded, gently stroking her back, but looking as if he derived no pleasure at all from it. "Must have been playing the old cat-and-mouse game from the moment he heard your name. Waiting for you to make a move. More than likely he didn't realize I was involved, at first. Reluctant to believe it of his own son, and all that, even when the evidence pointed in my direction. He was two or three jumps ahead of us all the way. We hadn't a chance. My fault. I should have introduced you as Miss Arabella Clutterbuck."

"I don't think I'd like to be called Arabella Clutterbuck."

"It might have meant success, all the same. Now we're in bad with both houses. My old man knows we swiped the Rembrandt, and your old man thinks we tried to diddle him. It's going to take more than a few kind words and a bag of sweets to get everyone smiling and happy."

"Honey, maybe we should run away?"

"Run away?" John said in surprise. "Run away where?"

"I don't know. Anywhere, to get away from it all."

"No, no! Then your pop would cut you off with a dollar, and mine would cut me off with a shilling, and you can't get far on a dollar and a shilling nowadays. We'll see it out to the bitter end—and something tells me it's going to be gall and wormwood, whatever gall and wormwood may be. Nevertheless we'll see it out. There's bound to be a solution."

"Maybe it was Claude, and not your father, who's been sort of egging us on."

"Claude?" John threw off a snort of derision. "That bean-brain! Most of the time he doesn't know whether he's awake or not, and most of the time it makes no difference whether he is or not, anyway. No, no! The bird behind this is a master-mind, one of the deepest thinkers of all time. By the way, now that we're on the subject of Claude, how did you fare with him after I slunk off, muttering in my beard?"

"He locked me in my room."

"He did, what?" John grew red around the ears. "The

devil scald him! Is this the far-famed hospitality of our house? For two pins I'd pull him out of bed by the leg and work him into the floor like beeswax."

"It doesn't matter," Prue murmured, snuggling up against his knees. "He caught me signalling, so really he can't be blamed. Looking at it from the strictly moral angle, I was in the wrong and he was in the right."

"This has nothing to do with morals. The overgrown slug!" John gave his beloved a hug that bent her ribs like whalebone. "The hound! How was he to know you wouldn't do something desperate, like throwing yourself out of the window, or something? I'll bet that never occurred to him, the clot!"

"It didn't occur to *me*, either. But the question is, honey, what are you going to do? If your pop knows we took the Rembrandt, then there's no future in sticking around until he makes up his mind what to hit us with, or whether it's really a case for the cops. Any moment now he's liable to come down on us like a ton of coal. I feel the wise move for us is to get out from under."

"We're not too popular with *your* old man, either," John pointed out moodily. "In fact, I can't call it to mind that we're really popular anywhere just at the moment. A couple of outcasts—that's how we're billed. Social pi-dogs, and so forth. Untouchables. Not that that aspect of it has me unduly bothered. I'm not one to go around fawning on people for a kind word. What rankles with me is that I've failed again."

"You haven't!"

"Forgive me, my sweet, but I have," the lad said firmly, giving her another big hug as an outlet for the pressure of his emotions. "One more failure added to the list wouldn't bow me down in the normal run of business; but this time it was *you* I was trying to please, and with failure staring me in the face I've gone all cold inside."

"Your feet are cold, too," Prue murmured absentmindedly. "And they have an awfully odd smell." She sniffed a few times, then looked up at him in wonder. "It's like brandy."

"It *is* brandy."

"Were you wading through it, or what?"

"I rubbed a little on to ward off frostbite. One of these

sovereign remedies. All you need is a bottle of brandy—and, of course, a touch of frostbite. From there on it's all yours. What's left over can be taken internally. But as I was saying, I've failed again, and it hurts."

The beautiful young woman, who had been kneeling all this time, now rose impulsively to her feet and threw herself into John's arms with such abandon that she almost knocked him flat on his back out of the chair.

"You haven't failed!" she said huskily, her lips against his ear. "Or if you have, it's only because you weren't cut out to be a crook. You were wonderful! Nobody could have done it better. The luck was against you, that's all. And it doesn't matter if we've become a couple of social outcasts, or whatever it was you said. We still have each other, and that's what counts."

This brief statement, uttered in the most emotional tone and plainly coming straight from the heart, convinced John that matters could have been a great deal worse. His was a mercurial temperament. Nonchalantly shelving the thought that to his friends and relations he would henceforth be only a pi-dog, he gathered Prue into his arms, and, rising to his feet, held her close against his bosom. His lips sought hers, and her eyes closed as she yielded to the kiss.

So the lad stood for some moments, the only sound to be heard the muffled thud of two hearts that beat as one. Then, raising his head, and with his beloved light in his arms, he strode purposefully, if with a slight limp, into her room. As he passed through, he raised his left foot and kicked the door shut, but gently, for he had no wish to rouse the house.

CHAPTER SIXTEEN

THE Christmas tree in the hall had thrown out a rash of tinsel stars, coloured lights, imitation snow and similar junk. Suspended here and there were boxes, wrapped in gaudy paper and tied with ribbon, that looked as if they might contain valuable presents. The old grandfather was staring up at all this, without the suspicion of a sentimental tear in his eye, when Sally and Mr. Massey joined him. He nodded briefly in welcome, then gestured with his cigar, almost sticking it in the eye of an angel with a gilt trumpet and a twelve-inch wing span.

"Here we are!" he snorted. "Christmas Eve, and all that sort of rot, balderdash and fiddle-faddle! Peace on earth, goodwill to men, everyone loving his neighbour—or if he can't quite manage that, then at least his neighbour's wife. All and sundry stuffed with sentiment, good resolutions, and utter damn' nonsense."

"Why so bitter, Nunk?"

"This is the time when the scattered units of the family come together with love in their hearts, though perhaps last week they were ready to shoot on sight, and next week they'll be wishing they'd slipped a pint of rat-bane in the soup. Here we're at the one season of the year when the bosom is stretched to bursting with tender affection and we all feel like little children again. Some of us even get a touch of religion, though it wears off in a day or two, and no harm done."

"All this is leading up to something," Mr. Massey assured Sally. "He's not simply blowing off steam."

"It's leading up to this—that anyone who dropped in today would think we had bubonic plague." The old coot made another sweeping gesture with his cigar—he came very close to sweeping a decanter to the floor. "Claude's been in bed all day, snuffling like a terrier at a rat-hole. He caught a chill running around in the snow last night, and the latest bulletin is that his eyeballs are like burning coals in his head. Fortunately, it doesn't seem to have impaired his appetite— I've never known anything that did.

"Derek, of course, was in bed all day, too—thank heaven! He appears to be making a slow but steady recovery, though I am reliably informed he was very ill during the night. Almost incredibly ill, I might say, considering that since being put to bed yesterday morning he had been fed only a few spoonfuls of broth, which didn't give him much of a foundation to work on, what?"

"Must have been lying on his stomach," Mr. Massey explained tolerantly. "The food, I mean, not the youth himself."

"My information is that it was lying on the carpet."

"Nevertheless there's hope he'll be with us for the feasting tomorrow?"

"He may have a relapse," the old grandfather pointed out, looking on the bright side. "We're bound to rate a bit of luck some of the time, what? Then there's John." He brooded a moment, nibbling at his cigar. "And Prue," he added. "Both indisposed. Kept to their rooms all day. Place is like a dashed hospital ward. Nothing but invalids on all sides. Puts me in mind of a day in the family vault. General atmosphere exactly the same. Ideal for meditation on the world to come, and all that, but by no means the right note for Christmas Eve."

"How is John?" Sally asked sympathetically.

"I'm told the fever has abated."

"*Fever?* What fever?"

"He was running a slight temperature this morning," the old grandfather replied. "Nothing dangerous, you know—a fraction of a degree above normal. It appears he fell out of bed last night and bumped his head."

"Oh!"

"And he has quite a bump on his head to prove it. Dashed careless of him, what? So his nurse decided to play it safe, and kept him in bed for the day."

"I didn't know he had a nurse."

"Prue is his nurse," the old coot stated simply. "Hour after hour she sat by his bedside, holding his hand; and if ever I saw a human eye melt in yearning and tender passion and so forth, it was hers. She couldn't have made it any plainer that she loves him if she'd hired a radio station and gone on the air. It was a touching thing to watch—especially when she stroked his bump. He claimed it took away the pain."

"But how on earth did he manage to fall out of bed?" Sally asked in wonder.

"There's no trick in falling out of bed. The trick lies in doing it when there's a beautiful young woman in the room next door. Then she comes in and strokes your bump; and if you happen to be a handsome flibbertigibbet like John her heart goes bumpetty-bump and there's scarcely a thing she wouldn't do to show her sympathy. That's *my* reading of the affair. I may be quite wrong."

It was at this moment that a bell pealed somewhere far in the interior, and the old grandfather turned to glance at the hall door, as if, by switching over to his X-ray vision, to see who stood there.

"Haw!" he murmured. "Dashed odd! Eleven o'clock. Bit late for callers, what?"

Beale came shuffling into view, and in a matter of moments had turned the key in the lock, drawn back bolts at top and bottom, and uncoupled the massive chain. These preparations complete, he opened the door.

Into the hall, brushing Beale aside—but not in a really contemptuous way—stepped a short, broad, square-looking character who plainly had no time to waste on butlers. This gentleman wore a fur coat reaching almost to his ankles, and of so ample a cut that a family of full-grown bears must have gone to its making. The collar of this undoubtedly expensive garment was up around his ears, and on his head he wore a wide-brimmed hat pulled low, so that little of his features could be seen but two piercing eyes and a strong, broad nose that looked as if at some time or other it had been beaten flat with a bottle. From just above the collar a large cigar projected at an angle, presumably from his mouth, like an anti-aircraft gun searching for hostile planes.

"I beg your pardon, sir!" Beale said coldly, with a glance that would have taken the hide off a mule. "Pray be good enough——"

"Okay, bud; okay!" the newcomer interrupted. His glance had come to rest on the old grandfather, and his cigar quivered as if in his emotion he had bitten it to the bone. "I'm looking for a jasper called Leigh—Oliver Blair Leigh."

"I am Oliver Leigh," said the grandfather, stepping forward, but not very far. "And whoever you may be, sir," he went on courteously, "you are very welcome here at Scumton Hall in this season of peace, love, rejoicing, goodwill to men, and so forth—though frankly, my dear fellow, I can't see very much of you, because of your hat."

"What about my hat?"

"It's on your head."

"Yeah—that's where I usually wear it."

Despite this defiant reply, the visitor removed his head-gear, though with obvious reluctance, revealing a large, square head with a narrow fringe of hair around the sides but nothing at all on top. The warmth of the old grandfather's welcome did not seem as yet to have penetrated his crust. Not only was his glance morose, but there was something positively savage about the way he chewed his cigar. Several times he appeared to be on the point of expressing himself; but on each occasion his glance shifted to Sally, and he bit back the words. Finally, however, he went on the air.

"Certainly am pleased to meet you!" he said, advancing with hand outstretched, while at the same time looking as if his duodenal had perforated there and then. "Certainly is kind of you to make me welcome, Mr. Leigh. My name——"

"Just a moment, sir!" the old grandfather begged. He turned to Mr. Massey. "My boy, pray pour this gentleman a little brandy to take the chill from his bones. You *would* care for a little brandy, what?"

"Yeah—I'll care for it. Mr. Leigh, my name is Preston B. Goodrich, of Detroit, Michigan."

"*What?*" the old coot cried, on an incredulous note, at the same time drawing back a little to get a better look. "Not *the* Preston B. Goodrich, automobile manufacturer, oilman, hotelman, steelman, wood-pulp man, and all the rest of it? Not *that* Preston B. Goodrich?"

"Why not?" Mr. Goodrich inquired, rather coldly. "Yep, that's me." He took the glass from Mr. Massey, bowed the head briefly in acknowledgment, and without further procrastination sank three-quarters of the fine old liqueur brandy at a gulp.

It did him good. His eye brightened, and a ruddier hue stole into his cheek, which up to that moment had looked rather like an over-ripe grapefruit.

"Yep, that's me!" he stated again, on a much firmer note, as if wishing the old grandfather would give him an argument about it. "I guess you remember the name, huh?"

"Yes, indeed!" the old grandfather assured him, reaching out for the decanter. "Drink up, my dear fellow! You need a little something to get the blood stirring in your veins. When

173

you came in just now you put me in mind of the lone survivor clawing his way down from the mountain-top in a howling blizzard." He turned courteously to Mr. Massey. "Blizzards *do* howl, don't they, my boy?"

"Yep. Like wolves."

"I thought so. In the press reports, they are almost invariably referred to as howling. The blizzard that did not howl would be a poor specimen indeed." He poured a generous measure into the Goodrich glass, and another into his own. "One has to take precautions in such weather, what? And about the best precaution to take is a toothful of brandy."

Here he knocked off to give the big oilman a frank and winning smile.

"You know, of course, that your charming daughter has been with us for the past week or so?"

"Yeah," Mr. Goodrich nodded, with an inscrutable sort of glance. "I know."

"What a beautiful child she is!"

"Yeah. Where is she right now?"

"I rather think she's in bed. Better not disturb her, my dear fellow—she felt a little under the weather today. Nothing serious, let me assure you. Just the merest chill. But she was anxious to be in top form for tomorrow, so she stayed in her room. Very wise of her, what?"

"Yeah. Yeah, very wise." Mr. Goodrich took a quick snort to keep his blood on the move. "Maybe I could come down and see her in the morning, huh? Huh?"

"My dear fellow!" the old grandfather protested, looking hurt. "What, are we to turn you from our door on a night like this? No, no! Perish the thought! We can do better than that, I hope. You must stay the night. In fact, you must stay as long as you wish. If you have a case, Beale will fetch it at once. You have? Splendid! Beale, fetch this gentleman's case, and see that his car is put under cover."

He took his guest by one arm, and led him over to the hearth, where the Yule log burned brightly with the aid of a half-hundredweight of coal.

"Warm yourself!" he begged, as if anxious for the tycoon's health. "Take off your magnificent coat, and let the heat soak in. By the way, I haven't introduced you."

174

He beckoned Sally and Mr. Massey, and made the introductions, which the great man acknowledged politely but without any real warmth. It became plainer and plainer that Preston B. Goodrich was a man of few words, and that already he had used most of them. He seemed content, while the old grandfather prattled on, to dart keen glances in all directions, without offering any comment either on his surroundings or on his host's remarks. Meanwhile he absorbed such brandy as was pressed on him—and for some reason or other, possibly because it was Christmas Eve, the old grandfather was at his most hospitable.

Eventually, however, Mr. Goodrich showed a mouthful of gold in a wide yawn, and confessed a desire to hit the hay. The old grandfather personally escorted him upstairs, and the sound of his pleasant conversation, and of the tycoon's answering grunts, died away.

Sally and Mr. Massey were left alone, with an empty decanter and a dying fire.

"I wish it was all over!" Sally said abruptly, staring into the embers.

"You wish what was all over?"

"Everything. I mean, Christmas, and the business of the missing masterpiece, and so forth. I want to get away."

"But you have to wait for Claude, what?" Mr. Massey asked, after a brief silence.

"No, I don't have to wait for Claude." Sally gave a little snort of laughter; and when she turned to look at Mr. Massey he noted with approval that her eyes were dancing. "I told him what I think of him," she said simply. "And I feel ten years younger. It's been growing in me for years. If I hadn't obeyed the impulse something would have carried away. It was a sort of pressure building up and up until I felt ready to burst."

"So today you blew your top?"

"Not exactly. It was more like a safety-valve. I told him a few things about himself, but in a polite sort of way. I mean, I didn't call him a fat slug, or a bonehead, or anything like that. I kept within bounds."

"Tell me, what was the immediate cause of all this?"

"Nothing much," Sally answered casually. "Principally,

I suppose, it was because he has a bad cold in the head. He snuffled. It's a small matter; but it was just that much too much. I couldn't face it. To sit there for hours at a time, looking at a man lying in bed, with his eyes watering, and listening to him snuffle—I felt I'd reached my limit."

"The dirty dog wanted you to work on Christmas Eve?"

"Oh, yes! Christmas Eve or Christmas Day, it's all one to him. He's a glutton for work—giving other people work, I mean. So then something seemed to snap, and all the barriers went down. Standing there, looking him right in the eye, I told him what I thought of him—in a ladylike way, of course."

"How did he take it?"

"He sort of swelled up, and went purple in the face," Sally answered thoughtfully. "As if he'd been connected to a free air pump at a garage. It was an impressive performance, but bound to be bad for his heart. I felt sure he was going to burn out a valve. But he came down to size again in a few moments, and stated at some length—he's always too verbose —that if I held so poor an opinion of him he didn't see how he could keep me on as his private secretary, and I had better look around for another situation, as loyalty was the first essential, and so on. That's what it boiled down to, though it took him about ten minutes to say it. He didn't seem to realize I could be loyal to him while still facing up to the fact that he was a pretty poor piece of work. So I replied that if it was all the same to him I'd quit at once, as my nerves were worn ragged, and he agreed that perhaps it would be as well, since I no longer had his confidence. I then left the room, skipping like a lamb and with a song in my heart. I should have done it years ago."

"Three years ago," Mr. Massey agreed, leaning over to slip an arm around her waist. "Three years ago, when I was mooning around with a yearning look in my eye. Think of all the wear and tear on your nervous system you'd have saved if you'd up and told him what you thought of him then. But I think you were a little bit dazzled by the brightness of his future."

"I was not!"

"You saw yourself as private secretary to the Prime Minister, or perhaps the Chancellor of the Exchequer," Mr.

Massey said firmly, ignoring her attempts to remove his arm from around her waist. "You were held in the spell of his yaketty-yak. It's taken you three years and a bit to see him for what he is, a pompous bladder of hot gases, devoid even of that mite of rat-like cunning needed to make a successful politician."

"It has not! I always saw him like that—or something like that, anyway. After the first few months I knew that even if he did manage to get himself elected he'd spend his time warming the back bench. But it was a good job, and I met interesting people, so I stuck it out. As for that yearning look in your eye you mentioned just now, I didn't notice it. All I could see was a jealous gleam. As if anyone need be jealous of Claude!"

"You weren't just a teeny-weeny bit fascinated by him?"

"No!" Sally said coldly. "I wasn't! If I want to be fascinated by someone, I'll pick a human being, not merely a poor imitation. But at the moment I'm not conscious of a wish to be fascinated by anyone, human or subhuman. My one desire is to get away from Scumton Hall and everyone in it as soon as possible, and I'd leave at once if I weren't afraid I'd be suspected of swiping the Rembrandt."

She made another effort to remove Mr. Massey's arm from around her waist, but it clung like the leg of an octopus. If anything, the pressure increased.

"I love to see your eyes flash like that!" Mr. Massey remarked. "You look as if you wanted to bite someone, and bite him good."

"Yes—*you*!"

"What have *I* done?"

"You thought I was in love with Claude!"

"No. I thought you were dazzled by the prospect of becoming a great man's secretary."

"That windbag!"

"Something warned me I'd be wasting my time asking you to come to Canada," Mr. Massey confessed nonchalantly.

"You could have taken a chance. Your time wasn't worth much, anyway."

"Besides, I couldn't have paid your fare."

"I could have paid my own."

"I'm glad you didn't suggest that."

"You didn't give me a chance to suggest anything. You didn't ask me to go."

"I'd probably have fallen in with the idea," Mr. Massey continued, giving her a big hug, then absentmindedly kissing the back of her neck. "Then I'd have been a man with a wife and responsibilities, and I'd have had to stay in the city and hold down a steady job."

"If you could get one," Sally said, on an aloof note. "So, not having me along, you didn't have to hold a job?"

"I wasn't tied down."

"I'm so glad I can't be held responsible for tying you down!" Sally threw off a snort of amusement mingled with annoyance. "No wonder you've been so reticent about your career! Reading between the lines, it looks as if most of the time you were on the bum."

"I moved around," Mr. Massey agreed, refusing to take offence. "Here one day, there the next, and so forth. Another advantage was that I was able to drop everything and come back here for Christmas."

"What did you have to drop?" Sally asked scornfully. "I don't know why you wanted to be here for Christmas or any other time. It's like a nut-farm."

"It seemed the best way of getting in touch with you," Mr. Massey explained. "It's a family custom with the Leighs to get together at Christmas. In the good old days, I understand, there could be up to fifty or sixty members of the tribe at Scumton for the festive season; but that was in the great-grandmother's day, when women knew their place and were kept in it, and broods of eight or ten were looked on merely as a good beginning."

"Let's leave that out of it," Sally suggested, on a more friendly note. "Do you really mean you came all that way just to see me, or are you coming over all sentimental because it's Christmas Eve and you have half a pint of brandy in your pipeline?"

"I mean it. Otherwise I'd be wintering in California, or possibly Hawaii."

"Maybe you could thumb a ride to California; but how would you bum a berth to Hawaii?" Sally relaxed a little under the pressure of his arm. "You don't have to answer that one—not if it means giving away trade secrets. I don't suppose it occurred to you to wonder why *I*'m here, did it?"

"I took it you'd be with Claude."

"The only reason I'm with Claude," Sally said in a low voice, staring into the fire, "is that I regarded him as a sort of link with the family and you. So long as I remained in touch with the family, there was hope that I'd get any news about you that was going. I couldn't very well write and ask the old man for the latest bulletin. I have a little pride. I was here last year and the year before, and there was no news at all. You hadn't written. You'd simply vanished into the wilds like an earwig in a sponge. If there'd been no news of you this time I'd have given up hope. A girl can't wait on and on just because of a few words from a young man who probably didn't mean them, anyway. You said you loved me, and asked me to wait while you went to Canada and made our fortune—and then you spoiled it all by some reference to Claude, and before I could give you my word we were scratching each other's eyes out. But I waited, anyway."

"And now you'll reap your reward," Mr. Massey pointed out, giving her a big hug. He threw off a snort of amusement. "The faithful heart comes into its own, what? As in all the best movies."

"It was nice of you to give up your winter in Honolulu on the off-chance of seeing me," Sally said formally. "But now that we've reached this stage, I'd like to have something definite to go on. Something to get my teeth into."

"You've got *me*."

"It may come to that later. The question is, are you proposing marriage, or do I have to wait another three or four years before you get around to that?"

"I've already proposed. You remember? Three years ago. Now I'm awaiting the favour of a reply."

"You haven't changed your mind?"

"Why should I? I've got the best on the market."

"Suppose, in a weak-minded moment, I agree? Do you push off into the wilds again, with your pack on your back and your shooting-iron under your arm, with one eye lifted for Redskins and the other turned inward on a vision of the girl you'd left behind? Is that how the script goes?"

"No, no!" Mr. Massey said earnestly, giving her another big hug by way of emphasis. "Nowadays I run a private plane."

"You run a private plane? You mean you pilot a plane for some wealthy citizen whose time is worth money?"

"*I* am the wealthy citizen."

"*You?*"

"Me. And I don't really need to dash off into the wilds any more. Certainly not very often. I'd have lots of time to stay home around the house and watch the little ones grow up. Lots of time for wintering in Honolulu and New Mexico and such-like haunts of the idle rich, too. Lots of time for enjoying life. I've made my pile. It's big enough to keep you and me and the children in modest luxury for a long time to come. Bigger, in fact, because it's growing all the time."

"You're sure you haven't had too much brandy?" Sally asked. "It sounds like a pipe-dream. As a matter of interest, possibly to the police, how did you come by all this wealth?"

"I sold my mine."

"I didn't know you had a mine."

"You should have guessed. I went to Canada to find a mine, and I found one."

"Gold, or what?"

"Uranium."

"Oh! The stuff they make bombs with?"

"That's the stuff. It took me a little time to locate the one I wanted; but in the end I pinned it down. I got a down payment of a few million dollars, and in case I run short I get a cut on every ton of ore mined for the next fifty years."

"I don't know whether to believe you or not," Sally murmured. "It might be rather nice to be married to a wealthy man, and winter in Honolulu; but I'd made up my mind to go back with you, anyway, so——"

She stopped there, not because Mr. Massey had crushed her to his bosom and was covering her face with scorching kisses, but because from upstairs there came a yell that sounded as if someone's throat was being cut an inch at a time.

CHAPTER SEVENTEEN

SALLY and Mr. Massey, being young and fit, arrived on the scene in good time to see Mr. Goodrich, in a suit of pyjamas with palm-trees all over, rush at the old grandfather as if to strike him senseless to the floor. It was evident at a glance that the honoured guest had left his room in a hurry, though he had taken the trouble to close the door behind him. Some powerful emotion had turned him purple in the face and made his eyes bulge out and the veins in his temples swell like bicycle tubes.

"Murderer!" he bawled, shaking a fist under the old grandfather's nose. "Low-down, crooked bum! So you thought you'd get rid of me, huh? For two cents I'd take you apart and stomp you into the floor!"

"My dear fellow!" his genial host protested, maintaining his customary nonchalance in face of this outburst. "Pray calm yourself before you blow your cork. Have you had a nightmare, or what? When you came out with that dreadful yell just now, I thought you'd been stabbed to the heart. It put me in mind of the good old days when a sinister figure was liable at any time to step from behind the arras and plunge a stiletto into someone's back. It *was* a nightmare, what?"

"It was no darn nightmare!" Preston B. Goodrich said, squeezing the words out between his teeth. "You tried to murder me, you old crook!" His tone went up a point or two. "There's a rattler in my bed!"

"You mean a rattle, what? A toy much in favour with very young children, which when shaken produces a sound that appears to give them some aesthetic satisfaction. But I'm dashed if I can imagine how one got into your bed. We haven't had a baby in the house for years. And besides, why make such a fuss about it?"

Mr. Goodrich had listened to all this with the closest attention, though plainly he found it difficult not to interrupt. His powerful hands worked as if he already had them around the old grandfather's neck and was wringing it out like a dish-cloth. So menacing was his demeanour, and so murderous the gleam in his eye, that Mr. Massey found it difficult to understand why he had not got down to the good work before now.

"The hell with you and your rattles!" he snarled, still keeping the teeth close together.

"It's not my rattle. I got through with such toys many years ago. Nor have I yet reached the stage of playing with them again."

"I said a *rattler*, you old fool!" Mr. Goodrich took in a deep breath, and continued as if calling a neighbour on the other side of the mountain. "A *rattlesnake*!"

"Come, come!" the old grandfather protested mildly. "You're not in Arizona now, rolled in your blankets under the light of Western stars, with the cattle chewing the cud all around and the coyotes howling on the ridge. We don't have rattlesnakes in these parts. Too dashed cold for them. They couldn't stand it, even in a fur coat. No, no, my dear fellow! It was a nightmare. Better get back to bed before you catch a chill."

"So it can pin me good, huh?"

The old grandfather turned courteously to Mr. Massey.

"Rather odd how this talk of snakes keeps popping up, is it not?" he mused. "Have you remarked it, my boy? Every so often the subject somehow creeps into the conversation. First one of the maids claimed to have found a snake in Derek's bed, and now our friend here accuses me—indirectly, of course—of slipping one of the jokers into *his* bed with the intention of having him bitten to the bone. Bit of a mystery, what? Could it be that we have a ghost snake about the house?"

"Ghost snake, my eye!" the tycoon snorted. "When I got into bed, I felt this darned cold thing against my feet. So I pulled back the sheets, and there it was, a snake as long as your arm and as thick as your wrist, and with a mean look in its eye."

"It rattled at you?"

"No, it didn't rattle at me."

"Perhaps its rattler is out of order, due to the cold. There is a poker in your room?"

"Yeah, there's a poker in my room, though I didn't see a thing to poke with it."

"Tomorrow you will have something to poke with it," the old grandfather promised. "Meanwhile, with your permission, I'll borrow it for a few moments. If there is indeed a snake in your bed, it will be my duty and my pleasure to beat it out as flat as a carpet, even if it means supplying you with clean sheets immediately afterwards."

"Yeah?" Mr. Goodrich said, on a reserved note and with a curl of the lip. "Well, brother, I hope it bites you as you meant it to bite me, only better. I haven't had a hearty laugh in a long time. This way."

"I am well aware of the location of your room," his genial host assured him, without meaning any offence, or certainly not much.

In his haste, though pulling the door behind him, Mr. Goodrich had left it a few inches open, and now it occurred to him that his bedfellow might have slipped out of the room when nobody was looking. Politely motioning the old grandfather into the lead, he dropped back a little, darting keen glances from side to side, though actually there was no cover around for anything larger than a beetle.

The old grandfather seemed to have no such fears. Stepping boldly forward, he pushed the door open and entered with a confident step, conveying the impression that he had been dealing with rattlesnakes all his life and thought nothing of mopping-up a clutch or two before breakfast. Having with one sweeping glance assured himself that his prey was not lying around on the floor, watching for a chance to nip the first passer-by, he advanced to the fireplace and lifted up the poker, an old-fashioned model about three feet long and an inch square, looking more like a fence-post than something for stirring the fire. With this formidable weapon in his right hand he approached the bed, humming softly to himself, while Mr. Goodrich, who had taken up a strategic position in the doorway, watched the drama unfold with a hopeful gleam in his eye. Grasping the bedclothes firmly, the old grandfather jerked them back. At the same moment he raised the poker above his head, ready to bring it down in a blow so powerful that no snake on the receiving end could hope to remain in one piece.

All this was so much window-dressing. He had not expected to see a snake. He was, in fact, convinced that the honoured guest had had a nightmare, and it had occurred to him that this was quite a normal thing with Preston B. Goodrich, possibly because he worked too hard. The fact that there actually was a snake in the bed took him so completely by surprise that he stood staring at it as if turned to a pillar of salt. He could scarcely believe his eyes—which was all that saved the sheets.

It was at this dramatic moment, even as the quarry lay exposed to view, that Derek entered the room, shouldering Mr. Goodrich aside without even a word of apology. At sight of the snake, so soon to be reduced to a couple of feet of jelly, he uttered a piercing cry. This yell, rising so unexpectedly behind him as he took his stroke, threw the old grandfather off balance, and the poker missed its victim by inches. Before it could be raised for another swing, Derek rushed forward, snatched up the snake—which appeared to have little or no interest in the proceedings—and crushed it to his bosom.

"Lay off, you old fool!" he hooted. "You leave Joe alone!"

"Dear me!" the old grandfather said mildly. "That's Joe, is it?"

"Yeah, this is Joe."

"He would appear to be the undemonstrative kind, what? One sees no evidence of his undoubted joy at your appearance —and you can take it from me, my boy, your appearance saved him a few multiple fractures. Tell me, how did he come to be in Mr. Goodrich's bed?"

"I put him there," the lad answered sullenly. "I had to keep him somewhere, hadn't I? How was I to know this old bum would be moving in? Maybe you don't know a snake has to be kept warm in weather like this. And that young stinker Alison was looking everywhere for him."

"Doubtless to give him a hot-water bottle, what?"

"She said she was going to feed him to a hedgehog."

"Hedgehogs don't move around at this time of year, either. However, it was a kindly thought—so far as the hedgehog is concerned, at any rate. Joe might not have appreciated her motives, though."

The old grandfather paused a moment, looking Derek over with a thoughtful eye.

184

"Your grandmother will be overjoyed to learn of your miraculous recovery," he remarked. "So timely, too! Had you come to your senses a few minutes later, you'd have found Joe rendered down to a handful of slime with perhaps the odd eyeball floating around, and I feel sure the fate of your pet would have cast a gloom over the coming revels. Now be good enough to return to your room, taking Joseph with you."

"I can keep him, huh?" Derek said eagerly. "Huh? Huh? Can I keep him?"

"So far as I'm concerned, my boy, you're at liberty to keep boa-constrictors. In fact, I'd gladly get you one if I could—a big one, and hungry."

"Say, won't that snake bite him?" Mr. Goodrich asked as the lad departed, tucking Joe inside his pyjama jacket for greater comfort.

"I'm afraid not," the old coot answered, with a sigh. "It's a grass snake, and perfectly harmless." He turned on a winning smile for his guest. "So you see, my dear fellow, you misjudged me. I really wasn't trying to murder you, you know. We Leighs cut out that sort of thing quite a while back."

"Yeah." As if conscious for the first time of Sally's presence, the tycoon reached out for his dressing-gown, and put it on. Meanwhile he bent on his host a morose and brooding look, and it was obvious some thought was working in his mind. "Where's Prue's room?" he demanded suddenly.

"Prue's room?" said his host, somewhat taken aback. "Just a few doors along, my dear fellow. Why do you ask?"

"Because I reckon I'll drop in and have a word with her."

"Now?"

"Yeah. Right now, brother."

"Haw! Rather late, don't you think? Why not wait until morning? Give her a pleasant surprise for Christmas, and all that."

"Now!" Preston B. Goodrich repeated, with a certain inflexibility of tone. "Never mind the pleasant surprise angle, pal. What I'd like to know is how she can sleep through the racket that's been going on around here for the past quarter-hour."

"More than likely she didn't sleep," the old grandfather explained tolerantly. "But you couldn't expect her to rush out in her nightie, either. She's a guest, not one of the inmates. Must observe the conventions, and all that."

"Yeah, yeah!" Mr. Goodrich nodded. "I understand. Which is her room, bud?"

"I told you she was indisposed, did I not? Didn't like to mention this before; but it may be something catching, you know. Measles, or mumps, or something. Never can tell. Best to be on the safe side, what?"

"I'll take a chance. Just point out the door. After that, pal, you can go jump in the lake."

"Never let it be said that I came between a father and his child at a sacred moment like this," the old coot replied, bowing to the inevitable with a good grace. "Step this way."

"Better tag along," Mr. Massey whispered to Sally. "I have a hunch murder might be done any moment now."

Mr. Goodrich wasted no time on conventional formalities. Having knocked once at his daughter's door, he turned the handle and walked in. Normally the door would have been locked; but Claude, on unlocking it that morning to free his prisoner, had thoughtlessly dropped the key in his dressing-gown pocket and gone back to bed. Next moment the fond father had switched on the light, and a moment after that a cry of emotion broke from his lips. It was not a cry of joy and thankfulness at seeing his only child again. It was a lion-like roar of fury at finding that his child, who now sat up blinking at him, had a young man in bed with her.

"*Pop!*" she hooted. "Pop, don't go black in the face! We're *married*!"

It stopped the fond parent, who had been gathering himself together to leap forward and take John by the throat, as if he had been hit over the head with a mallet. And while he stood dazed, with Mr. Massey watching him closely, there came faintly through the night the sound of bells.

"Hark!" said the old grandfather, cupping one hand to his ear in a completely unnecessary gesture. "The old village bells! It's Christmas Day! Peace on earth, goodwill to men." Turning, he clasped the outraged parent's hand. "Let us go downstairs, my dear fellow, and have a little drink to cement our newfound relationship. Believe it or not, this is as great a surprise to me as it is to you—or very nearly, at any rate."

"We'll be right after you," Prue added as her old man wavered. "There's a little explaining to do all round."

.　　　.　　　.　　　.　　　.

"It all began very simply," said the old grandfather, fondling his brandy goblet, which was full almost to the brim. "Some years ago, being short of ready money—and of all the other kinds, too—I resolved to sell the Rembrandt, regarding it as something I could part with without a tear; but first I took it to London to be cleaned. The bird who undertook the job gave the picture some sort of test—X-ray and infra-red, I believe he called it. At any rate, he discovered it was not a genuine Rembrandt at all, but a very fine forgery.

"As you will readily imagine, this dumbfounded me more than a little, and it would be no exaggeration to say I was in despair, or very close to it."

He paused briefly to wash the dust from his throat, and then continued.

"However, I am not one to remain bogged down in despair, and before long I recalled that only a few months before, an extremely wealthy person from South America, of Spanish extraction, who had recently made an enormous amount of money in some manner he left to my imagination, had offered to buy the picture, being anxious to acquire a few Old Masters for a new residence he was then building—as he put it himself, regardless of expense. So I wrote this worthy citizen and gave him the glad news that the picture was his if he still felt in a buying mood, and sat back to await his reply. Meanwhile, I commissioned this cleaner feller to have a copy made in the best manner, and he was good enough to inform me that nothing could be simpler.

"The original duly went to South America. I gave no guarantee of authenticity. I contented myself with stating that numerous experts were of the opinion that it was a genuine Rembrandt. I am not a swindler. I do not sell goods under false pretences."

At this point the old grandfather paused briefly to peer at his newfound relation with one eyebrow raised, almost as if he would welcome comment; but Preston B. Goodrich, catching his daughter's eye, sat tight, though he seemed to swell a little in his chair.

"The next was an Australian," the old coot continued, having first lubricated his vocal cords. "He had been informed, by this cleaner laddie already mentioned, and who was now a sort of junior partner in the enterprise, that I had some valuable paintings for sale. I tried to get him to take the portrait of my grandmother; but he preferred the Rembrandt. I asked for a month to think it over. In that month, I had two more copies made. I am no financial wizard; but it seemed to me that business was picking up. There was a demand to be supplied.

"You were the third," he said, turning courteously to Mr. Goodrich, who sat sipping his brandy in a moody sort of way. "I informed your agent I was not at all anxious to sell. Agents are trained men. Principals usually are unfitted to remark the difference between a Rubens and a railway poster, a Titian and a toothpaste ad. But the more I tried to put him off, the more bullheaded he became, and finally I let him have his way. He scarcely looked at the painting before handing over his cheque. I complimented myself on having found my niche."

"You'd found a bunch of suckers!" the honoured guest growled. "That's what you'd found!"

"Now, Pop!" Prue said fondly. "You never gave a sucker an even break yourself." She turned to her father-in-law, who was looking her over with an approving eye. "I'll go on from there, Dad. I met John at Oxford, and we sort of fell for each other right away. He started telling me all about his home and everything, and of course he mentioned the Rembrandt. That tied him up with the Leigh that Pop had bought his copy from, so I got mad and told him it was all washed out between us. He asked why, and I told him I didn't want any part of the son of a swindler, and he said you weren't a swindler, and I said any man who sold fake paintings was a swindler, and Pop had been told his picture was only a copy, but he could do nothing about it, and the genuine Rembrandt was

188

still hanging in Scumton Hall. So then John got all steamed up and said if I married him he'd guarantee to get the genuine article for Pop by fair means or foul, but we'd try foul first because he didn't see how we could pull it off otherwise. So we sort of sneaked off and got married."

"Just to get a darn picture!" her old man snorted, but not on a really aggrieved note. "Pooey to pictures, anyway!"

"No, Pop!" the beautiful bride said softly, with a sidelong glance at her handsome husband. "Because I love him. And *you*'ll love him, too, when you get to know him."

"I guess so," the doting parent agreed, but without looking at all convinced. "Only thing is, honey, how am I to get to know him when you're over here and I'm back home without my chicken, huh?"

"We'll go back with you, Pop. You can give John some sort of a job, and he'll learn the business from the ground up. Then when you feel like retiring he can step right into your shoes."

"Ahuh! If that's how you want it, honey, that's how it's going to be." Preston B. Goodrich turned to his son-in-law, and bent on him the sort of glance he used on a junior executive who wasn't getting out the work. "How would you like to start in the foundry, son?"

"Whatever you say, Pop," the young man replied agreeably. "The foundry it is."

"As I was saying," the old grandfather remarked, regaining a toe-hold on the conversation. "The mistake you made, my dear, was in giving your own name. Had you given a different name I shouldn't have suspected a thing—or certainly nothing in connection with the Rembrandt. As it was, however, I drew the inevitable conclusion, and you were under the closest observation from the very first moment. I saw you take the painting—this old house has its secrets, you know—and I had a very good notion of where you hid it. I found it next day, and, having locked the gallery, switched the Rembrandt for the portrait of my grandmother, a work of no great artistic merit."

He paused briefly to rinse the dust from his tonsils, then continued.

"It may interest you to know that meanwhile my grandson,

Derek, a lad of singular promise, having chanced upon a reproduction of the Goodrich Rembrandt, if I may call it so, in an American art magazine, was attempting to blackmail me, in the belief that my wife knew nothing of the sale." The old grandfather laughed tolerantly. "It shows a highly commendable spirit, of course, and I have no doubt the boy will go far; but in this instance he was mistaken. I had kept Martha fully informed of each successive transaction as it developed, and I must say I received from her nothing but encouragement and sound advice. She has a very fine head for business."

"You knew we were married, Dad?" Prue asked, giving him a searching look, and blushing a little as at some inner thought.

"I had my suspicions," the old coot admitted, without giving anything away. "And I can say, with my hand on my heart, that John's choice of a bride meets with my warmest approval. Had he searched the wide world over he could not have found a more charming, more beautiful, or more lovable girl—and I'm damned if I know how he did it!"

This graceful tribute went far towards melting the industrial tycoon's heart, and, rising impulsively, he clasped the old grandfather by the hand.

"And he's a fine young fellow, too!" he said earnestly. "Yes, sir! I'm proud to have him as my son. After a year or two in the foundry I'll see he gets a move up. Ten-twelve years from now he'll amount to something."

"He amounts to something right now," Prue murmured fondly.

"Yeah?" said her old man, politely but with little real enthusiasm. "Such as what, honey?"

"Such as the father of your first grandson," the lovely bride replied, blushing, so far as could be seen, all over. "Due some time in July, unless I've counted wrong. It's all right, Pop—we've been married four months."

"God bless my soul!" the old grandfather sighed, peering into his goblet, while Preston B. Goodrich did his best to embrace both Prue and John at the same time. He turned to Mr. Massey, being careful to lower his voice a peg or two. "How I hate and despise this mawkish sentiment, my boy!

Between me and you and the decanter, it makes me sick in the stomach. I think I'll go to bed."

. . . . .

"He's a wily old fox, what?" Mr. Massey remarked, slipping his arm around Sally's waist as the old grandfather led Mr. Goodrich from the room, with Prue and John following on their heels. "Let's sit a few moments, if you're not too tired."

"It's getting a bit late," Sally pointed out, while at the same time sinking on to the couch. "We unemployed young females have to get to bed early so that we can get up early to look for a job."

"You won't be unemployed for long," Mr. Massey assured her. "Let me plan your future. First of all, we go through the formality of getting married."

"Only the formality?"

"Next, we push off on our honeymoon. That's where the formality ends."

"Where? I mean, where do we honeymoon?"

"West Indies?" Mr. Massey suggested. "Florida? Arizona? Mexico? Hawaii? Just say the word. They're all within easy reach of our magic carpet."

"I didn't know you had a magic carpet."

"I have millions of them. Other people call them dollars." He turned to her, and kissed her ear. "Let's make it soon. I've waited three years."

"So have I," she whispered. "As soon as you like."

He took her in his arms, and was about to crush her to his bosom in the good old-fashioned style when something caught his eye. Bending, he gripped a bare ankle, and pulled.

Alison came out from under the couch without a struggle. Rising to her feet, she adjusted her nightie, which had crept up around her waist. She was not covered with embarrassment. Her glance was cool and aloof as she looked her captor over.

"How did you get in here?" Mr. Massey demanded, maintaining a firm grasp on her nightie.

"I came in," Alison said simply. "I heard Gran'pa say you were all coming down, so I got here before you."

"Why?"

"I wanted to know what was going on. Nobody ever tells me what's going on. I've got to find out for myself."

"Did you take away the ladder when we were in the loft the other afternoon?"

"Yes," Alison replied frankly. "I wanted you to blame Derek. I hoped you'd knock hell's bells out of him."

"Why shouldn't I turn you over my knee and knock hell's bells out of *you*?"

"No, please!" Sally begged. "Let her go. Run along to bed, Alison."

Released, Alison moved off without any display of emotion. But she halted in the doorway, and turned to look back. A smile slipped across her features.

"I hope you have a lovely time on your honeymoon," she said, and in a moment was gone, closing the door softly.